# THE BLESSED AND THE CURSED

# THE BLESSED AND THE CURSED

JADE MUSTO

Peridot Publishing

For all those whose stories haven't been told.

## Prologue

Blossom placed his overflowing basket of flowers gently on the ground, trying his best to crush as few of the new growths as possible. He hummed quietly to himself as he replaced a few of the cuttings that had fallen out and knelt in front of the new sprout that he had spotted. He was always excited to see a new type of flower in the meadow. The rolling field was awash with colour year-round thanks to his diligence, and he cared for each new bloom with the same level of dedication that a parent cares for their child.

Closing his eyes and tilting his head towards the sun he whispered the word that came as naturally to him as breathing, asking for Sun's blessing in a tongue that few had ever heard or understood. Warmth surged through him, turning his pale pink hair golden with its glow. His eyes shone with that same golden power when he opened them again. He looked down at the small sprout with a smile. Reaching out a single finger to transfer the blessing, he caressed the delicate bud. He watched with an awe that never waned, no matter how many times he did this, as the sprout grew before his eyes. He could feel the power of Sun's blessing thrumming under his skin as the new flower unfurled its leaves. Bright blue petals formed from fresh buds until it stood proud and fully grown amongst its siblings.

"Blossom."

The distant shout caused him to flinch. The residual power of Sun's blessing receded to his chest where it mingled with the remnants of the other blessings that he'd taken that day. His soft curls returned to their natural blush pink hue, the unnatural glow of his eyes disappearing as his power waned. In his excitement he'd forgotten his mother's golden rule, the one that had been hammered into him every time she caught sight of his power.

*Never let anyone see that you are Blessed, not even me.*

He didn't understand her fear and she had always refused to elaborate further when berating him. To him the blessings were a good thing. They let him grow food for them, let him heal himself and his mother should either of them grow sick, but his mother made it clear that no one else would see it that way. Bad things would happen to them both if someone should see him using his power, and as vague as that threat was it was usually enough to keep him vigilant. His excitement had simply overridden his fear this time.

He turned, still on his knees, ready to shout an apology down the hillside to their little cottage, but the sight that lay before him caused him to freeze. Three large men with skin paler than he'd ever seen stood at the base of the hill. Two of them were restraining his mother as she struggled against them whilst the third began making his way towards him. That was when he realised that the call hadn't been an admonishment, but a warning. He caught his mother's terrified gaze as she screamed the last word that he would ever hear her say.

"Run!"

## Chapter 1

Blossom's eyes snapped open, his heart pounding in his chest as he tried to remember where he was. The death grip he currently had on the bedsheets lessened gradually as he took in the sight of the dark blue canopy above him. He turned his head towards the glass doors on his right, the moonlight streaming through the half-open curtains highlighting the familiar trappings of his bedroom. He took a few deep breaths as he ran his hands gently over the soft cotton of his bedsheets. His pulse slowly returned to a normal rate and his breathing finally evened out enough that he was no longer gasping as he woke fully, leaving the nightmare behind.

He pushed himself into an upright position with a quiet groan. He placed a cool hand against his forehead as the headache that always accompanied that particular nightmare began to make itself known, pressing at his temples with a relentless ache. Tossing the covers back he flung his legs over the side of the bed, running a hand through his hair before standing. He pulled the glass doors to his balcony open, breathing in the cold night air gratefully. The last vestiges of winter were still refusing to relinquish their grip even as the spring buds were sprouting, and the air was sharp with the taste of frost. Blossom stepped out into the night with a shiver, his thin nightshirt doing little to protect him from the wind. Tilting his head back towards the sky he held onto the stone railing that surrounded his balcony. Rocking backwards and forwards on his heels he continued to shake the remains of the nightmare off, taking comfort in the grounding cold that seeped into his bare feet. He took another deep breath and opened his eyes, staring at the star speckled blackness above him. It was a full moon.

A familiar urge grasped him, and he returned to his room briefly to grab his coat and boots. Tying the sash of his coat tightly around his middle he began to climb up the strong vines that surrounded the balcony doorway. He'd spent years cultivating the vines to a thickness that could easily hold his weight and they now snaked up the palace wall to the rooftop, offering enough handholds that he could make the climb blindfolded.

Blossom paused when he reached the roof, taking another deep breath of cold air. Looking back over his shoulder he gazed out at the rolling hills and well-maintained forests that made up most of the royal ring of Vaten. It was a clear night, and with the moon as bright as it was Blossom could almost see the towering stone wall that separated the palace and its immense grounds from the rest of the kingdom. He shook his head and turned back to the task he had set himself. A few more steps up the gentle slope of the roofs edge and he soon found himself traversing the various chimney stacks and parapets that littered the rooftop until he reached his usual haunt, the northernmost spire. He jumped nimbly to the iron walkway that surrounded the spire. The walkway had been built once the palace guards had realised that no number of reprimands or threats could keep Blossom off the rooftops, so they'd opted instead to provide more stable footing.

Blossom placed his hands on the slate tiles of the spire, giving himself a stability that wasn't needed but was welcome none the less. Looking up he found the moon hanging directly above him, exactly as he knew he would. Asking for blessing had become so second nature now that Blossom didn't even need to say the words aloud. He simply closed his eyes and seconds later felt the cool energy of Moon's blessing rushing into him. His skin glowed a brilliant white as his muscles relaxed and the tension in his head began to ease. He rested his forehead against the spire as the blessing settled, cool and cleansing in his heart, replenishing the well of power that dwelled deep within his chest.

"Bad dream?"

As the familiar voice floated from behind him Blossom opened his eyes but didn't turn around, his gaze focused on the dark tiles in front of him.

"Bad memories." He replied, his nails digging into the concrete at the sides of the spire. Why did Asher have to be here right now? Blossom shouldn't have been surprised, the prince had an uncanny knack for knowing when he would be on the rooftops, but Blossom hadn't even known that he'd returned from the southern barracks. He wasn't due back for another week at least.

He let out a sigh. What had happened that day hadn't been Asher's fault, he knew that. And truthfully most days he believed it too, when he wasn't still raw from those final images of his mother. When he was awake and rested enough to push down the toxic words that had been whispered into his ears so often since then. But something about that dream always reopened the old wounds.

Asher had been the reason for the raids. He was the reason why Blossom had been bought to the palace, brought into a kingdom completely alien from his own, but he'd been a child when it had happened. They both had been. He'd blamed Asher initially, but the hurt had become less and less as the years wore on.

Now he'd spent more time in the palace with Asher than he ever had in that little cottage by the meadow, and there were very few days when he even thought about his old home. But even now, 12 years later, there were moments. Moments when he was feeling particularly vulnerable, or Asher was being particularly irritating that the urge to throw the old resentment back in the prince's face became almost palpable.

Blossom sighed again and turned round to face his oldest friend. Asher was here now, there was no point dwelling on it. "When did you get back?" He asked, freezing when he saw the state that Asher was in.

The prince was sitting across from him, his back pressed against a chimney stack, his arm resting nonchalantly on one raise knee. He was still in his riding clothes, the dirt from the road covering him like a second layer. The tired smile on his face answered his question for him and any previous annoyance vanished. Asher had clearly come to the rooftop to see him as soon as he had returned. Why he had decided to return in the middle of the night was the bigger mystery.

Blossom's gaze zeroed in on the prince's neck and before he realised that he was moving he'd practically marched over to Asher, covering the distance between them in only three strides. Crouching in front of him he tugged at the other man's collar, loosening the ties that held it closed against his throat. His eyes widened as he took in the familiar, black, ink-like tendrils of his death mark. Usually contained to the spot just above his collar bone they were now nearly at the prince's jawline.

"Asher, why didn't you come back earlier if it had gotten this bad?" He demanded.

"I didn't want to bother you. You'd subdued it just before I left so I should have been fine for another week. I honestly didn't realise that it'd grown so much." Asher responded with a shrug, that infuriatingly calm smile still on his face.

Blossom shook his head, he knew how painful the mark was when it was spreading, there was no way Asher wouldn't have felt it. "It's getting worse, like it's building up an immunity or something." He placed his palm on the side of Asher's neck, covering as much of the mark as possible. "Just be thankful that it's a full moon or we'd be making a trip to the lake to get Water's blessing as well for a mark this big."

"You make that sound like a bad thing."

"Shut up and let me concentrate." Blossom snapped, worry making him short-tempered. He closed his eyes and summoned the power of Moon's blessing, letting it pulse from his fingertips and into the mark. His eyes snapped open again when he heard Asher gasp and felt a dark force, like a wall of sentient resistance, pushing back against the blessing.

"What was that?" Asher asked breathlessly, a sheen of sweat had broken out across his brow, and he was panting like he'd just finished sparring.

"I don't know." Blossom responded slowly, looking at his fingers in confusion. The death mark was just as big as before, his power hadn't affected it at all. It was building up a resistance. Even worse, it was fighting back. Blossom had a feeling he knew why, but he pushed the thought down as he stood.

"Fuck, hang on a minute." He hurried back over to the spire, calling

Moon's blessing to him again. Holding it in his throat, he made his way back to his friend. He'd only ever had to do it this way once before, when he and Asher had first met, and he'd had 8 years' worth of death mark build-up to contend with. He tried to banish the image of the young prince, unresponsive and shivering, from his mind. Focusing instead on the version of Asher that was right in front of him.

He cupped his hand over the mark again, and briefly locked eyes with Asher, trying to mentally communicate to him what he was about to do, before leaning forward and sealing their lips together. He focused on reopening the connection that he and Asher shared. The one he'd been forced to sever years ago when the whispers that he was becoming too powerful had threatened to separate them for good. He concentrated on pouring as much of the blessing through their connection as he could, juggling the need to subdue the death mark curse with the need to preserve his own life by not bonding them completely. He focused on the fear of what would happen if he slipped up, using it to ignore the way that Asher sunk into the kiss, ignoring the way his own heartbeat skipped and sped up at their touch.

Blossom began to feel the tug at the back of his eyes that meant that he was overextending himself and pulled away. Landing ungracefully on his back with a huff, his limbs suddenly weak from exertion. He took a few deep breaths, watching them puff out above him like smoke in the cold night air as he allowed the tremors in his hands to pass before pushing himself up onto his elbows.

Asher tugged at the collar of his shirt, exposing his neck again. "How is it?" He asked, not looking Blossom in the eye. He appeared uncharacteristically bashful all of a sudden, the blush that adorned his cheeks visible even in the darkness.

Blossom let out a shaky sigh and smiled for the first time that evening. "Good." He said, standing and helping the prince to his feet. "It's the smallest it's been in years." It was true, the death mark had reduced to the size of a copper piece, no bigger than a button. "Even if we have to do it this way from now on, you won't need another blessing for at least a month I should think. You won't need to rush back in the middle of the night again." Blossom smiled proudly, expecting a similar reaction from the prince but Asher simply responded with a snide.

"Oh good. Blessing forbid that you should have to kiss me any more than you absolutely have to." Blossom froze, at a loss as to how to respond. The prince hadn't made mention of their arrangement for almost a year and whilst Blossom had become adept at simply laughing him off, he was out of practice. An uncomfortable silence filled the night air until Asher sighed. "I'm sorry, that was low." He muttered as he ran a hand through his already messy hair and looked down at his feet.

Blossom stared at his friend, feeling lost and far too tired to deal with the emotions that this conversation was going to bring up. "Asher I...you know I..." He stuttered over his words, unsure what he was even trying to say. He fell silent again when the prince reached out and placed a hand against his cheek, a mirror of the blessing touch, and Blossom felt his chest tighten with worry that the prince was going to kiss him again.

With a gentle nudge Asher bought their foreheads together and Blossom breathed a sigh of relief. It was a peace offering, something they'd been doing since they were children, a show of trust and comfort in once touch.

"Flower." Blossom raised his eyes at the old nickname, one he hadn't heard since they were teenagers. Pale pink meeting warm black as they looked at each other. "Would you ever let me kiss you just to kiss you?"

Blossom felt himself pull away, taking a step back to put some distance between them. "Asher don't do this." He begged quietly.

"Do what?" The prince responded, his own voice barely above a whisper.

"You said that you'd stop asking me things like that."

Asher shoved his hands in the pockets of his riding trousers. "I said I'd give you a year to think about it. It's been over a year Blossom."

Blossom gaped silently at him as he tried to think of a response. It was true, he'd had over a year to think up a good enough reason to put an end to their arrangement. But there wasn't one.

"I think I should be allowed an answer." Asher said finally, locking eyes with him.

"I can't." Blossom said, his words coming out before his brain processed what he was saying. It wasn't a rejection, not really. Just like all the other times, too scared to tell him the truth but unable to lie outright.

The prince smiled at him, and Blossom felt his heart clench at the sadness that he could see in it.

"It's okay Blossom. I understand."

Blossom shook his head, hand reaching up to clasp Asher as the other man turned away, fingers curling around the prince's wrist. How could he understand? How could he possibly understand when Blossom himself had never really understood why he had to say no. Was he even saying no, or was fear just keeping him mute like it always had? He opened his mouth but the only thing that came out was a gasped "I'm sorry".

There were so many things he was saying with those two words. 'I'm sorry I'm rejecting you again.' 'I'm sorry that I'm not allowed to let myself feel that way about you.' 'I'm sorry it was me the universe chose for you.' And even with all of that, it still wasn't enough.

Asher rubbed a thumb under his eye, and it was only then that Blossom realised that he was crying. "I understand." Asher said again before pressing his lips to Blossom's forehead. "I'm sorry too."

Blossom felt a sob tear from his throat as Asher turned from him but this time the prince didn't stop, instead he silently made his way along the rooftops back to his own room, leaving Blossom alone in the cold night air.

Taking a few shuddering breaths to try and stem the flow of tears that stubbornly refused to stop, Blossom once again lifted his face towards the sky. But this time he felt no relief, no calming power. Not that he expected any, Moon didn't give its blessing in multiples, even to him.

## Chapter 2

"Rise and shine beautiful."

Blossom groaned at Emma's cheerful sing-song voice, glaring at her from the safety of his bedcovers, which he burrowed further into when she made her way over to him after flinging his bedroom curtains open.

"And a good morning to you too, you look like shit by the way." Emma said lightly as she plonked herself down next to him. She crossed her legs atop his covers, her sunny disposition not wavering in the slightest in the face of Blossom's sour mood.

He had never been a morning person, even as a child. A fact that Emma knew all too well after ten years of service, but after he'd spent half of the night crying Blossom was even less happy about the wake-up call than normal. "I'm not getting up today." He replied sulkily, covering his head with the covers.

"Did you take Fire's blessing before bed or what? You're not usually this crabby during a full moon. In fact, this is usually the only time of the month that I can get a civil word out of you before breakfast." She snapped her fingers and stood up again, causing Blossom to peak out at her from his impromptu nest. "I know what will cheer you up, Asher's back. Arrived back sometime last night apparently."

"Yeah, I know." Blossom replied sourly. The reminder of last night's blessing caused him to curl up even tighter under the covers, until they were suddenly whipped away from him. He glared up at Emma, who tucked the bedsheets under her arm with an air of finality.

"How many times petal, your glares aren't intimidating when you have the colouring of strawberry pudding." She tilted her head, her brows creasing in concern as she finally took in the state of his puffy eyes. "Did you and Asher have an argument or something?"

He rolled over so that his back was facing her, hugging his knees to his chest. "It wasn't an argument." He could practically hear her rolling her eyes at his statement.

"Right." She elongated the word sarcastically. "So it was just that stupid thing that you do where you pretend that you don't love him, despite how much it hurts both of you, and then you both mope around the palace for days. Blossom you're 20 years old for blessings sake, and you've been betrothed to him since you were ten so just man up and accept it already. You're both such idiots that you're fucking made for each other either way."

"It's not that simple." Blossom grumbled before letting out a startled yelp as Emma smacked him hard on the ass.

"Oh yes it is, you big baby. Now get up and I'll draw you a bath, maybe Water's blessing will get you to cheer up."

Blossom felt a small smile creeping onto his face at her words. One of the things he'd always loved about Emma was that she never over-indulged him and made it clear when she thought he was being ridiculous. His face fell again when he remembered the real reason for his tears last night but with a shake of his head resolved to push them away for now. Let Emma continue thinking he and Asher were just playing some kind of juvenile game, it was better than letting her know the real reason why he kept rejecting him. He sat up and stretched as Emma disappeared further into his chambers, the sound of running water following soon after.

He made his way over to his bathing room, pulling off his nightshirt as he walked and dropping it into the waiting basket by the door as the large, claw-footed tub filled with steaming water.

"Lavender or rose water?" Emma asked, holding up two large jars of bathing salts, not in the least perturbed by Blossom's nakedness.

Blossom rubbed a hand over his eyes with a yawn. "Rose water, the king's taking us on a procession of the lower towns today and lavender will just make me more tired." He stopped when he realised what he had just said. That was why the prince had returned last night, they were supposed to ride the royal procession with the king today in preparation for the turning of the season. Which meant that his plan of Avoid

Asher Today was completely shot, as was his constant plan of Avoid King Silas. The plan that had been in place for the last ten years.

He groaned internally. Today was going to suck.

He climbed into the bath as Emma finished sprinkling in the bath salts, sinking into the steaming water with a sigh. He could feel Water's blessing running gently into him. There wasn't enough of Water's spirit in the bath for a full blessing but there was just enough to sooth him. He rested back against the porcelain, looking up at the ceiling until a tut from Emma causing him to tilt his head towards her.

"Oh petal, could you look any more pitiful?" She cooed as she knelt next to the bath. "Why do you insist on hurting yourself like this? Even if Asher did something to annoy you, your spirits are so resonant that continuing to reject him like this is going to destroy you."

"I don't want to talk about it anymore." Blossom muttered, staring at a spot on the wall so that he didn't have to look Emma in the eye.

"I know. I just thought that your excitement at being able to go outside of the royal ring for the first time would have prevented this. I also thought that Asher being gone for two weeks would make you less likely to stomp on his heart the second you saw him again." He felt gentle fingers running through his hair as he frowned. "You had that dream about your mother again, didn't you?" He nodded silently, his brows creasing when she spoke again. "You know Asher didn't ask for you to be separated from her, it's not his fault."

He huffed and pushed himself from the bath, wrapping the soft cotton robe that Emma held out around himself as he muttered. "I know that. I know the raids were to save his life, I know I shouldn't be mad at him for that."

"So you are mad at him?" Emma asked in disbelief. "I really thought you'd gotten over this."

"No I'm not mad at him." Blossom bit out feeling like he was going in circles. He couldn't remember exactly how many times they'd had this conversation, but he really wasn't in the mood to have it again, especially when he knew how weak his own arguments were.

"Then why petal?"

"No." He shouted, turning to face her. He was heartsick and angry, and he didn't need Emma trying to logic away the turmoil that he was going through. Especially when she didn't and couldn't have all of the facts.

"Blossom." She warned, her tone suddenly serious, reminiscent of many childhood scoldings. "Tell me the real reason why you keep rejecting him."

"I have." He shouted again. "I haven't even rejected him, not really. I just can't, I don't want to do this right now." He knew he sounded like a petulant child, but Emma was getting scarily close to the truth, and he knew that if she pushed now he'd tell her everything and he couldn't do that to her. Emma had been more of a mother to him than anyone had and if she knew what was really going on in his head, what had really been happening for more years than he could fully remember now she'd do something about it, and he couldn't let that happen. Because if she did something to save him or protect him then she'd be taken away from him, just like Asher would be if he gave in. He had to push them away just enough so that they wouldn't be gone completely, but ten years of fighting and lying had pushed him so close to the breaking point that he knew he couldn't hold out forever.

"Blossom." She said again, more gently this time.

"No, stop it." He cried, cradling his head in his hands, the remnants of Water's blessing turning sour in his chest. He could feel the toll of last night's blessing and the emptiness that he'd been left with after using almost all of his power breaking down that last barrier. "I'm so tired of it all. I love him so much, but I can't, I can't feel that way. I'm not allowed to." He keened.

"But why can't you?"

Somehow, he got control of his emotions enough to answer with the lie that had been drilled into him. The fear of the truth overriding his exhaustion as it always did. "Because he's the reason why my mother is dead." He screamed, but it wasn't until he saw the look on Emma's face that he realised that the last question hadn't come from her. He spun around, absently noting the dark circles under Asher's eyes before taking in the equally dark expression on his face. Blossom opened his mouth to say something, what he didn't know, but before he could think of anything Asher had grabbed his wrist and was roughly yanking him through the doorway and back into his bedchamber.

The prince slammed the bathing room door shut behind him and Blossom was about to remark on how rude it was to lock Emma out like that when another thought occurred to him. "Why are you here?" He asked. The prince should have been getting ready with his father, not standing in Blossom's bedroom on the opposite side of the palace.

Asher stopped suddenly as though he hadn't expected the question. He shook his head, anger ebbing from him as he stepped into Blossom's personal space. "You ask me why? When you're falling to pieces right in front of me?"

Blossom flinched as Asher rested a hand against his cheek, for a split second he'd been certain that the prince was going to strike him. A thought which he instantly realised was absurd, Asher may be much larger and more muscled than he was, but he had never been violent outside of the sparring rings. He was nothing like his father in that regard. "But how did you...?" He trailed off as Asher let out a bitter laugh.

"I don't know what you did to me last night. But ever since the blessing I've felt like complete shit."

Blossom's gaze instantly dropped to the spot on Asher's neck, he could easily see it, exposed as it was in his loose under-tunic but the death mark hadn't grown.

"Yeah, I thought it was that at first too. But then I felt your anguish as if it were my own. I don't know how I knew it was your feelings and not mine, but I had to check that you were okay."

Blossom's eyes widened as realisation sunk in. "Shit." He whispered. The connection, when he'd reopened it, he must have gone too far.

"Why what did you do?"

Blossom shook his head before closing his eyes and calling the power that Water's blessing had given him. He pushed gently at the connection, smiling in relief when only a tiny bit of power bled through. Just a small breach. He hadn't bonded them, not completely. Asher must have felt his emotions because they had been so intense. "It's nothing." He said, opening his eyes. "Only a temporary side effect, I had to use so much power to seal the mark that some of it's still lingering."

Asher didn't seem convinced, but he dropped his hand anyway. "Well, I guess that's good then. And at least now I know why you've been rejecting me for all these years." He walked away from Blossom to rest his hand on the door to the bathing room. "Or why you say you're rejecting me."

Blossom blinked. "What do you mean? That is why. I know that it's not fair Asher, but I just can't forgive you yet."

Asher smiled at him, no joy in the expression whatsoever. "So you say. But even if it is temporary, I can feel what you feel now so we both know that that's bullshit." He pushed the door open before Blossom could reply. "Get him dressed, we leave in half an hour." He ordered Emma, throwing one last angry look Blossom's way as he stormed out of the room.

"I don't think that I've ever seen the prince so angry before." Emma said, a hand on her cheek as she looked at the now closed bedroom door in shock. "What exactly was it that you said to him?"

Blossom hummed absently but didn't respond to her question, too busy replaying Asher's last few words over in his mind. How much had he given away in these last few hours of their connection? How much had the prince figured out?

## Chapter 3

Blossom allowed Emma to dress him in a kind of haze, letting her manoeuvre him like he was a doll, his mind so fixated on panicking that he didn't even realize what she'd dressed him in until she stepped back.

"All done petal." She said softly, placing his brush back on the side table.

He blinked down at himself, taking in the dark blue robe with its familiar patterns of swirling golden trim. The robe ended just below his knees, simple brown breeches and brown riding boots keeping the attention on the tailored richness of the blessers coat. "Why am I in the royal colours?" He asked, looking at Emma in bewilderment. He was used to the pattern and the fit of the robe with its high collar and sinched waist. He had worn one just like it almost every day since coming to the palace, the colours changing depending on the season.

A white and silver robe for winter, pink and copper for spring, green and gold for summer and red and black for autumn. He should be in spring robes right now, having changed out of winters robe just before Asher had left for the barracks 2 weeks ago. The dark blue that he was now draped in was new, close to what a moon blessed would wear if it wasn't for the golden trim.

"Because you're going on royal procession silly. The king ordered it; I imagine it's to ensure that the people know who you belong to. No blessed alive is allowed to wear this colour except for King Silas."

Blossom frowned as the words sank in, hunching in on himself in discomfort. His first trip outside the palace walls in over a decade and he'd be doing it dressed as the king's pet. He figured that he shouldn't be surprised by this but it did little to prevent the sour feeling in his stomach. "No one is allowed to wear my colours either." He said help-lessly, plucking at the sleeve of the new robe in frustration. The only reason why no one was allowed to wear his colours was because no one had ever found another nature blessed child, so he knew it was a moot point even as he spoke. He vaguely remembered being dressed in this kind of blue robe for the first two years of his stay in the palace until an appropriate colour had been decided upon, but he was in no hurry to return to that system.

"And I'm sure that's something that the king is absolutely thrilled about." Emma said sarcastically as she gently ushered him towards the door. "It's only for today Blossom, so try not to let it affect you too much and try to enjoy yourself okay? If you ask me, you should be wearing Asher's colours instead but that's another conversation entirely."

⌘

After dawdling a while longer in the palace hallways Blossom made it to the courtyard just as the horses were being saddled. The large stone expanse already so crowded with nobles, steeds, and stable hands that he had to take a longer route than normal to get to where his and Asher's horses stood. Asher was already astride his mount, a black behemoth named Coal, who would have been intimidating if Blossom wasn't already well versed with how much of a soft touch the horse was. Beside him stood Blossom's own horse, moving skittishly from side to side as the courtyard continued to fill with more and more people. She was Coal's sister, a sandy coloured mare that Blossom had named Daffodil when he had been gifted her as a child. The prince had mocked him relentlessly for it as they were growing up, so Blossom had kept the name just to spite him. Asher gave him a cursory nod as he made his way towards the prince, his all-black attire causing his legs to almost meld with Coal's body.

"Just a second there boy." A familiar boom rose from behind him causing Blossom to flinch visibly, his hand resting on the pommel of his saddle.

"Yes, your majesty?" He heard Asher snort from behind him at his formality as the king strode over.

"I didn't see you at the hearth this morning. Who's blessing did you last take?"

Blossom pulled his shoulders back, trying to minimise the difference between their heights but still falling a few inches short. One of his many gripes growing up had been that his Castillan heritage meant that he was always one of the shortest men in any group. This had not been helped by the fact that he was always surrounded by Vaten natives who all seemed to be 6 foot at a minimum. He looked up into the king's amber eyes and said with as stable a voice as he could. "Water's blessing your majesty."

The king sneered at the word. "Water's blessing. A lot of good that will do against anything. I should have known that you'd show up here with some simpering blessing like that." He snapped his fingers and four servants approached through the crowd carrying a large cauldron filled with burning coal. Coal bought directly from the king's hearth no doubt.

King Silas was fire blessed, a designation denoted by his bright red hair and amber eyes, and he staunchly believed that no other blessing carried enough power to be of much use. A belief that he made sure to remind Blossom of at every opportunity.

Blossom stared at the cauldron numbly for a moment as the mounted nobles watched on in curiosity. He was trying to think up a suitable excuse to stop himself from having to take Fire's blessing when the king suddenly grabbed a fistful of his sleeve and dragged him forward, causing him to almost stumble into the cauldron itself.

"Take it." The king commanded, stepping back and crossing his arms, using his broader frame to loom threateningly over Blossom.

Blossom sent a withering look his way before pushing up his sleeves and thrusting his hands into the flames. He felt his fingers close around a few pieces of coal as Fire's blessing surged through him, crushing the embers as his body warmed. The power raged violently through his veins, the glow emanating from his hair and eyes tinged with orange, giving off the illusion that he was burning from within. When he could stand no more he staggered backwards with a gasp, finding his feet just in time to prevent himself from falling.

"Nothing like it is there boy?" The king crowed, slapping him heartily on the back.

Blossom shook his head mutely, trying to ignore the way Fire's blessing roiled in his stomach as he coughed, a small plume of smoke gusting out of his mouth at the action. He turned back to his horse and looked up to see Asher gazing at him in concern, his hand fisted in the material of his shirt just above his heart. Blossom mounted Daffodil in silence, hoping that the prince would remain mute whilst the power settled down. He hated taking Fire's blessing, especially when it was from the fire that dwelled within the king's hearth, it was violent and worked on anger.

The king shouted a command once he had mounted his own steed at the head of the group of riders and the procession moved off. As Blossom waited for the people in front of him to move, he felt a hand grasp his and looked over as Asher leaned towards him.

"Is it always this painful?" He whispered.

"Fire is." Blossom replied shortly. He kicked his horse into a slow walk without another word, the movement pulling his wrist out of Asher's grip.

⌘

Asher stared after Blossom for a few seconds until the man behind him spurred him on to move. Kicking Coal into a trot he soon grew level again with his oldest friend, the world's only nature blessed. The man who had saved his life when they were both children, all those years ago. The man he knew that he would marry one day regardless of what Blossom said. The man he had been in love with for years. The man whose pain and suffering were currently radiating through his own chest so strongly he almost couldn't breathe.

"You said that this was only temporary right?" He asked as he pulled level with Blossom, rubbing a fist into his chest, trying to sooth the burning that had started the second Blossom had stuck his hands into that flaming cauldron.

Blossom gave him a sideways glance. "Yeah, don't worry. *You* won't have to feel this for much longer." He placed extra stress on the word 'you' and Asher dropped his hand as guilt quickly replaced the burn. He saw the side of Blossom's lip quirk and frowned.

"Oh, so it goes both ways huh?"

"I don't know what you mean." The lip quirk had turned into a full smile, the one that lit up Blossom's entire face. The one he'd been seeing less and less as the years went on.

"Don't do that." Asher said, turning away from him, trying to ignore the warmth that had filled his chest. Warmth that felt suspiciously like mirth that wasn't his.

"Do what?"

Asher sighed; on the one hand he'd been happy when he'd realised that he'd been experiencing Blossom's feelings. Especially the random rushes of love he got when Blossom looked at him, the fluttering of butterflies in his stomach when he touched him. On the other hand, it was making the discrepancies between what Blossom felt and what he said incredibly obvious, and it was really beginning to confuse and annoy him.

"Be all cute like that when I'm still mad at you."

Blossom's smile dimmed slightly but that didn't do anything to change Asher's opinion because now he had a pleasant blush adorning his lovely caramel skin.

They rode in silence for a while, leaving the main palace grounds behind and heading into the wilder hunting woods at the bottom of the hill. The woods hid the towering stone wall that separated the palace from the rest of the kingdom from normal view. If you weren't following the well-treaded road that split the woods in two you could spend hours riding or walking through them before catching even a glimpse of the royal ring. After just over an hour of gentle riding the trees began to thin, and the parade came to a halt before a sweeping stone gateway. An ornate wooden door emblazoned with the royal seal and inlaid with large gems representing each of the blessings beginning to creak open as they approached.

Asher heard Blossom take a deep breath and felt a surge of unfamiliar nerves flutter through his chest. "Are you okay?" He asked as Blossom stared at the slowly opening gateway.

"I haven't been through this gate since I was eight." Blossom said, not taking his eyes off of the view now being revealed to him.

Asher looked back at the gate, his eyes following the sweeping line of the palace walls until it disappeared beyond sight as realisation dawned. "Blessings be." He whispered. He'd only ever seen the wall as a glorified garden fence, something that you walked past when leaving your home. Only now, feeling the awe and apprehension seeping through whatever power continued to linger between them, could he see it for what it really was, a way to keep them separated from the rest of his people.

The parade began to move off and Asher found himself reaching for Blossom's hand again. Surprisingly Blossom didn't pull away this time, instead he squeezed Asher's fingers as they rode under the gateway and into Kilan, the capital city.

At the sight of the royal procession a deafening cheer rose through the crowded streets of the city. As they made their way to the parade route Asher found himself paying more attention to Blossom's awe-struck face than the adoring crowds.

## Chapter 4

Blossom couldn't remember the last time that he had been outside the royal walls, but he could vividly remember the last time that he had stood in front of the towering wooden gate. He had been ten years old, his tiny frame dwarfed by the sweeping stone wall as he stared up at the shining gems embedded in the door. Tears streaming down his face as his aching body heaved with sobs, his hastily packed satchel lying forgotten at his feet as he pounded on the wood begging to be allowed through.

It had been summertime and the weather had been warm, the dirt of the road dry and dusty as he finally collapsed to his knees. Giving up on getting any answer from the other side of the door he had cried in the walls shadow until the sound of hooves reached his ears. Sniffling he had looked up to see queen Lila, silhouetted in the sunlight above him. That was how he most often remembered her, a large comforting presence, her kind smile shadowed by the radiance of the sun.

"My darling boy, what's bought you so far out here?" She'd asked, scooping him up into her arms and placing him before her in the saddle.

"I don't want to go back." He'd whispered, looking down at the raw pink skin on the palms of his hands. Blisters and burns marring the soft skin. "I want to go home."

"Okay, let's go home." Lila had responded after giving him a strong hug. Turning her horse back towards the palace, she bent down and retrieved his satchel. "Asher has been searching for you for hours. He'll be so happy to know that you're safe."

Too tired and too small to argue Blossom had simply looked longingly at the closed gate. As it grew smaller the further away they moved, he wondered if he would ever again see what lay on the other side.

⌘

The city of Kilan was a riot of noise and colour, already a bustling cacophony of movement on any normal day the population had almost doubled in readiness for the first royal procession of the year. The streets had been strung with multicoloured banners and bunting, the side-alleys and squares that split from the main king's road filled with stalls selling mementoes and hot food. The gathering crowds of excited citizens occupied every spare space along the road, holding up flags and banners emblazoned with their families' blessings. Blossom squeezed Asher's fingers again, trying not to be too overwhelmed by the sheer number of people crowding the streets, all of them cheering and shouting as they passed.

As they slowly made their way down the pre-marked parade route, the king waved regally at the head of the procession. Asher followed his father's lead and also began waving and nodding, seeming to take great pleasure in the renewed excitement that it seemed to cause the onlookers.

"Should I be doing that too?" Blossom asked.

"I'm sure they'll love it if you do, most people are here to catch a glimpse of you anyway." Asher smiled at him warmly and Blossom could feel the other man's pride swelling in his own chest.

Swallowing down his apprehension Blossom tried out a wave, a genuine smile splitting his face seconds later when a group of young blessed waved back at him emphatically. They continued to traverse the city in this manner, always heading in the general direction of the second kingdom wall. As they rode through the slowly thinning crowds of bright colours Blossom's eyes homed in on a group of people dressed in very familiar robes.

"Asher." He hissed, reaching across the gap between them and tugging on the prince's hand. Asher leant towards him as they pulled level with the group, who all promptly bowed towards them, their pink locks on full display. "There are 5 nature blessed here. No one told me that there were any more. Why haven't they been brought to the palace?"

The prince glanced over his shoulder at the group as they continued to ride and frowned as he recognised the sigil on their robes. Stitched into the back of the pink robe was a tree in full bloom, its roots rising up to join its branches, forming a full circle of one plant. "They're not nature blessed Blossom."

"Yes they are, they have natures spring colour." Blossom gestured to his own hair, frowning when Asher smiled indulgently at him.

"Just because they have the same hair colour as you doesn't mean that they're nature blessed."

Blossom looked back at the group in confusion, locking eyes with one of the younger members before they all bowed again when they noticed him watching them. The young boy had had bright blue eyes. "Wait, how is that possible?"

"They dye their hair." Asher said with a shrug as though it was the most common thing in the world.

"Why?" Blossom couldn't think of a single reason why anyone would pretend to be nature blessed; they'd be found out as soon as someone asked for a blessing from them.

"They're Blossomites."

Blossom blinked, growing more confused by the second. "They're what?"

Asher sat up straighter in his saddle, no longer waving as he became suddenly uncomfortable. "There is a growing movement of people in the kingdom that believe that the appearance of a nature blessed child is a sign from the blessers."

Blossom tilted his head to the side as he considered this. "A sign of what?"

Asher sighed. "They believe that you are the blessers chosen one. A child born not of other people but of the blessers themselves, and that you have been sent to us to bring about a new age. They believe that your ability to receive blessings from each deity and that my..." The prince took a breath. "...my cursed state shows that the reign of the royal family is at an end and that you and those that follow you should be in control."

Blossom hummed in thought, dismissing the theory instantly, but looking at the king's back as they continued to ride another thought occurred to him. "How long have these people been saying this?"

Asher shrugged again. "A few years, I think. I honestly don't know all that much about it beyond what I told you. They're not a big group and most people don't believe what they say so don't go getting a big head about it."

Blossom smiled at him briefly. "Wouldn't dream of it."

If the group had only been around for a few years then that didn't explain the king's attitude towards him, although it probably didn't help.

The crowd continued to thin as they reached the outskirts of the capital city. The city of Kilan was also surrounded by a sweeping stone wall. The secondary kingdom wall was made out of dark fired stone instead of the white quartz of the royal ring, but it was no less intimidating in its size and scale. The wooden door set into this wall was plain, its only defining features being the heavy deadbolts and small guard door set into the bottom. The guard door opened as they approached and a city guard in bright red livery appeared through it, having been summoned by some lookout atop the wall. He gave the king a sharp salute before turning to a large lever set into the ground. He grabbed the handle of the lever and, heaving his body weight behind it, pushed it forward.

Blossom watched as the bolts on the gate began to move, he had seen similar counter-weight bolts back at the palace but never on this scale before and the door swung open on silent hinges a moment later. Blossom knew that the land beyond the wall was much more sparsely populated, filled predominantly with small farming villages separated by large swathes of rich fertile land. Not that Blossom had ever seen it in person, but he remembered from the lessons that Emma had given him as a child.

They rode slowly through worn dirt tracks as the sun continued to climb into the sky. At about midday, after traveling through 3 villages, each time stopping briefly whilst the king made short speeches and presented his son and Blossom to the few residents, they came to a halt.

At first Blossom couldn't see any reason for them to stop, it seemed to him that the king had halted them at a random point in the road but as they pulled off of the path and down a much less travelled track, he could hear the sound of voices close by. They crested a small hill and he found himself looking down into a grassy clearing. Before them stood a large tent in the king's colours, besides which a long wooden table ladened with food and drinks had been set up.

A crowd of people were gathered at the periphery of the camp-ground, and they all erupted with cheers as the royal procession arrived. Blossom looked over at Asher in a silent question.

"There's no way to visit all of the southern villages in one day, and my father didn't want all of us to be away from the palace for that long. So he sent out word that those who would want to see us should come here."

Blossom looked back at the crowd, there had to be at least a hundred people in the field, if not more. "Is the king going to hold an audience with all of them?" He asked in disbelief, that would surely take a day at least and the sun was already past its peak.

Asher snorted in response and dismounted his horse. "Hardly. This isn't a tour to hear from the masses."

Blossom frowned as he dismounted as well, handing his reins to a nearby servant. "Then what is it for? I thought we were here so that you could learn first-hand how a king rules his people. Isn't that why you've been away so often lately?" He hurried after Asher, pausing just before the prince turned to look at him as he felt a sudden jolt of bitterness from him.

"Blossom you can be really naïve sometimes." Asher said with a sigh.

Blossom bristled at the comment but deflated just as quickly when Asher stepped close to him and plucked at his sleeve, dragging his attention back to the royal colours that he was draped in.

"Obviously we're here to show you off, my father thought it was time for the people to see you."

The nature blessed frowned, was the prince jealous that Blossom was to be paraded around as some kind of favoured pet?

As if he could read Blossom's thoughts Asher pulled him close and whispered in his ear. "I just wish that we were being presented as a pair, not as two separate objects owned by my father. The people expect it." He added the bit at the end as Blossom reddened, panic rising in him at the thought of having to deal with another confession so soon after this morning's outburst.

"You wish I was in black." He said before he could stop himself, instantly regretting his words as Asher smiled. He should have just brushed Asher off, it was the safest thing to do, especially with the king striding towards them.

"Always." Asher responded simply and Blossom hated how easy it was for the prince to speak about his feelings. How he never seemed to have to second guess them or worry how his declarations may anger others. "But I guess that can wait until our wedding day." He added, taking a step back.

"Come now you two, you are keeping the crowd waiting." King Silas practically shouted as he reached them. Blossom flinched inwardly as the king indelicately grabbed hold of his upper arm, steering him towards the gathered onlookers with an unnecessarily tight grip. He led them to the tent where the crowd were notably better dressed, his hold on Blossom remaining unforgivingly tight. "Lords and Ladies, please allow me to introduce my son and heir Prince Asher, and the royal blesser."

Blossom had to physically fight with himself to not roll his eyes, of course the king would only deign to speak to the nobility, many of whom already knew him from their time at court, so the introduction was completely pointless. As Silas finally let go of him and fell into conversation with the nobles, he allowed his eyes to wander back to the crowd of peasants. He smiled as he spotted a small golden haired child hovering at the edges of the glen. He placed a hand on Asher's arm and inclined his head towards the visitor in an unspoken communication of where he was going. The prince nodded and Blossom made his way over to the little girl, who was now joined by a woman that he assumed must be her mother.

"Good day sun child." He said by way of greeting, crouching in front of her. "Good day." He said again with a nod to the woman.

"Good day your grace. I apologise, Sola only wanted to see you. You needn't have worried yourself about coming to greet us."

"Nonsense." Blossom replied with a warm smile before turning his attention back to the child. "It is fortunate that we should meet now as it appears that you will be joining my classroom soon. How old are you Sola?"

"5." She whispered shyly. "But I'm nearly 6."

Blossom's grin widened. "So I'll see you again in a few years when you come to the palace."

Sola nodded but a cough caused him to look away from her and up at the woman, who was looking down at him pleadingly. "Your grace, may I speak with you?"

Furrowing his brow in confusion Blossom stood. "Of course, what troubles you? Forgive me I don't believe I know your name. And please don't call me your grace, I am not royalty."

The woman shifted uncomfortably, looking from Sola to Blossom and back again. "I am Liza your grace, sorry I mean master Blossom. It's just that I'm afraid that Sola cannot come to the palace to train with you at your school. We are not rich and do not have the money to send her or buy her the supplies that she will need."

Blossom's mouth formed a small 'oh' in realisation before his previous smile returned. "My good woman, we supply everything that she will need. The future of all of our blessed children is in the kingdoms interest so the kingdom will provide for them. Sola will have room and board with other blessed children her age, as well as her deities' robes at no cost to you. And if you are worried about the travel then I will send one of the carriages to pick her up. We often send carriages to those in the further reaches, she would not be travelling alone."

Blossom forced himself to stop talking as Liza looked a bit stunned at the information, he had a tendency to ramble excitedly when it came to the blessing school. He made a mental note to ask Asher why this information wasn't readily available when they returned to the palace.

"So I can go to the palace?" Sola asked, gazing up at her mother hopefully.

"Yes my darling, I guess you can." Liza's eyes were glistening as she smiled down at her daughter, taking hold of her hand and giving it a squeeze.

Blossom was about to bid his farewells with a smile when the young girl addressed him again. "Why is your name Blossom?"

Her mother shushed her, but Blossom simply smiled. "It's okay. I understand that my name is unusual in this kingdom. You see Sola where I come from parents name their children after the blessings that nature has laid on them. But when I was born my mother didn't know what to make of me." He crouched so that he was eye level with her again. "No one had ever heard of a child being born with pink hair before. She knew that I must be blessed and as I was born during the spring season with the blossoms in bloom, she decided to call me after them."

"She thought that you were blessed by Spring?" Sola asked.

"Or the trees." He responded.

Sola looked pensive for a moment before speaking again. "Why are you dressed like the king? I thought that you had special colours."

Blossom's smile faded a bit at the reminder, but he tried to keep his voice upbeat as he responded. "Usually I do, but this is a special occasion. It is my first trip outside of the palace in a long time and the king wanted to make sure that everyone knew which house I was a part of. He's very proud of me you see, and he wanted others to know that." The lie felt bitter on his tongue, but he managed to smile throughout.

The little girl looked confused. "But I thought that you were prince Asher's husband. You should be wearing black then."

Blossom chuckled in an attempt to hide his blush and the unease suddenly knotting his stomach. Why were so many people bringing up Asher's colour today? "We are not married yet." He said simply, standing back up to his full height.

"But..."

"Hush now Sola, we've taken enough of master Blossom's time."

Just as he was about to respond Blossom felt a presence behind him and Liza and Sola fell into a bow.

"Your majesty." Liza said with a reverent whisper and Blossom felt his heart sink, sure that the king had made his way over to admonish him.

The gentle hand at the small of his back banished that idea but caused him to tense up for a different reason.

"Ladies." Asher said with a charming smile, his arm snaking further around Blossom's waist as he spoke. "I'm so sorry but I need to steal Blossom away for a moment."

Liza didn't respond beyond continuing to bow as Asher steered Blossom away.

"Mr prince sir?" Sola pipped up just as they were beginning to walk away.

Asher turned back with an indulgent smile, and Blossom could tell that he was trying not to laugh as Liza shushed her daughter again. "Yes little one?"

Sola suddenly seemed unsure of herself now that Asher was looking at her and scuffed at the floor with her shoe.

Asher knelt in front of her in much the same way that Blossom had only moments before. "It's okay, what was it you were going to say?" He asked, his voice gentle and soothing.

Sola seemed to be chewing on the inside of her cheek as she gathered up the courage to speak before finally blurting out. "You should marry master Blossom soon; he doesn't want to be in the king's colours."

Blossom felt his face heat up as Asher smirked at him from where he was kneeling.

"Don't worry little one, the next time you see master Blossom we will be married, I promise." Asher said with complete sincerity. He stood back up again and nodded at Liza before turning towards Blossom and beginning to lead him back towards the gathered nobles, his hand continuing to rest like a brand on his lower back.

"Now you'll have to marry me or else make me a liar." Asher whispered as they walked, mirth making his words light.

"We must have one of the guards or servants speak with her before we leave. Her daughter requires one of the carriages to get to the palace and she is almost of an age to join my classroom." Blossom said as Sola waved at their retreating backs, pointedly ignoring the prince's remark.

Asher nodded, the indulgent smile still on his face as he said. "I do love how invested you are in every blessed child that you meet. It makes me dream of the day when I can see you interacting with our own child."

Blossom felt his insides go briefly cold at the words, especially when he caught the king's eye. He gave a long-suffering sigh. "Asher please." Blossom pinched the bridge of his nose as the prince raised an eyebrow at him in question. "Let's not do this today."

He tensed up as Silas strode over to them, the intense anger in the king's gaze putting him instantly on guard. He silently begged Asher to drop his hand and hoped helplessly that Silas hadn't heard what the prince had just said or any of the conversation that they'd had with Sola.

"Come with me boy. There are people that you should meet." He said loudly, his voice jovial enough that many of the people gathered would have been tricked into believing that he was simply being friendly. But Blossom had witnessed this charade far too many times to be taken in by it and he tensed even more as the king steered him away from Asher with an arm wrapped tightly around his shoulders. It was only through years of practice that Blossom was able to keep from reacting physically to the searing heat shooting across his shoulder blades, invisible flames stabbing at him where Silas' fingers dug into his upper arm. He didn't need to look to know that he'd end this day with yet another series of welts in the shape of hands or fingers.

Blossom only vaguely paid attention to the names and faces being paraded in front of him as Silas kept a firm grip on his shoulders. The king looked completely at ease as he chatted with various lords and ladies from the outer towns, dropping his arm only when they reached the feast table. Just as Blossom thought that he could relax

Silas suddenly pressed a finger into the centre of his back, sending one last pulse of fire through his heart, stirring up the well of power that Blossom had managed to subdue on the ride and causing him to gasp audibly.

"Are you okay?" Asher asked in a whisper once they were seated. "It felt like father's power activated yours or something." The prince reached out to place a hand on his shoulder in comfort.

"I'm fine, just don't touch me please." Blossom replied, holding out a hand before him as though to push Asher away.

The prince's hand fell to his side, hurt flashing across his face and through Blossom's chest as he turned away. Asher didn't make another attempt to touch him or engage him in conversation, but he continued to send him worried looks as the feat wore on.

Blossom stared resolutely at his plate for the entire feast, though he didn't touch anything put in front of him. The day had been looking up when they'd first arrived, but this was closer to what he'd come to expect over the years, and he admonished himself for lowering his guard. He played the part of a dutiful and well-behaved pet as Silas bragged and brayed beside him, trying not to let Fire's blessing explode out of him as his shoulders continued to throb.

## Chapter 5

The rest of the day passed in a blur as Blossom drew into himself. He wasn't asked to do much, of which he was thankful and the few nobles that tried to talk to him seemed appeased by his simple nods. Asher also didn't attempt to talk or touch him again which Blossom was also grateful for as he spent the ride home focusing on their bond. Using gentle pulses of Fire's blessing he burned away at the breach, feeling himself hollowing out as Asher's emotions left him.

He hadn't realised how cold he'd been since he'd severed their connection all those years ago, but he figured that if he had survived with it for this long then he could live like that again. He could put up with a little emotional distance to keep Asher close to him. Emma's words from earlier that morning returned to him unbidden.

*Your spirits are so resonant that continuing to reject him like this is going to destroy you.*

He hunched his shoulders and stared resolutely at Daffodil's back. He knew that she was right, their disconnect was already allowing the death mark to get stronger. But as he glanced briefly at Asher, the prince's features sharp in the glow of the setting sun, the wrench in his gut told him that he wasn't yet strong enough to allow that connection to open again.

⌘

10 years earlier

"Here we are darling. Home." Lila said softly as she pulled her mount to a stop.

Blossom looked around wearily. He had thought that the queen would take him all the way back to the palace, but she had stopped just outside the inner ring. He was about to ask her why they had stopped when a small, black-haired boy appeared from one of the archways.

"You found him." Asher cried happily, running up to his mother's horse.

"Indeed my little prince, safe and sound just like I said he would be."

Blossom felt strong but gentle hands under his armpits, just before he was lifted from the horse and deposited almost directly into Asher's arms.

"Here you go. One little flower for one little prince."

Blossom looked back up at Queen Lila, her features once again obscured by the descending sun behind her.

"I have to go and speak with the king, you two go and play. Try to stay out of trouble."

He felt a hand on his arm and turned just as Asher bumped their foreheads together.

"Where were you? I couldn't find you." The prince asked quietly.

Blossom shrugged by way of an answer, not sure if he should tell Asher why he had been at the palace gate.

"You hurt?" Asher continued, looking down at Blossom blistered palms.

Blossom shook his head, nudging Asher with the movement.

The prince didn't seem convinced but after a moment of comparing his own palm to Blossom's he relented. "Guess not." He said before brightening considerably and tugging Blossom in the direction of the grassy hill that led down to the blessing lake. "Come on. The rabbits have had their babies and they're out of the burrows now."

⌘

As the sun began to sink behind the mountains that surrounded the kingdom, the royal procession once again passed through both sets of wooden doors. Their return received far less celebration than their departure as many people had already retired to their homes with the lengthening of the day. Soon enough the palace was looming ahead of them, an imposing silhouette on the surrounding landscape, it's spires and battlements a holdover from more violent times.

Entering the courtyard, the now tired horses came to a stop, their coats wet and steaming from exertion. Blossom slid down from

Daffodil's back, patting her flank absently before she was led away by one of the stable hands. He took a deep breath to steel himself and gather his nerves. As much as he didn't want to, he needed to speak with the king about the blessed children that he watched over. He had to check that Sola's mother's ignorance was an outlier.

As he made to leave the courtyard Asher stepped in front of him, appearing out of the darkness like a shadow. Blossom stopped, staring at the prince's chest, not able to meet his eyes yet, as he shifted from foot to foot.

"You were right."

"About what?"

"The side effects. I can't feel what you feel anymore."

Blossom hummed in agreement but didn't say anything more as he sidestepped around Asher and instead followed the king out of the courtyard. "Your majesty, can I speak with you?"

The king looked over his shoulder as he walked, but not at Blossom, past him to where Asher was still stood. The prince had his back to them both, his broad shoulders slumped after Blossom's brush off. Silas smiled at him, but it didn't reach his eyes. "Certainly, come with me. We will speak by the hearth."

That caused Blossom to halt briefly, his fists clenching at his sides. Nothing good ever happened around that hearth. He sighed and continued to follow the king, after Asher's speech about children this afternoon he would have been summoned to that room sooner rather than later anyway. He travelled the familiar halls of the palace, always trailing a few steps behind the king like a ghost. They walked past the throne room where he had first met Asher, through the grand hall where both he and Asher had had their coming-of-age celebrations and into the dark, foreboding room where he'd been bought far too many times over the years.

Unlike every other room in the palace, which was practically bathed in opulence, the hearth chamber was sparsely decorated. The walls were a dark bare stone stained black with soot. The only piece of furniture was a worn blue chair, that must at one time have looked regal but now sat threadbare and sad by the fire. The majority of the room was taken up by a large stone fireplace, the mantle standing a good 3 inches higher than Blossom's head it consumed almost one whole wall. The king's hearth.

It had first been commissioned and lit by one of Silas' mothers a year after he had been born. His orange eyes inspiring her to provide him with a constant well of power. He'd been the first fire blessed of the royal line, and as such there had been no permanent dwelling for Fire's blessing within the palace grounds as there had been with the others. Such as the blessing lake for Water's blessing and the stepped gardens for Earth's blessing.

"Well, well, well. This is the first time that you've sought out a teaching." Silas said, sitting down in the chair and holding his hands over the flames crackling in the fireplace as if he wanted to warm them. The unnatural glow of his eyes and the fire that wound up his arms belied that.

"I...uh..." Blossom swallowed. "I didn't."

The king shot him a warning look. "Spit it out boy."

Blossom felt himself stiffen at the commanding tone, standing to attention the same as any of the guards would have. "I want to ask what it is that we are doing to ensure that all blessed children can come and learn here. I met a mother in the glen today who didn't know that we would care for her child. She thought that her daughter would have to miss out on learning how to properly harness her powers because they were poor." His words came out rushed in his hurry to get this conversation over with and leave the room.

The king laughed as though Blossom had said something particularly funny. "The ones who need to know already know."

"What are you saying?" Blossom asked, shifting uncomfortably in the increasingly warm room. The king had begun to radiate heat now as he drank in Fire's blessing as easily as breathing.

"Did you really think that we bring every peasant that happens to be blessed into the palace? What is that girl going to do once she learns how to ask for and use her blessing? Help her family's crops grow?" He laughed again, the words sneering on his tongue.

Blossom couldn't see anything funny in what was being said. "But..."

"Enough." Silas barked, standing back up suddenly and causing Blossom to stumble back in worry. "There is a lesson to be taught here and it isn't the irrelevance of a farmer's daughter. Come here." He held out a hand towards Blossom, the gesture almost comically gentle considering the flames that continued to dance over his skin.

Blossom took a deep breath, trying to decide whether to push the point or not. Deciding to drop it for now and just get his punishment over with, he clenched his fists to try and stop them from shaking and stepped forward.

## Chapter 6

Blossom slammed the door to his bedroom behind him, leaning back against the wood as his breath escaped him in shallow gasps. He'd already been close to hyperventilating upon leaving the hearth room and the sprint to his own room had finally sent him over the edge. He could feel his heart pounding in his chest, his blood rushing through his ears, and the recently re-ignited Fire's blessing roiling violently in his gut. He raised a hand to his forehead as a painful sob escaped his throat, he could feel his hand trembling and pushed his palm harder against his head as he continued to dissolve into panicked sobs.

He'd gotten past this, he thought angrily, raising his other hand to his head also and tugging roughly at his hair. For the past two years he'd endured his punishments without ending up like this and he hated that he could picture the king's satisfaction if he realised just how badly today had affected him.

When he opened his eyes again, his vision fuzzy through the build-up of tears, he stared blankly at the material of his sleeve as it hung directly in front of him. As he took in the dark blue and golden silk draped over him his panic was overcome with anger and revulsion. He pushed himself away from the door, tearing his robe off and flinging it onto the bed with a scream, unable to stand it touching his skin anymore. Standing now in only his brown breeches he ran his hands roughly through his hair as he screamed again, anger and sadness mixing with the ever-present fear that dwelled in the back of his mind.

He looked around his room with what seemed like new eyes, taking in the dark blue bedcovers and drapes to the golden phoenix symbol hanging over his door. The mark of the king's ownership was everywhere. He couldn't remember ever feeling this disgusted with the hand that the blessers had dealt him, like his skin was crawling, the buzz of power beneath his skin replaced with unclean bugs. He felt Fire's blessing rising in his lungs and clenched his fists, his nails biting into the soft flesh of his palms. If the king was so intent on him utilising Fire's blessing then so be it, he'd show him what he thought of this violent power.

He let out another loud scream as he thrust his hands forwards, flames leaping from his fingers and curling around the drapes hanging from his bedposts. He let the blessing consume him, sending all of his power into the flames as his eyes blazed and his skin burned until, like a cup emptying itself of the last few drops of water, it ran out.

Ever since his first blessing, Blossom had always maintained a small well of power. Topping it up with each subsequent blessing until he had a mix of every deity's power. Unable to separate them from each other unless he filled himself up with a specific blessing, as he had done today. As he came back to himself, his senses slowly returning as though he was waking from a dream, the yawning emptiness inside of him pitched him forward and he fell to his knees. He watched with a detached numbness as the flames continued to spread, catching now onto the curtains and rugs, trying to catch his own breath as the room filled with smoke.

"Blossom?" A pounding sounded from behind the door, a vaguely familiar woman's voice reaching his ears. "Blossom, sweetheart." The voice was closer now and he felt small but firm hands on his shoulders. "Come on petal."

He was pulled to his feet in a sort of trance and bodily dragged out of the burning room, where he vaguely registered the press of multiple bodies and voices but couldn't distinguish anything concrete. That was until a familiar dark shadow crouched down in front of him.

"Blossom? Blossom look at me. Are you hurt?"

Blossom simply stared vacantly at Asher who was currently haloed by the flames behind him. He couldn't answer, everything felt too heavy to move, his arms lying uselessly on the floor by his side, his tongue stuck sluggishly to the roof of his mouth.

"Your majesty, the water blessed need to get in there to put out the fire."

Blossom didn't know who spoke, too focused on Asher's concerned face. Why did he look so worried? It wasn't like his own blessing could hurt him, yeah sure he was currently paralysed on the floor but a quick sleep would fix that. The prince looked over at someone to his left just as Blossom felt his eyes beginning to shut, the effort of keeping his eyelids open suddenly too much to deal with. "Okay. I need to get Blossom out of here."

"Your majesty, we need to question him this is..."

"No." The prince snapped, taking off the riding coat that he was still wearing and placing it over Blossom's shoulders.

"But your majesty..."

"I said no. I'm taking him away from here, can't you see that he's burnt? Emma keep an eye on them and retrieve anything personal that didn't burn. Set up a place for him to sleep tonight down the hall, we'll figure something more permanent out later."

Blossom didn't hear Emma's response as Asher lifted him to his feet and began to guide him down the hallway, people rushing past them in a blur as they seemed to move in slow motion. He leant his full weight against Asher as the prince practically carried him through the palace.

"Blossom I need you to talk to me. Are you hurt?" Despite being right next to him Asher's voice seemed to be coming from underwater and that thought seemed to wake something in his brain.

"Lake." He breathed, his voice coming out in a rasp.

"What?"

"Take me to the lake."

A hand gently cupped his cheek and tilted his head up until he was looking into Asher's concerned eyes. Asher looked at him silently for a moment, his dark eyes scanning his face intently as Blossom focused on figuring out if it was possible to swallow without any saliva. "Okay." He said finally, slinging one of Blossom's arms over his shoulder he changed direction and began leading him down the stairs and out of the palace.

The sun had set fully whilst Blossom had been with the king, and the grounds were bathed in cool moonlight as they made their way down the grass verge towards the Blessing Lake. Whilst you could see the lake from the palace it was a good 20-minute walk from the courtyard to the water and the pair made the walk in silence. Blossom's breathing begun to return to normal as the fresh evening air banished the last of the smoke from his lungs.

As they got closer to the water Blossom began to feel a tug in his chest, like the sudden emptiness inside of him was reaching for the power that lay in the lake. He pushed himself away from Asher even as the prince tried to hold onto him and staggered towards the lake. He knew how deep the lake was, had spent many a summer day swimming its depths with Asher when they were young, but right then as his bare feet touched the cold water, all he wanted to do was keep walking.

Taking a deep breath he walked a few more steps, until the water lapped at his middle before forcing himself to stop and holding out his hands. He gasped as Water's blessing rushed into him, tilting his head back in bliss as his heart began to slow and the burning sensation left behind by Fire's blessing ebbed. He opened his eyes, staring at the moon hanging above him. He didn't need Moon's blessing as well right now but as he looked, he felt the gentle surge of healing power pool in his gut. A large smile split his face; moon had never gifted a blessing without being asked before.

"Blossom?"

He turned at the quiet sound to find Asher stood on the shore, worry still clearly evident on his face. Blossom continued to smile at him, tension bleeding from his shoulders as Water's blessing continued to work through his body. As he slowly waded back out of the lake, water dripping from the ends of his borrowed coat he saw Asher sit down as though suddenly exhausted.

"What happened in there Blossom?" Asher asked once he'd drawn level with him, the slight slop making it so that Asher didn't have to crane his neck too far to look at him.

Blossom shrugged, looking at a spot over Asher's shoulder, he always had a hard time lying straight to the prince's face. "Fire's blessing is volatile, I lost control. I didn't mean to..." He stopped when Asher stood back up and a hand once again cupped his cheek. Asher turned his face until Blossom looked him in the eye.

"Blossom, you've never done that before. You've never overexerted yourself like that. You were almost...empty."

Blossom pulled back with an exasperated snort. "So what, you feel my feelings for one day and think you know everything?"

"No that's not what I..."

"How do you know that I've never emptied myself before? What do you know of the blessings? What do you know of Fire's anger huh?"

Asher blinked at him, shocked at the sudden venom in Blossom's voice. Blossom knew he was snapping for no good reason, but the events of the evening had left him shaken and the feeling of Asher's concern was too much on top of everything else. He stopped ranting suddenly as a realisation dawned on him, he could feel Asher's concern, it was radiating off of him like a physical wave.

"What did you mean when you said that I was empty?"

Asher blinked again, stunned for a moment by Blossom's sudden turn around. "It was like you'd hollowed out or something. Like there was a space in you that shouldn't be there."

"But, but I fixed the breach. You shouldn't be able to feel me anymore."

"Is that really what you want to focus on right now? You tried to burn down your room, you got burnt in the process and you're worried about the fact that I could feel it?"

Blossom shook his head mutely, pushing at the connection to see which spot he had missed. He stepped back in shock as he felt his power rushing through the breaches that he'd spent so much of that afternoon closing again.

Asher clutched at his chest in surprise as he felt the power of Water's blessing pour into him. "What was that?" He gasped, almost losing his own footing.

Blossom couldn't answer right away, too shocked by what he'd done to say anything. Somehow the connection had gotten stronger, the holes in the barrier that he had erected growing even bigger than they had been before. At this rate it would only take a few more blessings before they were bonded fully.

"I can't...I can't fix this." He sunk to his knees on the soft ground, his shoulders throbbing painfully as he pictured what the king would say if he found out. What he'd do to him.

"Blossom? Blossom hey, listen to me." Asher knelt in front of him, rubbing his hands soothingly up and down Blossom's arms as though he was trying to warm him up. "That isn't important right now. You need to heal your burns. I don't know why you lost control; fuck I don't understand anything that has happened today, but I can feel how much they hurt."

Blossom took a few deep breaths, he could worry about how much Asher had felt later. The prince was right, he needed to heal himself. Maybe that was why Moon had given its blessing without him asking for it. He nodded and, with Asher's help, stood again. Asher stepped back as Blossom closed his eyes, pale white light emanating from him as he bought Moon's blessing to the surface, cooling his skin and slowing his pounding heart. He felt his shoulders relax and slowly opened his eyes again to see Asher watching him, a small smile on the prince's face.

"What?" He asked, although the rush of adoration that he could feel from Asher answered his question for him.

"You don't want me to say so I won't." Asher responded, stepping towards him. The prince tugged at the lapel of his borrowed coat. "Looks good on you though."

Blossom felt himself blush as he looked down, observing the black material draped over him for the first time. He found himself laughing but he couldn't quite put a finger on why. Asher joined him a moment later, the tension of the day and the previous night slipping away as they both dissolved into helpless giggles.

⌘

"Where am I going to sleep now?" Blossom asked, his gaze still fixed on the stars above them. They'd ended up lying on the grass as their laughter had subsided, the absurdity of the last 24 hours finally catching up with them.

"Emma should be fixing you up a place to sleep in one of the guest rooms for tonight. After that though, there's a spare room close to mine." Asher responded, looking at him out of the corner of his eye. "It would make more sense to move you into the family wing then to set up another permanent room in the guest wing."

"How much trouble do you think I'm going to be in? With the king I mean." Blossom asked, he had hoped to stay out of the hearth room for a while but couldn't see this going unpunished.

"Maybe some, but I don't think that father can be too mad at you. It only happened because you'd been training in Fire's blessing with him after all. I already thought it was a stupid idea to have a lesson when you were tired from riding, and I guess I was right."

Blossom pushed himself up onto his elbows, looking down at the prince in confusion. "What?"

"Well, that's why you joined him in the hearth room when we returned right?" Asher asked, turning his head slightly to look Blossom in the eye. "You always go there when you're taking lessons from him."

Blossom blinked, did Asher really believe that the king's 'teachings' were on how to better use Fire's blessing? He felt an odd sense of relief at the thought. So Asher genuinely had no idea what had been happening to him. He let out a short laugh. "Yeah, I guess he can't really blame me."

"Blossom." He looked back at the prince. "Is that not what's been going on?"

"No sure it is."

Asher sat upright; a frown etched onto his face. "You're lying to me." He said, his words a statement and not a question.

"No I'm not."

"Blossom, what are you not telling me?"

*A lot of things*, Blossom thought but instead he huffed and stood. "You're overthinking things Ash. Come on it's getting cold." He held out his hand to help Asher up and they began making their way back towards the palace.

## Chapter 7

Asher awoke just as the sun was beginning to peak through his curtains. With a groan he sat up and stretched, sighing when his back popped a few times. A heavy day of riding always left him feeling stiff the next morning and he'd had multiple back-to-back days of it now, so he was even more sore than usual. He made a mental note to spend some time in the training grounds after breakfast to loosen his muscles again.

The door to his bedroom opened unceremoniously a few moments later and Edwin, his valet, entered. "Good morning your majesty. Have you been awake long? You should have rung for me."

Asher smiled at the man, he was Emma's twin brother and whilst they shared the same coppery Castillan skin that was where their similarities ended. Edwin had inherited none of Emma's fire and force, instead he was consummately soft spoken and often rather nervous. Around everyone except his sister and the prince that is, Asher was the only one unrelated to him that didn't seem to make Edwin tremble.

"Don't worry about it, I've only just woken up. Tell me is Blossom awake yet? Or my father?"

Edwin was opening the dark curtains covering the door to Asher's balcony when he responded. "I have yet to see master Blossom, but my sister has gone to wake him. They have many preparations to make for the new group of blessed joining us next week I hear, so he will not be allowed to have a lie-in. Even though I told her that he should be resting after what happened last night."

Asher laughed at that, warmed by Edwin's small smile. "I'm sure Emma wouldn't let him sleep late even if there wasn't anything to do. You're probably right about him needing the rest though." He responded, slipping out of bed as Edwin finished opening all of the curtains and began to set out his clothes for the day. Even before he'd tried to burn down his room Asher had felt how worn-out Blossom had been.

"The king is already at breakfast, apparently we are expecting a surprise visitor, so he asked for an early wake-up call."

Asher blinked at the statement, taking the proffered loose trousers and stepping into them. "Who?" He asked but Edwin simply shrugged in response, helping him into a black cotton shirt. He wasn't surprised that Edwin was dressing him in training clothes, he'd been his valet for 10 years and often knew Asher's plans before the prince did. He was surprised by the news of a guest though, everyone who usually attended court had already been here for a few weeks, arriving as soon as the winter snows began to thaw.

"I cannot say, the other servants were only informed of it an hour or so ago and we were given no names, but they will be staying for a few days."

Asher let out a quiet 'huh'. He'd have to ask his father about it, along with the other question that had been niggling at him all night. Ever since Blossom had reacted so weirdly to the mention of his lessons with the king he'd been trying to figure out what else might be going on. There had been an uncomfortable undercurrent of fear that had rippled out from the blesser as soon as he'd bought it up. He knew that Blossom had always kept his distance from the king but he'd never realised that he was quite so afraid of him.

The king was the only one at the high table in the dining room when Asher entered, not that he was surprised, Blossom would be far too busy over the next few days to eat with them. What with preparing the blessers dormitories and clothing, ensuring that all who needed to be picked up were sent carriages and on top of that redecorating and settling into his new chambers. Asher was pretty sure he wouldn't see Blossom again until the welcoming ceremony at the beginning of the next week.

Asher couldn't help the smile or the warm feeling in his gut when he imagined Blossom's rooms being so close to his again. They had shared quarters as children, and it had been difficult for both of them when they'd been forced to sleep apart as they entered their teenage years. But his mother had insisted that it was unseemly for a betrothed couple to share rooms before they were wed and so they had been separated.

He raised his hand politely at a few of the courtiers as he passed, not wanting to get dragged into any gossip or petty squabbling before he'd had something to eat. This was his least favourite thing about being back at the palace, when he was out in the barracks or on a tour with his men he saw the real problems facing the people in his kingdom. The unrest in the outer reaches, the poverty of the lower villages beyond the secondary wall. Here there was just a bunch of spoilt nobles who held pointless grudges and stabbed each other in the backs over the smallest of things.

"Good morning father." Asher said, sitting to the right of the king and helping himself to a plateful of scrambled eggs and well-cooked sausages.

"And to you Asher." The king replied, looking up briefly from the letter in his hand to nod at him. "What is it I hear about the blesser being moved into the family wing?" He asked as he took a sip of steaming hot coffee, smiling briefly at a lady who had just entered as she curtseyed to him.

Asher rolled his eyes and held up his own cup to be filled. "Really father, I wish you'd just call him Blossom. He is going to be your son-in-law after all."

The king let out a 'harumph' and put the letter down. "Stupid name, we should have changed it when he came to us." He grouched.

"Be that as it may, it is his name and has been for the past 20 years so you might as well get used to it."

"Do you know how much you sound like your mother when you talk like that? She was all logic and rationality too."

Asher smiled proudly, Silas only spoke with such a gentle tone when speaking of the deceased queen. And whilst it hurt Asher to be reminded of her absence, it cheered him to know how much his father still loved and thought of her.

"But back to the topic at hand, he is not to be moved to the family wing. He is not part of the royal family." The king held up a hand as Asher went to interject. "Until the night of your wedding he will sleep in the guest wing with the other nobles and that is final."

"Fine." Asher huffed, shoving a forkful of egg into his mouth. "But you're not angry at him?" The king looked at him blankly. "For burning down his room?"

Silas let out a booming laugh and the hall fell silent for a moment as the courtiers waited to be included in the joke. "Of all the things that that boy does wrong, embracing the full power of Fire's blessing is not one of them. I burnt down many of these rooms in my youth, you have no idea the trouble I caused your grandmothers as I was learning."

Satisfied that Blossom wasn't going to be punished for last night he moved onto his next question. "So, I hear that we are going to have someone staying with us for a few days?"

The king nodded. "Yes, Lady Halberth and her daughter will be staying until the blessed arrive."

"Any particular reason?" Asher asked, wondering absently if his father had decided that it was time to re-marry. Lady Halberth was only a few years younger than the king and he vaguely remembered them getting along well the last time she had been at court.

"She is a noble lady who wishes to stay a while at court that is all." Silas responded, his tone suspiciously light. "Her daughter on the other hand is one of the rare water blessed. She was too young to come to court the last time Lady Halberth was here and too old to come and study when we opened the school, but she wishes to spend some time learning with the royal blesser. I expect you to make her feel very welcome and ensure that that boy devotes enough attention to her whilst she is here, I hear that she is quite beautiful."

Asher found himself rolling his eyes again, a habit that he'd fallen into the last time he'd had an extended stay at the palace. "Very subtle father. Blossom and I aren't even married yet and you're already trying to throw potential surrogates at us. Although I am surprised that you'd want a water blessed grandchild. Then again if Blossom were to be the sire, then the only thing that we could guarantee is that they'd be blessed. We don't know what deity would choose them."

The king slammed his, thankfully now empty, cup down. "Do not be vulgar." He snapped causing Asher to stare at him in shock and the hall to go quiet again. Not that the king seemed to care as he continued to speak loudly as though they were the only two in the room. "She is a guest in this house who has come to learn, not some brood mare for you to evaluate."

Asher didn't respond, too shocked by the sudden 180 that the conversation had taken. There had been no doubt about what the king had been insinuating so why was he suddenly denying it so angrily. He could feel his cheeks burning in shame as close to 100 eyes landed on him.

The king rose and loomed over him, suddenly very serious. "And your children with have royal blood. Do not let me hear you contemplating allowing that boy to father your heirs again." With that the king stormed out, closely followed by an entourage of chattering courtiers. The events of the morning left Asher so dazed that he didn't even realise that he hadn't gotten a chance to ask about Blossom's lessons until he had walked down to the training yard.

⌘

Asher soon found himself lost in the rhythm and routine of his usual knights training. He always felt more relaxed with a spear or sword in his hand, and far more at ease with the other knights and soldiers. He spent the morning sparring with the other people that he found on the grounds. His usual partner Lieutenant Kara Scaper wasn't sparring today having broken her arm during a jousting tournament a few weeks earlier, but she was still happy to shout advice and sometimes insults from the side-lines as he took on some of the newer recruits.

"Has your death mark reached your eyes or something? A novice could have blocked that swing." She shouted cheerfully as Asher took a hit to his shoulder.

"How much trouble did you get into with Emma when you came back with your arm like that?" He shouted back, grinning at the frown that settled over Kara's face. Emma was never very forgiving when her wife returned from tournaments injured.

"Not as much trouble as you'll be in if Blossom has to try and bless your head back onto your shoulders." She yelled, her good mood returning almost instantly.

He gritted his teeth and pushed back into the fight, ignoring the insults that his mentor continued to fling at him, knowing that she was only doing it to distract him. He had just gotten into a good flow when Edwin found him in a panic, panting and gesturing wildly back to the palace when he couldn't get enough breath to speak. As it turned out what Asher had thought of as only being an hour had ended up being three, he'd quickly lost track of time and the Lady Halberth was due any minute. Asher threw his sword to Kara, shouting an apology that he couldn't stay to help tidy up as he ran after his valet back to the palace. He knew how much trouble he'd get in for missing the welcome party.

A quick, cold bath later and he somehow made it to the palace steps just as an ornate silver carriage drew to a halt.

"You're cutting it close." Blossom whispered out of the side of his mouth, a polite smile plastered to his face, as Asher tried to catch his breath.

"Hello to you too." The prince responded as he straightened his black doublet and tried to smooth down his still damp hair. Blossom nodded at him with an amused glint in his eye. He reached up a glowing hand and ran it through the prince's hair, drying it with the warmth of Sun's blessing.

Asher was about to whisper a quick thanks but fell silent as the carriage door opened and an elegantly dressed woman began to walk up the palace steps, a delicate younger woman dressed in blue and silver robes following closely behind her.

"Your majesty." Lady Halberth curtsied lowly a few steps below the king. "My eternal gratitude to you for inviting us to your court. Please allow me to introduce my daughter Lady Amelia."

The young water blessed woman stepped forward and curtsied as well, her long blue hair falling in waves to her lower back.

"Lady Halberth, Lady Amelia. Be welcome in this house. Allow me to introduce my son the Prince Asher, and the royal blesser Blossom."

Asher stepped forward at the summons and bowed alongside Blossom. He was unsure if anyone else had heard the way the king had spoken Blossom's name, like it was something unclean that he was having to say, but if they did no one reacted.

As the king began to guide Lady Halberth into the palace, Asher and Blossom fell into step with Amelia who smiled at them radiantly. They both took a moment to introduce themselves less formally than the king had.

"It is such an honour to finally meet you master Blossom." She gushed as they ascended the stairs, her hands held up by her mouth as though to stop herself from screaming with joy.

"Please just call me Blossom. It is a pleasure to meet you too, our water blessed are few and far between and we value each and every one of them."

Asher felt himself frown as he was instantly forgotten by the pair in front of him, who took to talking about blessings and techniques as they walked. Most of the conversation went completely over his head. He was used to not always understanding blessing talk but not so used to being completely ignored. He coughed to get Blossom's attention and the blesser turned to look at him, as did Amelia who seemed annoyed at being disturbed, frowning slightly at him.

"This is where I must leave you. I should return to my own training." He said, a weak excuse and one that he knew Blossom instantly saw through if the furrow in his brow was any indication.

"Are you sure you don't want to join us on the tour?" Blossom asked. "It's not often that we get to show people of our own age around."

"It's nothing I haven't seen before, and I'm clearly surplus to requirements at the moment. I wouldn't want to get in the way. I will see you both at dinner, I do hope you won't think me rude if I do not continue to walk with you, my lady?" He bowed slightly as he said the last part.

Lady Amelia curtsied again in response, her smile polite. "Of course not your majesty, I would not want to keep you."

Asher turned on his heel and marched off back towards the training grounds, not sure why he suddenly felt so annoyed.

## Chapter 8

Blossom watched Asher's retreating back with an air of bemused confusion, the prince had been angry for some reason. He couldn't imagine why but it hadn't been directed at him, so he knew that it wasn't something that he had done. Blossom decided to put it out of his mind and refocused his attention on his guest. Lady Amelia had the same willowy limbs and pale blue eyes as most water blessed, and her dainty appearance made her look years younger than she was despite the fact that she stood eye level with him.

"Is there anywhere that you would especially like to see? You have had a long journey, so I do not wish to tax you by dragging you around the whole palace." He said with a smile.

"I would love to see the blessing school if that is okay?"

"There is nothing in the palace that you wish to see first? The blessing school is a bit of a walk away from the main grounds."

Amelia smiled with a shrug. "I'm sure I will be able to find my way around here soon enough. Once you've seen one grand house you've seen them all."

Blossom nodded, confused at the statement, but indicated for her to follow him anyway. The blessing school was why she was here after all, court life may not hold that much of an interest for her. "I'm afraid that it will be quite busy, we're deep in preparations for the next intake of blessed. The dormitories will be practically impassable, but the classrooms should be empty. I apologise in advance if we get waylaid on our way there though, there is still a lot to do."

"I am sorry if our timing is incredibly inconvenient. I told my mother that we should visit after or during the school year, but she was insistent that we come now."

"Nonsense, I am always happy to help when another blessed asks for it. Why else would I have been born nature blessed if not to ensure that all of our blessed can use and understand their power as fully as they are able."

Amelia beamed at his response, and they began walking through the palace, bypassing the halls and grand rooms with little more than a cursory glance. They cut through the palace and out onto the rear gardens, the blessing lake glistening beautifully in the distance, which Amelia excitedly asked to visit the next day. Blossom turned talk back to Water's blessings as they walked after it became clear that Amelia genuinely didn't care about any of the intricacies of palace life.

They descended through the stepped ornamental gardens that wrapped around the back and sides of the palace. Past the more practical vegetable patches and herb gardens and into the outer cloisters, which served as a smaller version of the royal ring and separated the palace proper from the palace grounds. As soon as they stepped out into the open they were suddenly waylaid by half a dozen frazzled servants who seemed to have been lying in wait for him.

"Please master Blossom, we cannot find the sun bedding and we have at least 14 new sun blessed joining us this year." One man shouted; his arms full of dark green, earth blessed sheets.

"Master Blossom, has a decision been made on individual trunks? Where are the scholars meant to keep their personal belongings?" Another asked.

"Master Blossom, master Emma is saying that some of the apprentices are staying in rooms of 6 I told her..."

"Please, please, please." Blossom said loudly, waving his hands to get everyone's attention. "Calm yourselves, these problems only seem so big because you are panicking. Now to answer your questions in order." He began to count off his fingers as he ran through the answers that he could provide. "The sun sheets are in the basement next to the sun robes which should also be brought up to the dormitories. The trunks arrived this morning and should be in the common room of the east dormitory. Now don't worry if there aren't enough, some of the children asked if they could bring their own and I said yes. It would be best for them to be stored on the scholar floor until we know who is arriving with their own trunk and then they can be handed out. Emma and I decided that there will be 3 dorms of 6 and 2 dorms of 5 on the apprentice floor, there is plenty of room for this and Emma has the lists of who will be staying where. Remember that she is my second in command and should be trusted, do what she says if you cannot find me."

Some of the servants had dispersed as Blossom answered their questions, in too much of a hurry to complete their tasks to focus on the whole speech. Blossom took Amelia's arm and addressed the remainder of the crowd. "Now if there are any more urgent matters that Emma cannot resolve can they please wait until after dinner, I have a guest to entertain but I will be available as soon as the family have finished eating."

The remainder of the servants bowed and dispersed, many muttering darkly amongst themselves, allowing Blossom and Amelia to continue towards their destination.

"Wow you weren't kidding." Amelia whispered as they began to descend the curved bank that led away from the palace, the gravel track crunching beneath their feet as they walked.

Blossom nodded, guilt rippling in his gut. He hated having to shirk his duties like this, but he couldn't face more of the king's wrath so soon. He just hoped that the servants knew that he wasn't brushing them off lightly.

He felt Amelia grip his arm harder and gasp as the entirety of the blessing school came into view below them. Two large square buildings bordered a wide stone walkway which ended at a round, open topped structure, behind which lay carefully tended, sweeping gardens. The gravel path led straight to it, blending almost seamlessly with the stone as they hurried down the hill.

The avenue before them was lined with trees, between which was strung colourful bunting and lamps. The two square buildings on either side were almost obscured by the greenery, but between the branches they could see flags emblazoned with each deity and blessing tapestries hanging from poles secured to the walls.

"These are the blessers quarters, we used to have those who shared a deity sleeping in the same rooms but that bred a kind of segregation that I wasn't comfortable with, so now we separate by age group. That way they are sharing with the people that they will be studying with. Children come to us when they turn eight, they spend two years as novices where they all share one large dormitory." He gestured to the shorter of the two buildings on the left-hand side of the walkway. "They then become apprentices for two years and finally scholars for another two years. When the children return to us for their third years and every subsequent year after that they are given smaller dorm rooms and allowed to choose who to share with." Blossom explained as they continued to walk down the avenue, this time gesturing to the building on his right, this one standing two stories higher.

The floor beneath their feet was a mosaic of blessing colours and symbols. Yellow tiles with a sunburst for Sun's blessing, silver tiles with a full moon for Moon's blessing, red tiles with a burning torch for Fire's blessing, green tiles with a mountain for Earth's blessing and blue tiles with a raindrop for Water's blessing. Every few feet a larger white tile emblazoned with the nature blessed symbol that Blossom alone was allowed to wear sat in the centre of the path. A tree bisected into 4 showing each of the seasons.

"And this is my school." Blossom said as they reached the end of the avenue, he pushed the large wooden doors open with a flourish. Blossom couldn't help the proud smile that split his face at Amelia's delighted gasp.

"It's wonderful, it is unlike anything I have ever seen. Certainly unlike any classroom I have ever seen."

"The blessings are a gift from nature, so to learn them we must be surrounded by nature."

The classroom was a sweeping open dome built of pale white stone. The walls dripped with various plants all in full bloom despite the time of year, and above them the ceiling opened to a clear blue sky. The centre of the room was emblazoned with the image of a golden sun, around which the moon phases were inlaid in shimmering mother of pearl. To the west of them lay a pool of clear water, fed by an immense waterfall that seemed to spring from the wall itself. On the eastern side a large hearth burned brightly, more open and less threatening than the royal hearth.

"We exist in harmony with each other so all of nature's blessings can be found here." Blossom said as Amelia wandered around the vast room in a kind of dazed awe.

"What do you do if it's raining?" She asked once she had stopped, gesturing up at the open sky above them. She'd gravitated towards the sparkling pool in her journey and almost seemed to be swaying towards the water as she spoke.

Blossom smiled. "We do this." He said, flicking a lever behind him. They both looked up as curved sheets of clear glass began to slide out of the tops of the walls, rising upwards until they met in the middle with a melodious tinkling sound. "Our water blessed often want the ceiling left open during the rains or a storm, but we only do that if it's a water specific lesson."

"This place is truly amazing." Amelia breathed, she settled down beside the pool, letting her fingers trail in the cool water, her eyes lighting up briefly as she asked for blessing.

"It is Queen Lila's design. She wanted to make a place fitting for so many blessed, one that shows the unity between the deities. And of course, she used her miraculous inventions to make it even more magical." Blossom made his way over to Amelia as he spoke, making the respectful death sign by touching his thumb to his forehead, which Amelia mimicked.

"May she be forever blessed." She whispered, the mood suddenly sombre.

"I have something else to show you." Blossom said, changing the subject as tactfully as possible. He waved Amelia over to him as he walked past the pool to the wall. He placed his hand on the wall and pushed, a hidden doorway appearing moments late. "There are six of these rooms, I show you this one because I think it will interest you the most." He said as Amelia followed him into the newly revealed room.

Amelia gasped again, her continuous wonder causing Blossom to glow with pride. This room was smaller than the main chamber and draped in ribbons of blue and silver. Shallow streams meandered their way around the floor and the walls were hidden by a constant cascade of bright, clear water.

"This is where the water blessed have their early lessons." Blossom explained, gesturing to the plump cushions laid on the few dry patches of stone around the room. "I cannot teach every lesson and so I focus on the older children. I do of course run a few lessons with the novices, but for the most part they are taught by someone who shares their blessing. I think it is important to learn from someone who has shared your experiences, who knows your deity as completely as you do."

Amelia lit up at the news. "Oh, do you think that I could one day be one of those teachers? I would love to help young water blessed realise their potential, it would be so much better than sitting at court or paying visits all day." She asked, catching hold of Blossom's hands in excitement.

"I don't see why not." Blossom answered and they exited the room again, the door sliding closed silently behind them. "There is a room for every blessing, and a room where Emma teaches." Blossom said pointing to different spots around the main chamber. "Emma is not blessed, she teaches maths, reading, writing, that sort of thing." He explained when Amelia looked blank.

"Can I ask you something Blossom?" She asked, running her fingers over the word engraved just above the water door.

"Of course." Blossom replied.

"What is the word for Nature's blessing? I have never heard of it, probably because you would be the only one to speak it."

Blossom smiled and gestured for her to follow him back into the centre of the room. "How about this, if you can pass one of the tests that I set my students at the end of their first year then I will tell you, sound fair?"

Amelia considered for a moment. "Sounds fair enough, what is the test?"

"Stand in the centre of the room." He waited for Amelia to do so before speaking again. "Now, I am going to name the blessers and for each one I want you to speak their word." He held up a hand when Amelia made to look around. "Speak their word without looking at the marks above their doors." He returned Amelia's sheepish smile with a kind one of his own as she turned back to him. "Speak their word and then speak it again in the common tongue."

He was pretty sure that Amelia couldn't read the markings etched into the stone from where she was stood but his smile widened when Amelia nodded and dutifully closed her eyes anyway.

"Let's start with an easy one, your deity. What is Water's word?"

"Haliana. Serenity." Amelia answered without hesitation.

"Good, and now Moon."

"Lunis. Healing."

"Correct again. What is Earth's word?"

"Tobenit. Strength."

"And Fire's?"

Amelia paused for a moment, frowning as she concentrated. Blossom didn't blame her; most people had a hard time speaking the word of the deity most opposite their own.

"Susini. Passion." She said at last.

"Wonderful and finally what is Sun's word?"

"Chilania. Nurture." Amelia said as she opened her eyes.

"Perfect score." Blossom said with a clap as he strode towards her. "Now, with those words in mind I will tell you Nature's word." He placed his hands gently on her shoulders before speaking again. "Ninehshim. Balance."

## Chapter 9

Asher waited impatiently in front of the dining hall for Blossom and Amelia to return from wherever it was that they had gone off too. They weren't late yet, but he'd been experiencing a nagging annoyance in the back of his mind since leaving them to their tour. The feeling hadn't been helped by the almost constant stream of happy emotions that he'd felt emanating from whatever Blossom had connected them with. He hadn't returned to training after leaving them and had instead been moping around the palace since then, trying and failing to get invested in court drama. Telling himself that whilst he was here, he should be learning how to relate to the people he'd be surrounded with as soon as he became king. He refused to acknowledge that what he was feeling was jealousy and he instead blamed it on what his father had said over breakfast, that he was simply unprepared to deal with the idea of surrogate suitors so soon.

The instantaneous way that Amelia had gravitated towards Blossom could have been completely innocent. She may simply be excited to speak to another blessed, especially one of Blossom's rank. Or maybe she was in on the king's plan to push a surrogate at them, it would explain why she had appeared so suddenly at court. It wasn't that he didn't trust Blossom, in fact in the entire time that they'd known each other Asher had never once worried that Blossom may prefer someone else to him. Even after the numerous times that he had shot down his advances it hadn't ever occurred to him that it was because he wanted someone else.

They were engaged after all and now he knew that Blossom loved him back his mind should rest easy. But it was only now occurring to him after seeing Blossom interacting with another blessed his own age that maybe the love he felt from the other man wasn't romantic in nature. Just as he was fixating on that last thought delicate laughter floated down the hall and he looked up to see Blossom and Amelia walking arm in arm towards him.

"Why is that so surprising?" Blossom was asking her with a chuckle, which caused another melodious laugh to fall from Amelia's lips.

"Why is what so surprising?" Asher asked, causing them both to look over at him.

"Oh your majesty, I didn't see you there." Amelia asked with a surprise that Asher was certain was faked. "I was simply asking Blossom which deity he believed would have blessed him if he wasn't nature blessed. It's a game that many blessed play, but I'm sure it sounds silly to you." Amelia responded, her tone suddenly formal and honeyed.

Asher frowned at her response trying to decide if he was just imagining her intentions as false, but inside a part of him was smiling, he knew this answer. "Moon's blessing right?" Asher said, looking over at Blossom who beamed at him.

"Exactly." He responded and Asher felt his heart swelling with Blossom's happiness.

"Oh you two. I'm sure he must have already told you that." Amelia said, leaning closer to Blossom, resting her other hand on his upper arm as she looked up at him. "We just seem so compatible that I was sure you'd say water blessed. But then again I'm biased."

Blossom laughed again, seemingly oblivious to Amelia's increasing closeness. "Well Moon and Water are sister blessings, much like Sun and Fire so you weren't far off."

"Or maybe you just don't know Blossom as well as you think you do." Asher said, surprising himself as well as the other two with how much venom was in his voice. "Shall we go in?" He added, trying to lighten the mood, inclining his head towards the dining hall.

Blossom nodded again but looked at him reproachfully as they entered as a group. The king and Lady Halberth were already seated at the high table, an honour that the king always reserved for the first night of a new courtiers stay.

Asher frowned as the king indicated for him to sit to his right and for Blossom and Amelia to sit on his other side. Lady Halberth was seated next to him, and he tried to engage her in conversation to try and ignore the annoyance growing in him as Amelia continued to touch Blossom brazenly out of the corner of his eye, giggling and tossing her hair as they conversed in hushed tones.

"Tell me your majesty, as an unblessed what do you think of master Blossom's blessing school?" Lady Halberth asked him, her smile warm and her tone genuine.

"I know that Blossom is very proud of his school and his students and so I am very proud of him in turn. But I admit that I am not very well educated in blessings myself so I couldn't go into the technicalities of what he teaches." He felt Blossom's eyes on him as he spoke.

"Can any unblessed truly understand the blessings? I swear, most of what my daughter tries to tell me goes completely over my head." Lady Halberth said airily, taking a sip of wine.

Asher laughed. "As you say my lady. But I do know that since Blossom started his school the quality of our blessers has increased greatly, you only need to look at our harvests to see it." He smiled at Blossom who flushed happily at the praise, smiling down at his plate.

"You see things the way a true ruler would." Lady Halberth replied. "His majesty was just telling me of your last excursion with the royal troop, you seem to be just as skilled at teaching as master Blossom is. I have been told that the knights regiment seems stronger than ever."

Asher smiled, glancing quickly at his father who nodded at him proudly. "Thank you my lady, it is an honour to represent to royal family and I strive every day to be worthy of my armour."

The rest of the meal passed in amiable chatter and Asher was happy to see Blossom so animated for once, even if he disliked how clingy Amelia was. He sighed as the deserts were bought and resolved to stop dwelling on it. His father had told him that their stay was to be a short one, she would be leaving the day after tomorrow and he wouldn't have to worry about it again.

⌘

"Asher, can I speak with you a moment? I have to go and deal with some problems relating to the school after this so it'll be short." Blossom said once the final course had been cleared away and the party were rising to leave and begin mingling with the rest of the court.

"Of course." Asher responded, frowning down at where Amelia's hand sat atop Blossom's own.

"I'm afraid that I must excuse myself for the rest of the evening my lady, but I will see you again tomorrow." Blossom said quietly, extricating himself from Amelia's grasp.

Asher followed Blossom out into the hallway, the din of the dining hall quieting as soon as the doors were closed. He led him down a few deserted hallways before pulling him into one of the recessed alcoves dotted along the wall. "What is wrong with you? You've been in a weird mood all day, it's starting to give me indigestion." Blossom asked as soon as he checked that they were alone.

"What do you mean? I'm fine." Asher responded, crossing his arms and leaning on the wall behind him. "Why wouldn't I be fine when a woman that I barely know is draping herself all over you?"

Blossom blinked before bursting out laughing, clutching at his stomach as he leant back against the wall. "That's what this is about, your jealous? Am I not allowed to have other friends?"

Asher's hands dropped to his sides, curling into fists subconsciously. "Of course not. I have no issue with you having friends Blossom. And if that's all it was it wouldn't bother me, but I'm pretty sure that friendship isn't what she has in mind." He raised a hand as Blossom opened his mouth to interject. "Look, I get that meeting you is a great honour for most blessed which may explain why she's flat out ignored me since she arrived, but I don't think so."

Blossom's brow creased. "So you're not jealous that I've made a friend but you are jealous that she wants to be friends with me more than with you?"

Asher threw his hands up in exasperation. "No." He shouted, looking around quickly to check that he hadn't drawn attention to them. "No." He said again, more quietly this time. "Look, my father has invited her here because he wants her to be a possible royal surrogate, a fact which she is blatantly aware of because she had been flirting with you all evening. And okay I know that we will need a surrogate when we are married if we are to produce heirs. What I don't like is how blatant she is being, we aren't even married yet and she's acting like she's trying to be your mistress."

"You cannot be serious." Blossom responded after a moment of staring at him.

"Are you trying to tell me that you haven't realised how much she's been hanging all over you?" Asher hissed.

Blossom shrugged in response. "She's just a tactile person, you're exactly the same."

It was Asher's turn to stare at him. "We're engaged Blossom, she's known you for 5 hours. Those two things are not comparable."

Blossom rolled his eyes. "What do you want me to do Ash? She's a guest here, I'm not going to be rude to her. And I'm slightly insulted that you seem to expect me to just because you have taken a disliking to her. And I'm even more insulted that you seem to think that I need to be warned away from her. Even if she was flirting with me, which I maintain that she isn't, why are you so worried?"

Asher crossed his arms again, staring at the ground. "I'm not saying be rude to her, and I trust you. I wasn't trying to imply that I don't. I wasn't even going to say anything, but you asked. I'm sorry, I just don't like thinking of you with someone else. And I want you to have friends, I really do, I hate leaving you alone when I go out to the barracks."

He felt a hand on his shoulder and looked up to see Blossom smiling at him. "Look, she's leaving soon so you just have to put up with it for a few more days. And if you're that paranoid that she's going to jump me or something then hang out with us tomorrow. We're going to the blessing lake for some lessons, it'll give me a chance to see you before school starts." Asher laughed quietly at that as Blossom paused. "Now I don't know what the king has told you, but I can guarantee that if she has been bought in as a potential surrogate, which I doubt, then it wasn't for me."

"What has my father said to you?" Asher asked, to which Blossom once again rolled his eyes.

"It doesn't take a genius to guess that the king would want you to father our children. And to be perfectly honest with you, the thought of having to sleep with someone else, especially a woman, kind of makes my skin crawl."

"Are you saying that you want to sleep with me then?" Asher asked with a grin, trying to lighten the mood.

"Shut up." Blossom snorted, pushing at the prince's shoulder. "So, are you finally going to admit it?" He asked.

"Admit what?" Asher responded, glad to see that they were back to interacting like they always had.

"That you were jealous."

The prince sighed, looking up at the ceiling. "Okay fine, I'm jealous."

## Chapter 10

Both Asher and Amelia were already at breakfast by the time Blossom arrived at the dining hall the next morning.

"Good morning, Blossom." Amelia greeted him with a gentle smile.

Blossom returned the greeting whilst ignoring the dark look that Asher sent the girl's way. He'd hoped that their talk last night would have stopped the palpable waves of jealousy that were emanating from the prince, but they were just as strong as ever. Knowing what the sour feeling was did little to stop it clenching in his own gut, and Blossom couldn't wait for Amelia and her mother to leave the next morning even if only to calm Asher down. At least Asher had admitted that it was nothing that Blossom was doing that was making him feel this way, so Blossom's own indignation had lessened somewhat.

"Have you decided whether or not to join us at the lake today Asher?" He asked, placing a placating hand on the prince's arm as he spoke. It should be incongruous enough for the king to raise no objections, but still he dropped his hand the second that Silas looked over to them.

"I think I will. If you have no objections my lady? I wouldn't want to get in the way of your lessons."

Amelia paused for a beat before smiling again. "Of course not your majesty. I would be delighted."

The small group headed down to the lake as soon as breakfast ended. Amelia's spirits high as the large expanse of glittering water came into view. She clutched at Blossom's arm in excitement, and he had to shoot Asher a reproachful look when he felt the now familiar stab of jealousy from him.

As soon as they were in reach of the water Amelia hurriedly pulled off her boots and practically danced into the shallows.

Blossom once again placed his hand on Asher's arm under the guise of using him for support whilst he removed his own shoes. "Be nice Ash." He whispered quietly.

Asher looked at him innocently. "I am being nice. I haven't done anything."

Blossom simply smiled at him and gave his arm a pat. "What are you going to do whilst we train?" He asked.

Asher shrugged. "I was just going to watch, is that okay?" Asher reached out as hand as though he was going to touch Blossom again but the blesser stepped out of his reach and began heading towards the water.

"That's fine by me." He called over his shoulder.

"Won't the prince get bored? There's not much for him to do here is there?" Amelia asked as he drew level with her.

"Don't worry about him. If he gets that bored then I'm sure he'll leave." Blossom replied absently. If boredom was what resulted from Asher's jealousy and paranoia, then so be it. "Let's begin shall we?"

They asked for Water's blessing together, both glowing briefly as the calming power washed through them. "Is there anything in particular that you wanted to learn whilst you're here?" Blossom asked once they had replenished their stores of power.

"I would like to know how to manipulate water more. I've only ever really used Water's blessing to sooth myself or others." Amelia replied skimming her hands over the still water.

"Fair enough." Blossom said, nodding. "Follow my movements." He raised one hand slowly, the water below it rippling before rising to meet his fingers. "Try to think of the water as a part of yourself. The way that your blessing is."

Amelia copied him. After nothing happened the first few times she huffed and slashed at the water.

Blossom laughed quietly at her childish behaviour. "Try not to think about it so much. This is something that your blessing already knows how to do. Trust it."

Amelia locked eyes with him. "Okay, I'm looking at you. I'm not thinking about it. We're just having a normal conversation." She raised her hand again. Nothing happened.

"You're still thinking about it." Blossom admonished gently. "But I think you're on the right track with talking to take your mind off of it. Talk to me about something completely unrelated, ask me questions. Anything."

Amelia took a deep breath, glowing again as she soothed herself with her own blessing. "Okay." She held her hands out parallel to the water and looked at Blossom again. "Do you think it'll be weird when you marry the prince?" She asked.

Blossom was caught off guard. He looked briefly over to where Asher was, confused as to why Amelia would be bringing this us so suddenly. Then again he had asked her to ask him something unrelated to what they were doing. "Why would it be weird?" He asked.

Amelia shrugged, raising one hand. A small, snake-like trickle of water rose along with it. Blossom didn't react, not wanting to break her concentration. "Because you were raised together. Wouldn't it be like marrying your brother?"

Blossom let out a small 'huh' before his features softened into a smile. "I've never thought of him as my brother. I don't think either of our feelings are familial. We were never raised as siblings, he's the prince and I'm the royal blesser. That's how it's always been."

Amelia hummed but didn't seem convinced.

Deciding to change the topic Blossom gestured to the column of water that Amelia had summoned. "But look, you've got it."

⌘

Asher sat down on the soft grass of the bank and watched as Amelia and Blossom began to glow with the soft blue light of Water's blessing. Amelia had been so excited upon seeing the lake and seemed genuinely happy to be following Blossoms instructions that Asher began to wonder if maybe he had been wrong. As they took turns controlling the water in the lake, first Blossom then Amelia, creating dancing streams of liquid in the air he found his focus wandering.

Asher's hand absently strayed to the mark on his neck, feeling the ever-present ache of it through his tendons. He laid back on the grass, massaging the tension in his shoulder even though he knew from experience that only Blossom's blessing would ease the tightness.

He hadn't been lying to himself when he said that he'd never worried that Blossom didn't love him. Even when he had rejected Asher's numerous advances there had been something that told him that Blossom was doing so out of some feeling of obligation. So what if Amelia wanted something more? Even if she did, that didn't mean that she was going to get it.

Asher winced slightly as he worked at a particularly tight knot in his neck. As he stared at the clear blue sky above him, soothed by the sound of moving water, he found his mind drifting back to the last time that Blossom had 'slipped up' and made his affection known.

It had been just after his mother had died, not long after their 16ᵗʰ birthday. Asher had been preparing for the funeral, more specifically the entombment. Trying to mentally steel himself to stand in the cold, foreboding darkness of the royal catacombs when Blossom had come and found him in his room. Blossom had dismissed Edwin and helped Asher into his funeral clothes himself, murmuring words of comfort and pulsing Moon's blessing into him with every little touch.

"This isn't something that you can heal Blossom." Asher had said once he'd realised what Blossom was trying to do, his voice coming out small and broken.

Blossom hadn't responded for a while, just stood between him and the mirror, watching him with a stricken expression. "I don't know how to help you." He'd said at last.

Asher had taken hold of his hands, pulling him closer. "Just be here with me, that's all you can do."

Blossom had leant up and placed a kiss on his cheek before wrapping his arms around him. "Always." He'd whispered. "I'll always be here."

Blossom hadn't let go of his hand through the entire ceremony, standing resolutely by his side until just after the feast later that night.

The next day, probably in an attempt to return to some semblance of normality, Blossom had gone with his father into the hearth room for a lesson. He hadn't seen him again for a week, and after that Blossom's little shows of affection had disappeared.

He looked up as a shadow fell over him, drawing him back out of his memories. Blossom was looking down at him in concern.

"Is it hurting?" He asked, his voice quiet and calm in a way it only ever was after taking Water's blessing.

Asher dropped his hand and sat up, shaking his head as he did so. "No it's fine, I was just lost in thought. Are you done with your lesson?" He asked, standing up and looking over Blossom's shoulder. Amelia was still in the lake, turning in slow circles, water swirling around her in a sort of curtain as she moved.

"No, I just wanted to check on you." Blossom responded, inspecting the mark on Asher's neck. "It doesn't look like it's grown much but I can bless it again if you want."

Amelia had been walking towards them as they spoke, and Asher found he couldn't help himself. He reached out and cupped Blossom's cheek, caressing the soft skin with his thumb.

Blossom batted his hand away with a scowl. "Asher don't." He said sharply.

Asher shrugged, trying to go for innocent and failing. "Sorry flower, there was something on your face."

Blossom was clearly not convinced and looked like he wanted to say something more, but his attention was soon diverted as Amelia looped her arm through his.

"Is everything okay?" She asked sweetly, but Asher was certain that he could sense an air of triumphant smugness about her as she and Blossom returned to the lake.

⌘

Despite promising Emma that their trip would be quick, it wasn't until later that evening that Blossom was able to join her in the blessing school.

"Sorry I've left you all day but there didn't seem to be a good time to leave, and Amelia insisted that I join her for dinner as it's her last night." Blossom apologised breathlessly.

Emma's smile was tight as she accepted the apology, but Blossom was pretty sure that her annoyance wasn't directed at him. "That's okay petal, but I'm afraid it's going to be another late one. We need to go over the schedules before tomorrow, it seems that there are some class clashes that we missed."

Blossom groaned but followed Emma to the room that she used for teaching. Taking a large stack of paper from the desk they settled in for a long evening of work.

It was close to midnight when Blossom finally dragged himself back to his room, closely followed by an equally exhausted Emma. They'd spent the last 4 hours making up for the rest of the missed day, and by the end had been running on nothing but adrenaline which had finally deserted them both as soon as they'd gotten back into the palace.

"The gall of that man, to spring this visit on us at such short notice." Emma groused as she helped Blossom out of his robe.

"I know." Blossom said with a yawn. "But what can you do?" Normally he enjoyed Emma's lack of reverence when it came to the king, but he was far too tired to engage further. "And besides we need all the water blessed that we can get."

"And you have to play host tomorrow as well right?" Emma asked as Blossom crawled under the covers.

He sighed as he settled down. "Yeah, but I think we're basically ready right? It's only for the morning anyway, they should be leaving after lunch."

"Yeah, we're over the worst of it, good night petal."

"Night Emma." Blossom replied, almost too quietly to hear as the room was plunged into darkness.

## Chapter 11

Blossom's eyes flickered open as he felt a presence in the room. "Emma?" He whispered as the empty side of his bed sunk, like someone had sat down. "What's wrong? What time is it?" He asked as he pushed himself upright. He looked towards his windows, but no light was peeking through so it must have only been a few hours since he had fallen asleep.

He turned to question Emma further but before he could say anything he felt a wet pressure against his lips. He scrabbled backwards, getting caught up in his bedcovers as he did so which resulted in him falling to the floor with a painful thump. He stumbled upwards and flicked a hand towards the candles on his bedside table which flickered to life a few seconds later.

Amelia was sat on his bed, dressed in a silky blue and silver nightdress. She was watching him with what seemed to be indulgent bemusement as he clutched his bedcovers to him.

"Amelia?" Blossom asked in shock. "What are you doing here? This is my bedroom, isn't it?" He looked around himself at the unfamiliar trappings of the room but recognised just enough to know that it was the empty suite he'd been given until his own room was repaired. He raised a hand to his lips as another thought occurred to him. "Did you just kiss me?"

Amelia crawled towards him across the mattress, her eyes hooded. "You know why I'm here Blossom." She crooned, the shoulder of her nightdress slipping down slightly as she moved. "I know you felt the spark between us."

Blossom backed away, holding one hand in front of him, the other still holding the bedsheets. "There must have been a mistake."

Amelia huffed as though he was being intentionally difficult and stepped off the bed, her movements fluid and graceful in a way that only a water blessed could move. "Blossom, you don't need to try and play hard to get. No one will know, I will slip away before the servants come. I bet none of the other courtiers even know which room you've been moved to." She advanced on him, tugging the bedding from his grasp with surprising force.

Left with nothing to cover himself but his thin nightshirt Blossom continued to hold his hands out to stop her as he backed even further away.

"No Amelia, you're mistaken. I don't want to do this. I'm...I'm engaged to Asher."

Amelia halted briefly, snorting as she said. "The prince?" She let out a cruel laugh, her previously sweet demeanour dissolving in an instant. "What does that matter? He's unblessed, even worse, he's cursed. He could never understand you like I can, you're being forced to marry him anyway, to keep him alive."

"You're wrong."

"What?" Amelia stopped her advance again, looking genuinely confused. "How can I be wrong? I saw how you spoke to him at the lake, you rebuffed every advance he made."

Blossom shook his head. "It's complicated, but all you need to know is that I love Asher. Blessed, unblessed, cursed or not. I love him, and he understands me far better than you ever could." Blossom stepped forward, attempting to edge around her and towards the door. "Please Amelia, leave now and we'll forget all about this." He said with a gesture towards the door.

Amelia stared down at her bare feet, her expression suddenly lost. "I don't understand, I thought you liked me. The king said that you were looking for a way out, I can offer you that. The prince can't hold you to your engagement if you want to marry someone else. If you bed someone else. King Silas said that he would support us."

Blossom sighed heavily. "Of course he's the one behind this." He huffed. "Look Amelia, I do like you. Just not in that way." He said awkwardly, reaching out to place a hand on her shoulder.

Amelia looked up at him suddenly, grabbing hold of his hand and yanking him towards her with more strength than he would have thought her capable of. Her skin glowed a faint blue and Blossom felt his muscles relaxing as she pulsed Water's blessing into him. "I can make you look at me that way, I can make you promise to marry me." She hissed, shoving him towards the balcony doors.

Blossom stumbled in shock, only regaining his footing when he practically collided with the glass of the doorway. He turned around, his limbs weak and clumsy with the residuals of Water's Blessing. He opened his mouth to try and respond but the air was driven out of him as Amelia threw herself at him, knocking him into the door. His head cracked painfully against the glass and stars sparked behind his eyelids causing him to slump against her briefly.

"Stop." He shouted as she clawed at his nightshirt, any kindness or gentleness gone from her features, replaced by a wild frenzy that distorted her pretty face into something monstrous.

"The king said that I could have you." She snarled, reaching down and grabbing him tightly through the cloth of his nightshirt.

Blossom shouted out again in pain and shoved her away, panic making him use more strength than he'd intended to. Amelia fell to the floor with a quiet 'oof' but was back on her feet within seconds reaching for him again. Blossom scrabbled behind him for the doorhandle and flung the balcony doors open. Pulling them shut behind him and holding onto the handles as he tried to think of a way out of this.

He looked frantically from left to right, there were no vines here and he hadn't taken Earth's blessing in weeks so he couldn't create footholds in the stone of the wall. The door rattled loudly as Amelia threw her slight weight against them, trying to force them open.

"He said you could be mine." She screeched; her eyes wild as she looked at him.

Blossom closed his eyes, collecting the mixture of blessing power inside of him into a tangled mess that might just about allow him to escape this. He whispered Nature's word under his breath and when he opened his eyes again they glowed, as did the rest of his body as he bought all of his power to the surface.

He locked eyes with Amelia who had stopped her assault on the door and was gazing at him in awe. He spoke Water's word as soon as he got her attention, calling her blessing to him and watched with a grim satisfaction as her power flowed out of her and into him in a steady stream of blue light. Amelia took a step backwards as though to try and break the connection through distance, but before she could her eyes dimmed and she slumped to the floor. He opened the door only briefly, to check that he hadn't gone too far and that Amelia was only unconscious, before heading back out onto the balcony and gripping the top of the doorframe. Ignoring how much he was shaking he hauled himself up and began to climb.

⌘

Asher wasn't sure what had woken him up initially, but as he looked around his darkened room for the disturbance he heard a knocking at the door to his balcony. Frowning he climbed out of bed and wandered over to the doors. He opened the curtains a crack before flinging them wide a second later when he saw who was on the other side.

"Blossom what are you doing here?" He asked as he opened the door, letting the other man in. He amended the question when he saw how panicked and shaken Blossom was. "What's wrong?"

"Amelia she..." Blossom collapsed onto the floor, his legs suddenly unable to support him, breaking down into tears that cut off whatever it was he was trying to say.

"Amelia what? What's wrong with her?" Asher asked gently, kneeling beside Blossom and wrapping his arms around his shoulders.

"She's in my room, she tried to..." Blossom trailed off, pressing the back of a shaking hand to his mouth as he sobbed again.

Asher's face darkened. "She tried to what?" He growled.

Blossom looked at him, his watery eyes wide. "You were right Asher. You were right. I'm so stupid."

"Hey, hey none of that." Asher sat more fully on the floor, pulling Blossom close to him.

"She wouldn't stop, even when I said no."

Asher felt his heart stop at the words, he could feel how much turmoil Blossom was in, the panic flooding through him.

"I escaped through the window." Blossom said, a bitter laugh escaping him as he spoke.

"It's okay, you're okay, you're safe now." The prince soothed, pushing down the anger boiling inside of him in order to properly comfort his friend. "I'll talk to my father. She won't get away with this."

Blossom laughed again, a quiet, broken sound as he rested more fully against Asher's chest. "Your father was the one who said that she could do it."

That caused Asher to pause, and Blossom too if the suddenly ridged set of his shoulders was anything to go by.

"What? She must be lying. My father made it clear that he didn't want a surrogate for you so why would he say that she could have you?"

Blossom looked up at him, searching his face for something that Asher couldn't guess at. "Forget it." He said quietly. "Just...just hold me. We'll deal with it in the morning."

Asher wanted to argue but Blossom sounded so exhausted that he relented. He grabbed hold of the soft black blanket at the end of his bed and covered them both with it. Lying back on the floor of his room he held Blossom close until the blesser fell asleep.

As he watched Blossom's sleeping face Asher couldn't help but remember when he had first been bought to the palace. The nightmares he'd had. He couldn't count the number of times that he had woken to hear Blossom screaming in the next room, the number of times that he had crept into Blossom's bed and held him until he slept. It had been the main reason why they had shared a room for so long, Blossom had been too exhausted to use his blessings to heal Asher until they had been allowed to share a bed, and his parents had considered it a small price to pay to keep their son alive.

Carding his hand gently through Blossom's pale pink locks he wondered how many nightmares the blesser had had after they were parted. Wondered if maybe the reason why Blossom had been moved all the way over to the guest wing had been to stop him from hearing his screams.

## Chapter 12

Blossom was in the meadow again, looking down at the bright blue flower that he'd just grown. There was something different though, something that told Blossom that this wasn't going to be like his usual dream. The first thing that tipped him off was that he knew that this was a dream. Despite how many times Blossom had revisited this site whilst asleep, he never knew that he was dreaming until he awoke again. The second thing was that as he stood amongst the flowers, he knew himself to be the same age and height that he was in the real world. A grown adult where before he'd always been a small child.

Blossom looked down at himself, his blessers robes seeming out of place in the colourful field of his childhood.

"Blossom." The call that he'd come to expect sounded from behind him, but this time it was a man's voice that called his name.

He turned slowly, not sure if he wanted to see Asher stood in place of his mother. He needn't have worried, as he turned the scenery around him changed and Blossom found himself in the great hall of the palace. He recognised the scene in front of him instantly, his and Asher's coming of age celebration. Asher was dancing with one of the noble ladies a few feet away, their steps practiced and easy.

"They look good together don't you think?" A voice floated from beside him and Blossom turned to find Silas leering at him, his expression smug and superior.

"Of course sire." He replied dutifully, just as Asher appeared before him.

He hadn't seen the prince move but suddenly they were both in the middle of the hall, dancing among the other nobles though he could hear no music.

"Asher." He whispered but the prince didn't respond, simply spun him around with a smile on his face. Blossom felt a hand press against his back and glanced behind him. Silas smiled evilly and he felt a jolt of burning pain between his shoulder blades.

"Why won't you love me Blossom?" He heard Asher whisper quietly and turned back to face the prince. He couldn't respond, the pain continuing to lance up and down his spine.

Couldn't Asher see what Silas was doing to him?

The prince seemed blind to the fact that his father was behind Blossom and instead pulled him closer, leaning in as though to kiss him. Blossom turned his head away. "Asher, please don't." He gasped, another jolt of fiery pain shooting through him.

"Why not?" The response was angry, it also wasn't in Asher's voice.

Blossom turned back to see that it was Amelia that held him now. Silas stepped away and the pain in his back stopped but was quickly replaced by the sharp stab of Amelia's nails in his arms. He tried to step away from her, to break the embrace but Amelia gripped him tighter, her face twisted into a snarl.

"You're mine. He promised me." She growled, her voice unnaturally deep and menacing.

Blossom shook his head and tried to step away again but his back bumped into a solid wall of muscle. He looked up to see Silas smiling down at him, the king placed his hands on Blossom's shoulders, keeping him still.

"No." He cried, struggling in Silas' iron-like grip, panic flooding through him as he realised what was going on. "No I don't want this."

Amelia ignored him, with a triumphant crow she began tearing at his clothes as Silas held him still. Blossom looked around the hall frantically as he tried to shield himself from the assault. The other nobles had stopped dancing and were watching the spectacle impassively. He knew without even trying that none of them would help him.

Blossom cried out again as Silas tossed him to the floor, his robes now in tatters. Scrabbling onto his back desperately Blossom looked up as Amelia advanced on him. "Asher." He cried helplessly, eyes searching the room for the prince. "Help me please."

Asher was stood next to his father, his face a picture of disgust but he made no move to stop what was happening.

Blossom reached out a hand towards the prince. "Asher." He shouted again, his voice hoarse as though he'd been screaming for hours.

Asher looked away, his lip curled in distaste. "Just accept it Blossom." He said, his voice far too loud for how calmly he'd spoken.

Blossom could feel tears running down his cheeks as he continued to try and evade Amelia's grasping hands. "Please help me." He sobbed.

Asher's head suddenly whipped towards him and he screamed his name again, causing the whole room to shake.

⌘

"Blossom."

Blossom's eyes snapped open and he sucked in a lungful of air. He felt like he'd been underwater, his nightshirt stuck to his sweaty skin, his chest heaving. Asher was leaning over him, worry etched into every feature. Still not quite out of the nightmare yet Blossom grabbed Asher's arms desperately. "Help me." He gasped, panic causing his words to hurt as they forced themselves from his throat.

"You're okay, you're okay. It was a dream." Asher soothed, pressing their foreheads together, hands on either side of Blossom's face. "It was all a dream. I've got you flower, you're safe."

Blossom felt his vision blur as tears welled in his eyes. He was vaguely aware of the fact that he must have already been crying in his dream, judging from the wetness on his cheeks. He couldn't bring himself to care too much though as he clutched Asher tighter and sobbed into his shoulder.

Gentle fingers petted through his hair as the prince repeated 'I've got you' and 'you're safe' over and over until Blossom's breathing stopped hitching and his tears stopped falling. Asher pulled away from their embrace to look at Blossom's face. He rubbed his thumbs under Blossom's now puffy eyes, wiping the remains of his tears away. "Okay?" He asked with a small smile.

Blossom returned the smile with a watery one of his own and nodded.

Asher's smile grew slightly, happy with the response. "Good. You're safe now, I've got you." He said again as though he knew how badly Blossom needed to hear those words. The prince leant in and pressed a kiss to his cheek and this time Blossom let him.

Tucking his head under Asher's chin and holding him tightly Blossom took a deep breath, relishing in Asher's warm, sleep mussed scent. "Thank you." He breathed quietly. Enclosed in Asher's arms Blossom drifted back into a, thankfully dreamless, sleep moments later.

## Chapter 13

"I'm sure that it's not what it seems like Ed."

"Then explain to me why they're both on the floor like that Em."

"I dunno, let's ask them shall we?"

Blossom groaned as he felt a foot pressing into his back, rocking him forwards slightly with the pressure. He briefly buried his face into Asher's hair with a grumble.

"Not a good wakeup call Emma." He sighed when Emma continued to poke at him, rolling onto his back and squinting up at her.

Emma bent over him, her hands on her hips and a small smile on her face. "It did its job and woke you up though didn't it?" She looked around the room in curiosity. "I have to say petal I didn't think that the first time I would be waking you and Asher up after a night together that I'd find you on the floor."

"It wasn't like that Emma." Asher said having woken up as they spoke, sitting up with a wince as his back popped. "But I agree with you that we should have slept in the bed."

Blossom had to agree, he could feel the stiffness in his joints as he stood up. He stretched his arms above his head with another groan, shaking his arms to try and regain some easy movement after lying on the hard ground.

Emma's smile had faded slightly as Asher had spoken. "I know your majesty." She said quietly.

Blossom frowned. "What's happened?" He asked, finally noticing Edwin wringing his hands behind his sister.

"You'll see soon enough." Emma sighed. "Come on petal, let's get you dressed. You two are going to have to have your stories straight when you go downstairs. We'll go through the servants hallways to stop you being seen."

Blossom and Asher both shared a worried look before Blossom followed Emma out of the room and back to the guest wing. Thankfully they didn't bump into anyone else on their way, servant or other whys. Blossom did not think that the other courtiers would believe his innocence as easily as Emma had.

"Emma what's happening?" He hissed once they were back in his room, gravitating towards the clothes laying atop his bedding. Emma had made his bed whilst he had been gone which he was thankful for, he didn't want any reminders of what had happened last night.

"The lady Amelia has accused you of trying to take advantage of her." Emma said matter-of-factly and Blossom took a step back from her in shock, dropping his trousers back onto the pile next to him.

"What?" He blanched. "She's saying that *I* assaulted *her*?"

"I'm not sure what play she is trying to go for, but the king is furious. There's talk of dissolving your engagement to Asher and forcing you to marry her instead."

"I...I...I never, I can't..."

"I know, I know." Emma soothed him, holding up a fresh robe for him to slip on. "Even if I hadn't just found you having a sleep over with Asher, I'm pretty sure that you've never shown any interest in women whatsoever. What were you doing in Asher's room anyway?"

"I had to get away from her, she broke into my room...she attacked me." Blossom replied, fastening the last of the buttons on his robe. He felt foolish saying it, Amelia may be of a height with him, but she was of noble birth, far more delicately built than he and had probable never done a day of physical labour in her life. If it came to explaining a physical altercation, he knew which one of them people would believe to be the aggressor.

But when he turned back to Emma, ready to continue to plead his case her face was like thunder.

"That little bitch." She hissed.

⌘

Asher was waiting for him at the bottom of the stairs by the time he left the guest wing, dressed in his stiff court attire which Blossom would usually blame for the look of deep discomfort on the prince's face.

Blossom smiled weakly at him as they drew level. "I get the feeling that this is going to be the worse court assembly we've ever been too." He whispered, his words coming out in a trembling breath.

Asher didn't respond verbally, simply nodded and took his hand reassuringly as they made their way to the throne room.

"If I'd just listened to you and been more on guard this would never have happened." Blossom said quietly as they walked, comforted by the dry warmth of Asher's hand in his.

Asher stepped in front of him causing him to stop suddenly so that they didn't collide. "Don't you dare say that." He said, cupping Blossom's face with both hands, squeezing his cheeks together slightly as he forced him to look at him. "This isn't a case of who was right and who was wrong. I'd give anything to have been wrong about her if it meant that you didn't have to have gone through what you did last night. You trusted her and she betrayed that trust, that is on her not you."

Blossom smiled up at him, he couldn't remember the last time he'd gotten so close to breaking the king's rules, but he desperately wanted to kiss the prince right then, so much so that he felt it like a pressure in his chest. Before he could cave Asher rested their foreheads together for a brief moment and then continued walking.

King Silas, lady Halberth and lady Amelia were already waiting in the throne room, which was unusually empty of courtiers. Amelia was sobbing loudly into her mother's shoulder and the King was glowering from his throne as though he wanted to set the whole room on fire. Though Blossom was sure that he could sense an air of triumph in his gaze. This confused Blossom, if Silas was trying to do what he thought he was doing then surely he'd need a larger audience.

"You keep that monster away from my daughter." Lady Halberth snapped once she saw them, hugging Amelia closer to her.

Asher pulled Blossom behind him, shielding him from the distraught woman. Blossom was hurt initially but the look of righteousness on

Asher's face and the anger he could feel through their connection soon made him realise that it had been an act of protection for him not for Amelia.

"What is the meaning of this?" The prince demanded, his hand still holding Blossom's even though the action pulled his arm in an uncomfortable direction.

"Careful of your place Asher, and careful of who you choose to protect. This boy is standing accused of a heinous crime."

"Is this a trial?" Asher countered. "I see no other people here to stand in judgement and I want to know what he is being accused of."

Blossom got the sense that Asher knew exactly what he was being accused of but wanted to hear the words from Silas' lips first.

"My daughter was invited into that man's room after dinner last night under the guise of a blessing lesson and when they were alone, he threw himself on her like an animal."

"Why would I invite you to my room for a lesson when we had spent the whole day at the lake?" Blossom asked as he peaked over Asher's shoulder, so baffled by the statement that he forgot the grievousness of the accusation for a moment.

"You will remain silent boy unless I command you to speak. We will not hear your lies until lady Halberth has finished." Silas snapped and Blossom felt Asher's grip on his hand tighten but neither of them responded.

"You invited her as a ploy to get her alone in your room of course." Lady Halberth thundered like the answer was obvious.

Blossom's mouth snapped shut as he tried to decide the best way to plead his case without enraging the king. He only hoped that Silas would allow him to speak before declaring his sentence. He knew that the king was well aware that this was a false accusation, just as he knew that he would need evidence concrete enough that the king would have to relent in order to save face.

"Your majesty may I speak?"

The whole room turned to where Emma was stood in the doorway, her brother hovering nervously behind her.

"Can you not see that we are busy here Emma, can it not wait?" Silas responded.

"I realise that your majesty, but it cannot wait. What I have to say is in relation to the accusations being laid on Blossom."

The king's eyes narrowed, he studied Emma's face as he weighed up the benefits of allowing her to say whatever it was she was going to say. "Speak." He said at last.

"Blossom was with me at the blessing school until midnight last night, we walked there together after dinner. There are at least 5 other servants that can testify to that, so there is no way that he asked lady Amelia up to his room."

Amelia had stopped crying whilst Emma spoke and was glaring at the other woman over her mother's shoulder, her eyes suspiciously dry.

"Amelia? You said that it happened right after dinner." Lady Halberth said, leaning back from her daughter to study her face.

Amelia looked from her mother to the king, who held her gaze silently. She finally looked back at her mother and broke down again. "It was after dinner, but much later." She sobbed, her cries loud and dramatic. "It was all so awful that I got mixed up. He told me to wait for him until he was done. That he would be too busy to meet me any other time. It was early in the morning when it happened." Somehow through her sobs her words were completely audible.

"That's a lie." Asher shouted causing Amelia to hiccup in surprise.

"Asher remember your manners. You cannot accuse a noble lady with no proof just because your so-called fiancé has attacked her."

Asher glared at his father. "That's not what I'm doing. I know for a fact that Blossom didn't assault Lady Amelia."

The king sighed in exasperation. "And how do you know that?" He asked.

"Because he spent last night in my room, with me."

"What?" The king roared, standing up and storming down the steps towards the two of them. Blossom took a few steps backwards in fear, dropping Asher's hand in his hurry. "Why was this boy in your room?" Silas continued to shout; the previous accusation completely forgotten.

Asher stepped in front of Blossom again as though he could physically protect him from his father's rage. "He didn't feel safe in his own room." He replied, sending a poisonous glare towards Amelia. "You know how bad his nightmares can get. We did nothing but sleep I promise, Edwin and Emma found us this morning."

"Your majesty, what about my daughter?" Lady Halberth asked, annoyed at being so quickly forgotten.

King Silas spun around. "Begone from my court." He shouted causing both Lady Halberth and Amelia to flinch in shock.

"But your majesty you said..."

"I said begone. Your lies have been revealed for what they are and you are no longer welcome here. Step foot on these grounds again and you will be hanged."

The two women sat in shock for a few seconds before the king took a menacing step towards them and they were sent scurrying away out of the throne room through one of the servant's entrances.

The king turned back to Blossom and Asher, his face dark. "You two are not to sleep in the same room again, am I understood? I don't care what he is *afraid* of." Silas said, drawing out the word afraid in a simpering mimicry of a scared child.

"Yes your majesty." Blossom said with a bow, just happy that this had blown over so quickly, and glad that he hadn't had to risk Silas' wrath for it to do so.

"Get out of my sight." Silas snapped.

"Not yet Father, I need to have a talk with you." Asher said in response as Blossom began to back out of the room.

⌘

"Asher I am disappointed in you." King Silas said gravely once Blossom had left and the throne room contained only the two of them. "You could have bought scandal down upon this family by allowing that boy to share your bed."

Asher looked at him with furrowed brows, trying to determine whether he was being serious or not. "Surely Blossom being found in the same bed as his intended would be less of a scandal then him assaulting some visiting noble."

The king said nothing, but Asher got the uncomfortable feeling that he didn't agree with him.

"I am very busy today Asher, and this ridiculous farce has already pushed back some very important matters. What was it that you wanted to say?" He asked, making his way back to his throne and sinking down onto it as though he was suddenly very tired.

"I want to set a date for the wedding." He responded.

The king looked up sharply. "What?"

"We're of age now and have been for a few years. I'm not sure why you have kept insisting that we put it off, but it is time that Blossom and I were married."

The King's eyes narrowed. "We will not speak of this now, not after what has just happened."

Asher blinked. "But that's exactly why we should speak of it." He exclaimed, striding towards the throne as he continued to speak. "If Blossom and I were already married then we wouldn't have even had to consider her accusation because she would have had to have been in our betrothal suite. She would have had to have broken into the family wing on the other side of the palace and she would have had to have done it whilst I was there. It would have been so much easier to disprove."

The king sighed and lapsed into silence. "Wait until you are both 21 and then we will set a date." He said finally. "The school year is about to start and there is no time to think of this now."

Asher wanted to argue but reconsidered after a moment, this was the closest he had gotten to a confirmation of their wedding since his mother had died. "Very well, thank you. Good day father." He said, turning to leave but stopping as another thought occurred to him. "Why were you so ready to believe that Blossom would do such a thing anyway?"

Silas snorted dismissively and waved his hand in the air. "That boy may have been raised here but that doesn't change what he is. You have been blind to his flaws for far too long but I do not have the time or energy to explain them to you now."

Asher stood frozen in place. "What do you mean 'what he is'? You're blessed as well, surely you don't mean that the blessed are more likely to attack someone."

Silas laughed, a short sharp sound that caused Asher to cringe away instinctively. "It has nothing to do with him being blessed. Forget I said anything and go about your day, we will put this behind us for now."

Asher was torn between pushing the matter and wanting to be away from his father, he'd never heard such a cruel sound coming from the man before. Deciding to do as Silas said he turned on his heel and walked quickly to the door.

"Oh and Asher." The prince stopped by the doorway and turned back, his stomach clenching with unease.

"Yes?"

"If you see that boy, which I'm sure you will. Tell him that I wish to speak with him in the hearth room after lunch."

## Chapter 14

Blossom stepped back to admire his handiwork, he'd spent the last 10 minutes trying to get a series of blessing banners to hang straight and was finally satisfied with his work. "What next?" He asked as Emma came to stand next to him.

"I think we're done petal." She responded, her gaze sweeping over the main blessing chamber. It had been draped with brightly coloured flags and ribbons to celebrate the arrival of the new blessers, every bare patch of wall or floor now covered like the world's largest and most ostentatiously wrapped gift.

"Really?" It was just past 2 and Blossom felt his heart sink slightly when he remembered the message that Asher had delivered a few hours earlier on his way to the training grounds. "Then I best go and meet with the king I guess." He said with a resigned sigh. "Will you be okay if I leave you?"

Emma placed a hand on his shoulder and smiled encouragingly at him as she gently pushed him towards the door. "We'll be fine petal. Best go ahead and get your scolding over and done with. I'm sure it won't be too bad now that he knows that you're innocent."

Blossom wondered if she knew just how apt her analogy was as he began making his way back to the palace, and how inaccurate her final statement had been. He stopped frequently on his walk under the pretence of checking this or that was perfect for the coming week, trying to stretch out the mile that separated the blessing school from the palace.

⌘

He wasn't sure if it was due to his nightmare or if it was simply because of what the king had tried to do, but as Blossom made his way past the great hall he couldn't help but remember the last time something like this had happened. It had been his and Asher's 19<sup>th</sup> birthday and as usual a lavish ball had been thrown in their honour. Or Asher's honour. Ever since queen Lila had died Blossom's birthday had been more of a footnote to the main festivities. Not that he minded all that much, Asher never failed to make sure he felt included, and he almost preferred the quiet birthday dinners he had at Emma and Kara's.

Just like their coming-of-age celebration the year before Silas had wasted no time in throwing every noble and foreign royal that was even close to Asher in age at the prince. Asher had been completely un-aware of the ploy and had happily danced with guest after guest under the assumption that it was simply the polite thing to do. It had been near the end of the ball when the ballad of courting had begun to play and Silas had leant in close to him whispering about how much better suited Asher was with the man he had been dancing with, the third son of the Shotsen queen, ruler of a small kingdom that shared their northern boarders.

Blossom had wearily agreed, ever since queen Lila's entombment and his subsequent punishment he'd been trying harder and harder to ignore Asher's advances, rebuffing them more vehemently than before. He hadn't had a chance to say anything more as Asher had interrupted them, holding out his hand as he asked Blossom to dance.

"I thought you were dancing with prince Karken?" He'd asked des-perately, trying to telepathically signal to the king that he wasn't doing anything to encourage Asher.

"I'm not going to dance the ballad of courting with anyone but you Blossom." Asher had replied simply, taking his hand and leading him to the middle of the hall. "You seem tense, you haven't danced much tonight."

Blossom had known that Asher had simply been making small talk, but his response had been rushed and slightly panicked sounding. "I just like watching you having fun with other people. You've never danced with so many nobles before."

Asher had grinned at him. "Jealous?"

Blossom had stolen a look at the king and the fury written across his features had prompted him into saying. "Asher can we make a deal?"

"What kind of a deal?" The prince had responded, his smile not wavering.

"Well, you're going away for a while with the knights soon and as it's the first time we're going to be apart for that long I was wondering if we could…" He had trailed off at the mischievous glint that his words had sparked in Asher's eye. The prince had no idea what he was about to say, and it caused Blossom's heart to contract painfully. "…could we stop talking about getting married?" It hadn't been what he'd wanted to say, not exactly. But he couldn't bring himself to ask Asher to dissolve their arrangement completely.

"What?" Asher had asked incredulously, so stunned that he'd missed the next step in the dance and trod on Blossom's foot. Blossom had winced but said nothing about it. "Why?"

Blossom had shrugged, he didn't have a good reason. Not one that he could tell Asher anyway. "We've been engaged for years now, we were promised to each other before we ever even had the notion of what that would entail. I just think now would be a good time for a break, see if this is something that we actually want."

He'd expected Asher to argue with him, but before the prince had a chance to respond the music changed and he was swept away by the other dancers. Asher found him later that night, his face a mask of determination. "Fine." He'd said, confusing Blossom briefly as to his meaning.

"Fine?"

"I'll give you one year Blossom." Asher had refused to look at him as he had spoken. "For one year I won't mention it. Won't flirt with you. Won't even touch you more than needed, but you have to promise me one thing in return."

He'd been so relieved that his plan had worked, so happy to have a temporary reprieve from the king's wrath that he'd agreed readily. "Anything."

The flinch that had gone through the prince at that word was almost enough to cause him to call it off, but Blossom had kept his mouth shut. "After a year, when my feelings haven't changed. Because they won't, believe me." He'd added the last bit when Blossom had opened his mouth to disagree. "I want an answer to this question. Do you love me?" The prince had stared at him for a long time before speaking again. "Do we have a deal?"

Blossom had nodded, not trusting himself to speak.

⌘

The palace had felt cold after the warmth of the spring sun but as soon as Blossom stepped over the threshold of the hearth room, he instantly began to miss the coolness of the hallways. King Silas had stoked the fire to a fierceness that Blossom hadn't seen in years and sat shadowed by the brightness of the flames.

"The next time that you're planning on framing me for something in an attempt to keep me and Asher apart you may want to coach your conspirators better." He said by way of greeting, surprising both the king and himself at his boldness.

"How dare you." The king growled, stalking towards him. "How dare you speak to me like that. I am your king." He grabbed Blossom by the lapel and dragged him towards the fire.

"You're right, I'm sorry. After all I have no proof that you told Amelia that she could 'have me' despite her explicitly telling me that. My apologies your majesty." Blossom replied. He had no idea why he was responding to the king's actions today so differently from all of the other times that Silas had done something to him, but instead of the fear that he usually felt during one of these sessions Blossom felt nothing but a white-hot rage. "Although I have to say that you're change of tact was something I didn't see coming. Throwing someone at me instead of Asher."

He stumbled backwards suddenly as the king quickly slapped him across the face, but before he could fall Silas had grabbed hold of his shoulder, digging his nails into the still tender flesh.

"On your knees." He demanded pushing down on Blossom's shoulder.

Blossom sunk to his knees in front of the fire, staring at the flames. Still dazed from the slap he didn't resist as the king moved him, feeling a throb in his cheek where the large ring that Silas wore had struck him. He felt the king's hand at his back, deceptively gentle as heat began to spread through him.

"It would do you good to remember that you are here because of my good graces. It is only through the goodness of my own heart that I don't keep you chained up like a slave in the dungeons. You will be punished extra for talking back to me."

## Chapter 15

Asher stood beside Blossom on the steps leading to the blessing school as the avenue filled with excited children. The newest class of blessers were easily distinguishable in their common clothes, noble children in silks mingling with peasant children in rough spun wool. The older children were already wearing the robes of their deities, clumped together in their friend groups, catching up with the stories and adventures that they'd missed in their time away over the winter season.

"Children." Blossom called, his voice carrying clear across the crowd. The students turned almost in unison at the sound and began to make their way towards him, a sea of green and yellow intermixed with the rarer blues, reds, and whites. "To those of you returning welcome back, to those of you entering your first year with us then simply welcome. I hope that you find your time at this school informative and rewarding."

There was a round of applause and a few cheers from the older children, and Asher couldn't help but grin back at them before his attention refocused on Blossom. He always loved the beginning of the school year because it meant that he could see Blossom in his element, the look of pride on the blessers face almost radiating its own light. He'd never been this involved in the school and had always watched from a distance in the previous years but being in the thick of it this time it was clear to see how much the students adored Blossom. "I am sure that you are excited to get to your dorms and begin unpacking and once I am finished you can do just that. But first a few of the customary announcements and introductions."

Blossom placed a hand on his chest. "As many of you will have guessed I am master Blossom." There were a few more whoops and cheers and from Blossom's smile Asher guessed that it was some kind of in joke with him and the older students. "This is master Emma who will be continuing your general studies, so those of you who thought that you would be able to forget about maths by coming here had better think again." He gestured to his left and Asher didn't miss the slight wince that crossed Blossom's face as he raised his hand.

Blossom had refused to talk to Asher about anything that had happened over the past few days, and it wasn't until this morning that he had even seen him up close. After confronting him about it Blossom had claimed that he'd gotten the dark bruise on his cheek from an accident that had happened during school preparations. A statement that Asher didn't believe for a second. He had instantly stormed down to the throne room the second he'd seen the injury, but in a sudden fit of wanderlust his father had disbanded court and departed for a month-long kingdom tour the day before school was to start so the prince hadn't had a chance to confront Silas about what had happened either.

Blossom had continued to introduce the rest of the gathered teachers whilst Asher had been lost in thought, and he tuned back in as Blossom gestured to him. "And my guest here is the royal prince and heir to the throne of Vaten, Asher."

The children all bowed in unison and Asher bowed back with a warm smile that he hoped would dispel the children's awe. He didn't expect reverence from the students.

"Prince Asher has generously offered to hold sparring lessons for those who want to learn to duel without the use of their blessings. They will be held once a week after the day's lessons have ended. Those of you wanting to avail yourselves of this opportunity should sign up on the registers posted in your common rooms." There was a general murmuring among the crowd at the news, and Asher could already pick out a few excited faces that he was sure he'd be seeing on the training grounds.

"Finally, on to the announcements. There will be a welcome feast in the great hall of the palace tonight as there is at the beginning of every school year, but for those of you who are new most nights your meals will be served in your dorm common rooms or in the blessing garden. The long day, or summer solstice as some of you from the western reaches may wish to call it, marks the end of your first term and as always a celebration will be held at the blessing lake, this is 2 months from now. And finally, today is a free day that you can spend settling into your new home and exploring the grounds but do not stray into the palace without an escort, keep to the school grounds which are bordered clearly by larger versions of these blessing stones." He held up a palm-sized pebble stamped with his symbol, the nature tree. "Classes will start at 9am sharp tomorrow so don't stay up too late."

Blossom smiled indulgently like he knew that most of the students wouldn't listen to his last directive and clapped his hands once. "So with the formalities out of the way the only thing left for me to say is that the school year has officially begun. Now go and have fun, dinner will be served at 6 o'clock."

There was another loud cheer and the crowd descended into anarchy as students ran this way and that trying to get to their dorms.

"Would you mind helping for just a few moments whilst we settle everyone and make sure they all know where they are sleeping?" Blossom asked him quietly, as though he was afraid that Asher would say no.

"Of course." He replied brightly. "I meant it when I said that I want to be more involved. I'll help wherever I can."

⌘

Blossom entered the returning dorm building where the apprentices and scholars stayed. He'd sent Asher into the novice dorm with an armful of timetables and welcome packs and had his own arms full of sets of timetables for the final-year scholars. The returning dormitory was four stories to the novices two. The apprentices had full reign of the first two floors and the scholars the top two. The scholars were given a choice of single occupancy rooms or larger occupancy rooms where they could stay with their friend groups. Normally only those who wanted to study to become blessing teachers chose the single occupancy rooms and so there were only a handful of them at the end of each of the corridors.

He made his way slowly up the stairs to the scholars' dorms, squeezing himself past the tide of children and teachers until he reached the top of the building. He knocked on the first door he got to and pushed it open after getting a chorus of 'come in' from those inside.

"Master Blossom." The group of children, who were now closer to young adults he noted, cried out in glee as he stepped into the room.

"Good morning." He responded with a smile. "I have your timetables." He waved the stack of paper and chuckled at the group of well-intentioned groans that he received. "Come on now, are you not excited for your final year? You get your one-on-one lessons this year."

The 5 children climbed over the mess of clothes and other personal items scattered about the room to collect their timetables. The two sun blessed in the room crowing with delight when they saw that they shared most of their lessons.

"Do any of you have group blessing on Wednesday afternoon?" Kela, an earth blessed asked.

"I do." Firon, a fire blessed, said walking over to her and comparing his timetable. "And hey we have the same free periods on Monday and Thursday."

"Okay children, I have the rest of these to hand out. Do you think that you can get all of this cleaned up before dinner? You're creating a bit of a safety hazard here." Blossom gestured to the chaos of the open trunks on the floor. He received a chorus of 'Yes Master Blossom' and left with a wave. He continued to make his way through the rest of the shared and single rooms, answering questions and soothing those that he knew always needed a few more days to settle in as he handed out the rest of the timetables.

He knocked on one of the single occupancy doors at the far end of the dormitory and heard a quiet 'Yes?' from behind the wood.

"It's master Blossom, do you mind if I come in?" Blossom asked, pushing the door open when he heard an affirmative noise. "Hello again Selina." He said with a smile.

The smile was returned to him from behind a mop of dark green hair. "Hello master Blossom." Selina said, just as quietly as she said everything.

"Looking forward to your final year?" He asked as he handed over her timetable.

Selina nodded, biting her lip nervously. "I am...only..."

Blossom sat down on the edge of her bed, keeping a good few feet away from her, knowing that Selina wasn't overly fond of touch. "What's wrong?" He asked.

"I'm worried about the architect's exam."

Blossom had to bite his lip to stop himself from laughing. The architect's exam was one of three possible exams that the earth blessed took before leaving the school. Selina had been studying for it for over 3 years now, and despite her nerves Blossom knew that she would pass it easily. "Oh Selina you have months before your final exam, and besides if you continue to perform like you did last year then you really have nothing to worry about."

Selina nodded but didn't look convinced, staring down at her timetable dejectedly.

"Tell you what, how about I ask master Hotem if they would be willing to give you one on one tuition during a few of your free periods?"

Selina lit up, finally making eye contact with him as she asked. "Would you really?"

Blossom nodded, standing back up and making his way to the door. "It won't replace all of your free periods but I'm sure that they will be able to work something into the schedule. I'll go and talk to them now and they will let you know by the end of the week."

⌘

"Your majesty?"

Asher turned as best he could in the crowded hallway, clutching the remaining timetables and welcome packs to his chest to stop them from being knocked out of his hands.

"Oh hi Emma. How do you deal with this every year?" He asked as Emma practically climbed over the swarm of children to get to him.

"It's always best to let the first years find their beds first before handing out timetables." She said, slightly out of breath when she finally reached him.

Asher looked around as realisation sunk in, he'd been calling out random names that he found written on the tops of the sheets in the hopes that one of the children flowing past him would answer. "Ah, good to know. Blossom just asked me to hand them out, I didn't think beyond that."

Emma smiled, still sweating slightly, the press of so many bodies making the hallway much warmer than usual. "Give it another 10 minutes and it'll calm down. In fact, whilst it does I have to talk to you about something." She opened a door behind her and gestured him inside, grabbing a candle stand from the wall as she followed him.

"What is this?" Asher asked, looking around at the stacks of boxes and piles of books surrounding him.

"A storage room. It's easier to keep some of the teaching material in here than in the school building. That way we can lock the school up once lessons are done for the day, but we still have resources if the students need something after hours whilst they're studying."

Asher nodded. "Okay, do we need something from here?"

Emma shook her head and sat down on one of the boxes. "No, it's just a quiet place to talk, we're unlikely to be disturbed in here."

"Okay what is it?" Asher asked, also sitting down, placing the paperwork beside him as he did so.

"There's something wrong with Blossom." Emma said and Asher subconsciously touched his cheek in the spot where Blossom had been bruised. Emma nodded when she saw the action.

"He told me that it happened during preparations, he didn't catch something that was thrown to him or something like that."

"If it did happen then it wasn't when I was with him, and I was with him for almost all of the preparations. I think your father was angrier about you two sharing a room than we thought."

Asher's mind flashed to the large ring that his father wore, the royal seal emblazoned on the top. He'd been caught with it himself multiple times as a child and knew how much it hurt.

"There's something else too." Emma shifted where she sat, suddenly uncomfortable. "He hasn't let me dress him since that morning, and he makes me leave the room when he's having a bath."

Asher stared at her for a moment. "What are you saying?"

"I'm saying that either he's become very self-conscious overnight or there's something that's he's trying to hide from me. Some mark or injury that he doesn't want me to see."

⌘

Blossom stepped into the midday sun, his hands finally empty of paper. There were no more trunks to unpack or boxes to move, a fact that his throbbing back was very thankful for. He smiled as a frazzled looking Asher exited the novice dorms across from him. "Stressful huh?" He asked, his tone light and playful. "Thank you for helping out though, and it does calm down from here on out."

"Don't mention it." Asher responded wiping a sleeve over his brow. "I didn't realise how much work went into just getting them here."

Blossom laughed and gestured for Asher to follow him. "Come on, the teachers' lunch has been laid out in the garden, I think we've earnt a break." He stopped when a warm hand slid into his and tugged lightly. He turned to face Asher, an eyebrow raised in confusion. "What's the matter?" He asked as the prince stepped closer to him. He felt his cheeks growing warm at their sudden proximity. "Asher we're in public." He breathed.

Asher shrugged. "What are they going to see? Two people standing close to each other. Everyone here knows that we're engaged anyway, but that's not what this is." The prince reached up and brushed a thumb over Blossom's cheek, pressing gently on the tender flesh where the king had struck him.

He pulled his face away with a sigh. "Not again Ash, I told you that I'm fine. It's nearly healed anyway. One more dose of Moon's blessing tonight and it'll be gone."

The prince continued to look at him steadily as he dropped his hand and Blossom suddenly found it hard to hold his gaze. "Why won't you let Emma dress or bathe you? Is there somewhere else that you're hurt?"

Blossom paused, the comment causing his attention to return to the ache in his back. The one that had been there since his last visit to the hearth room. He'd been angry and resistant during his punishment, which had riled Silas more than he'd ever seen before and led to the lightning like burn that was currently branded up his spine. He'd been ready to break down and admit everything that had been happening to both Emma and Asher when it was over, but seeing the fury in Emma's face at the mark on his cheek he'd remembered why he'd kept silent for so long. He needed to protect them, from the king and from themselves. He could take Silas' wrath if it meant that Emma and Asher could stay with him.

He sighed and stepped back from the prince. "Nothing physical no." He sighed again, running a hand through his pink curls. "I need to go and apologise to her." He said quietly.

"What do you mean?" Asher asked and Blossom couldn't tell if it was in reference to the first or second thing he'd said. He chose to focus on the second.

Blossom crossed his arms defensively. "I just can't let anyone see me like that at the moment, not after what happened."

"You mean with Amelia?" Asher asked and Blossom winced. He'd hoped that Asher would come to that conclusion, but he still didn't want to lie outright.

"She violated me Ash, and she hurt me." He could feel tears forming at the back of his eyes at the pitiful look on Asher's face. Their connection had been dimming over the past few days, and he'd been actively blocking it when he could to stop Asher from feeling his pain, but right then he could still feel a pulse of sympathy and residual anger from the prince.

"Oh flower." The prince said, stepping towards him. He raised his arms to give him a hug but seemed to think better of it and let them fall back to his sides. "You don't need to apologise to Emma for that. Let me talk to her, I'm sure she'll understand."

Blossom nodded, a small smile tugging at his lips. "Thanks Ash."

## Chapter 16

The first few weeks of school went by in a blur and before he knew it Blossom was helping the final year scholars with their individual exam preparations.

"Okay Skyla, remember that you need to plant your feet. You are going to need continuous blessing to raise a structure this big, so you need to have a firm connection with the earth."

Skyla nodded and shifted her weight so that her stance was wider, and she was lower to the floor. Her strong back muscles tensing as she began to glow, the power of the blessing causing her usually moss coloured eyes to turn a more sea-foam colour as they focused on the wide space in front of her. Skyla was skilled enough that she didn't need to ask for blessing aloud and with a grunt thrust her arms upwards, the ground before her erupting in a series of columns and walls.

Blossom watched as a fresh sheen of sweat broke out across her brow as she clapped her hands together. The walls toppled towards each other, stopping just before they touched before gently resting against one another. Skyla held her stance for a few seconds more before releasing a breath and standing straight, her skin returning to its normal pale shade as the light faded.

Blossom walked around the structure in silence, running a hand along the rough dirt walls, sensing out any weak points where Skyla hadn't fitted the earth together properly. What stood before him was a defensive shield wall, one that earth blessed soldiers made on the battlefield to protect their comrades. Usually a pair of earth blessed would work together to make a structure this big and then continue to ask for blessing to move it along the battle ground. He took a step back and raised his left leg, slamming the sole of his foot hard into the wall. The structure didn't even wobble.

"Good." He said simply, Skyla wasn't one for over-the-top praise. He stepped back to the perimeter of the summoning ground and looked over to where Skyla was standing, her breathing still heavy with exertion. "Now move it."

⌘

Blossom helped Skyla off of the ground where she'd collapsed into an exhausted heap. "You're so close Skyla, another month or so and the protector's exam will be a breeze." Once she had steadied herself he began to guide her out of the garden and back into the school building. "Just remember, the protector's exam is a worst-case scenario, it's highly unlikely that you will have to maintain a structure like that by yourself for that length of time. And even more unlikely that you'll have to move it."

Skyla nodded mutely, looking over her shoulder back into the garden. "If I could just try one more time..."

Blossom held up a hand to stop her. "Not today. There will be plenty of time to try again, the worst thing you can do right now is overstretch yourself. You should take a warm bath and rest before your next class. In fact go and find River, he needs to practice for his therapy exam and right now you are the perfect test subject."

Skyla seemed hesitant to leave the training ground but finally gave a nod and headed off in the direction of the dorms. Blossom couldn't help but smile at her retreating back, stubbornness was a common trait in the earth blessed and it was a trait that Skyla had in spades.

Blossom rolled his shoulders, loosening some of the tension that had built up during the morning and looked around the main classroom. There were small groups of students dotted around the large chamber, some with teachers, some simply studying or practicing by themselves. He smiled again, he always felt happiest when school was in full swing, and the king's continued absence from the palace had allowed him to enjoy it more fully than he had before.

He didn't have any other students to mentor for the next hour, so Blossom decided to peak in on the little first year novices that were currently gathered in Emma's classroom. They were all sitting on the floor on large cushions as Emma carried a stack of workbooks to her desk. Given their relaxed postures and general lethargy they must have just finished their lesson.

"Master Emma, can you tell us the story of master Blossom and the prince since we've finished our maths?" One of them asked as they sprawled over the lap of their friend.

"The what now?" Blossom asked, stepping into the room properly.

Emma looked up at him in surprise. "Oh Blossom, I didn't know that you were there."

Blossom smiled at her and the rest of the students. "I was just passing by and then I heard that there was going to be a story." He said, settling himself on the ground next to the rest of the children who were now all looking at Emma beseechingly.

Emma sighed good naturedly as she sat down in her own seat. "You know the story though petal."

"Petal?" A few of the students cried incredulously causing Blossom to glare half-heartedly at the woman.

"Thanks for that." He said to which Emma merely shrugged innocently. "I don't think I've ever heard the story told before though."

"My daddy used to tell it to me before bed." One of the little fire blessed students piped up and Blossom looked around at the eager faces in surprise, was his life already being used as a bedtime story?

"Well now I have to hear it." Blossom said at last, looking back at Emma expectantly.

Emma sighed again but this time she was smiling. "Okay, okay if you insist."

There was a chorus of happy cheers and the students settled down even further into their impromptu nest groups. Emma waited until everyone was comfortable before starting her tale.

⌘

*A little over 20 years ago, the king and queen of Vaten conceived their first and only child. They had been trying for a child for many years and were so happy about the pregnancy that when it was close to the time for the baby to be born, they threw a lavish party to celebrate. It was during this party that* the queen went into labour. The queen was whisked off to her chambers where she gave birth to what everyone thought was a healthy baby boy. They named the new prince Asher, because of his ash black hair and because he was the son of the fire king.

Unknown to the people of Vaten at the very same time a little boy with pale pink hair and eyes was being born in the neighbouring kingdom of Castilla. A child with this colouring had never been seen before but his mother knew that he must be blessed by something and so named him Blossom, after the tree flowers that she could see from her window. A few days after he was born on the night of the full moon, baby Blossom began to glow with the white light of Moon's blessing. Blossom's mother took him outside the next morning and found that he glowed with Sun's blessing as well. To her surprise baby Blossom was able to take blessing from every deity and realising how powerful that would make him. How dangerous many would think him. She moved to a secluded spot right on the border between Castilla and Vaten to raise him in secret.

Whilst this was happening the new-born prince Asher was growing sick. On the same night that Blossom had taken his first blessing a dark mark had appeared on Asher's neck and that mark had been spreading ever since. There had been tales of marks like this appearing on people before and they were almost always fatal, so they had become known as death marks. Not willing to let his infant son die without trying to find a cure king Silas sent out a command that all blessed citizens of his country were to come to the palace to try and heal him.

Many came and many tried but the mark continued to grow and baby Asher continued to weaken. Knowing that only a blessed could cure him the king sent out soldiers into other kingdoms to bring back their blessed. Many of the neighbouring kingdoms were willing to help the king, seeing this as a good way to strengthen the bond between them but Vaten and Castilla had been at war for many years and so the Castillan king forbade any of his own blessed from crossing the border to try and help.

Growing desperate and believing that the blessed that could cure his son must live in Castilla king Silas organised a series of raids into Castillan territory and captured as many blessed as he could find, but still his search proved fruitless. It wasn't until 8 years later that a group of Vaten soldiers stumbled *upon the little cottage where Blossom had been living. Blossom had grown up separated from everyone but his mother, and he had no idea of the raids or the war that had be waging around him and so had no idea that he wasn't supposed to return with the soldiers to Vaten. When he heard that another little boy his own age was deathly ill, and that he might be able to help he went with the soldiers gladly.*

*When Blossom was bought to the palace prince Asher was almost dead. Most of his body had become covered in the death mark, so much so that even his eyes had turned black. Thankfully Blossom was able to use a mixture of all of the blessings that he had taken to fight the death mark, and whilst he couldn't get rid of it entirely, he drew it back to its original place on prince Asher's neck. With Blossom at his side the prince made a quick and almost full recovery and they have been together ever since, waiting for the day when they are old enough to marry and rule Vaten together.*

⌘

Blossom almost laughed when Emma finished talking. He knew that she had been simply reciting a bedtime story for children, but the watered-down nature of the tale truly baffled him. It appeared that some of the students agreed as a few raised their hands to ask questions.

"Yes Henley?" Emma asked, pointing to a small moon blessed child that sat to Blossom's right.

"Why did master Blossom's blessing work when no one else's did?"

"Because he could use all blessings stupid." A precocious earth blessed replied.

"No we do not call each other stupid Taka." Emma admonished. "Blossom would you like to explain?"

Blossom nodded. "It is in part because I am nature blessed. However there have been times when others have had death marks and a single deities blessing has cured it. The reason why I was able to help control Asher's death mark is because our spirits resonate with each other."

"What does resonate mean?" One of the sun blessed asked, raising her hand as she spoke.

"Everyone's spirit exists on a different plane. That is why some people are blessed and some people are not. For example, your spirit exists on the same plane as the sun. This means that your spirit will resonate with other sun blessed, it is a connection of sorts. Mine and Asher's spirit exists on the same plane, and it seems that ours are the only ones that currently exist there. I can resonate with his spirit, and therefore his curse which means that I can help to stop it."

"You will learn more about this when you become apprentices so don't worry if it's confusing now." Emma soothed when some of the students looked around blankly. "Any other questions before we break for next class?"

A few of the original hands went back up and Emma gestured to each in turn.

"What happened to your mother? You know when the soldiers came to take you away?"

Blossom's smile turned sad. "She didn't come with me." He said simply, not wanting to sour their concept of the bedtime story. "But Emma did, since coming here she has been my mother."

Emma blushed and her eyes turned watery as she smiled proudly at him. She shook her head in an attempt to regain her composure and gestured to the next child who had raised their hand.

"How did you bless the prince to take his mark away? My mummy says that you just put your hand on his neck, but my sister says that you have to hug him."

Blossom laughed at that. "Well now that the curse is mostly under control, I do just put my hand where the mark is, but when we first met I had to do more than that."

"What did you do?" several of the students asked, leaning forward eagerly when Blossom beckoned them closer.

He put a hand up to his face like he was about to tell them all a secret and whispered. "I kissed him." Laughing heartily when half of the children gasped in delight and the other half made disgusted noises at the mere thought of kissing.

## Chapter 17

"What a lovely day." Emma remarked absently, looking over her shoulder to ensure that none of the younger students had strayed from the pack. "Keep in your pairs everybody." She called, gesturing to a few of the scholars to corral the novices back into their lines.

They had been spending the morning touring the palace gardens in an ad hoc lesson about the balance of nature.

"You're right." Blossom replied, looking up at the clear sky as another impromptu lesson idea came to him. The last weeks' worth of lessons before the celebration of the long day often unfolded like this. Blossom felt it was more important for the new children to form bonds with each other and their older peers before their first bonding celebration, than to keep to the rigid structure of the past few months.

"Sun blessed." He called, turning to face the gathered students, there were a total of 120 children for this current school year and at least 40 of them were the blond haired, golden eyed children of the sun. A loud chorus of 'Yes master Blossom' rang out in response.

"Please can you all form a circle in the middle of the garden. Everyone else continue to follow master Emma back to the school, we will be doing blesser specific lessons for the rest of the day." He called, then more quietly so that only Emma could hear said. "Can you notify the other teachers when you get back?"

Emma smiled at him in answer and after a gesture to the students began walking again as the excited sun blessed scrabbled to form a circle.

"Now, how many of you have asked for Sun's blessing today?" A handful of the older children raised their hands. Blossom rearranged the circle so that the students who already had a fresh well of power were evenly distributed throughout the group. "Okay so today, as it is such a bright and sunny afternoon, we are going to practice group blessings." A general murmur ran through the group. "This will also help those of you who are struggling to ask for blessings by yourself and will be good practice for the upcoming festival."

He made a slow perimeter of the circle as he spoke. "Now which one of you can explain what a group blessing is?" One of the first-year scholars raised her hand. "Yes, Lola." Blossom nodded at her.

"A group blessing is where you all ask for the same blessing and share the power between you. It gives you more power than an individual blessing and opens you up for blessing transference."

"Well done, and who can tell me what a blessing transference is?" There was a longer pause and then a young first-year novice raised his hand. "Yes Aelius?" Blossom asked in surprise, transference was a concept that not many blessed knew of before they started at the blessing school.

"Is it when you use your power to like spark someone else's power?" He asked, making little star motions with his hands as he said the word spark.

"In a sense." Blossom responded. "Those who are blessed by the same deity share a link, this is why you are all able to ask for the same blessing. Each blessing exists on its own level in the body, with sun blessing existing here." Blossom pressed a few fingers to his forehead. "The link between you and your deity also exists between each of you, as well as all other sun blessed. Now normally this link is dormant, and you won't even feel it but if you have opened this link with another sun blessed then you can give them some of your blessing or activate theirs. Most sun blessed will link with each other during harvest time and activate each other's blessing to increase their power. This is blessing transference."

Her smiled at some of the blank looks he was receiving. "Don't worry if you don't understand it yet, it is a lot of information to receive all at once. Blessing transference is easier to understand once you have experienced it yourself."

"It's like this." Aelius said happily before grabbing hold of the hand of the person next to him and tilting his head towards the sun.

"No." Blossom shouted sharply, pulling the other student away from him and effectively breaking the connection between them. Aelius looked up at him in shock, as did many of the other students, Blossom never shouted at them. "I'm sorry Aelius." He sighed, kneeling down in front of him. "But you can't just force someone else to transfer with you, you could hurt them, or yourself."

Aelius looked like he was about to cry. "I'm...I'm sorry master Blossom. I...I just wanted to..." His bottom lip quivered as tears gathered in his eyes.

"Hey, hey, hey. Nothing happened, you're okay. No one got hurt, you didn't do anything wrong." Blossom soothed, pulling him into a hug. It took a few moments, but Aelius' tears stopped and Blossom was able to let him go and resume his lesson.

"Okay, before we continue let me reiterate. You cannot get hurt from using your own blessing, which I'm sure most of you know. A sun blessed will never be harmed from the warmth of their own deity's power. Just as a fire blessed will never be burnt from flames that they themself summon." The circle reformed whilst he spoke, the child that Aelius had grabbed shyly holding out their hand to him to show that there were no hard feelings. "However, that power can be used to hurt others. If you try to do a transference without the other persons consent, and even with consent if you are not careful then you can send too much power or take too much power which can be really harmful. Who here has used all of their blessing before and felt that nasty coldness?"

About two thirds of the students raised their hands.

"Okay now imagine inflicting that on someone else by taking their blessing away from them." He let the thought linger for a few moments before clapping his hands.

"Onto something much more fun. I would like you to hold hands with those next to you so that we have an unbroken circle."

The students did as they were told, a few blushing as they clasped hands. "Okay then, now we are all going to look towards the sky and on the count of three we will all speak Sun's word. Ready?"

"Yes master Blossom."

Blossom took a step back and began to count, he smiled as the group of children all began to glow, their faces lighting up with glee as sunlight streamed from their hair and skin.

"Well done." Blossom crowed as the group looked around at each other happily.

"Now that's not a sight you see every day."

The students turned in unison as Asher strode towards them.

"Master Blossom's blushing." One of the second-year apprentices whispered to her friend.

Blossom coughed self-consciously and looked away from the prince. Asher had clearly just come from training and had removed his tunic, leaving him in only his breeches, his bare chest still glistening with sweat.

"Are you all having fun?" Asher asked with a smile.

There was a series of nods before the child that had been next to Aelius asked. "Master Blossom? Could you show us proper transference with Prince Asher? It's how you cure his death mark isn't it?"

Asher grinned at him and stepped closer, taking hold of both of Blossom's hands. "Yes Blossom why don't we show them?"

Blossom rolled his eyes with a huff, hoping to distract everyone from the warmth that was still radiating from his cheeks. "Okay fine. But only because the mark has grown."

He waited until the sun blessed had moved closer before gently pulling his hands from Asher's grip and stepping backwards. He tilted his head back and silently asked for Sun's blessing, feeling its subtle warmth spreading through his limb's seconds later. There was a collective gasp from the novices, most of them had never seen a silent blessing before.

"Have I ever told you how beautiful you look when you receive blessing?" Asher asked with a disarming smile, which earned another collective gasp along with a few 'ohhhs'.

Blossom glared at him. "And have I ever told you not to make those kinds of comments in front of my children?"

Asher simply grinned at him, not sorry in the slightest and gestured to the mark on his neck. The mark hadn't grown anywhere near close to the size it had been that night on the roof, which was probably due to the breaches that Blossom had accidentally made. Somehow during the kings last punishment those breaches had closed enough that Blossom could no longer feel Asher's emotions, but the marks growth was still slower than it had been.

Blossom stepped forward and placed his hand over the mark, easily covering it with his palm. He gently stroked his thumb over the curve of the prince's jaw just to watch him flinch in surprise, a small retribution for making him blush so much earlier. He mentally scolded himself for the lapse in control, he needed to be careful, the kings continued absence from the palace was making him bold.

"Now Asher and I have done transference for years, so we already have a well-established power link." Blossom explained, trying to keep his tone professional. He took a breath and closed his eyes again, pushing the warm sun blessing through their link whilst also being careful not to reopen the breaches too much. He frowned when he felt a pushback, a dark energy similar to what he'd felt on the rooftop. More prepared for it this time he rolled his shoulders, keeping contact with Asher. He took another breath and forced the dark energy back with more of the blessing's power and opened his eyes to see the death mark receding beneath his fingers.

"If Asher had a blessing of his own and hadn't wanted me to do that, that would have hurt him." Blossom said as he dropped his hand. "But because he consented to receiving blessing and because I have done this before it helped instead."

Asher gestured to his neck as Blossom spoke and he couldn't help but laugh lightly at the man's theatrical movements. "You will learn more about transference in your third year here so don't worry if it's still confusing. You've all done very well asking for group blessing." The students beamed at him, and Blossom was just about to tell them that they should begin heading back to the school when Asher leant close to him and whispered in his ear.

"I thought you said that you'd have to kiss me from now on for that to work."

Blossom shoved him backwards with another huff. "Shouldn't you be hitting someone with a sword right now?" He asked with a smile.

"Of course, master Blossom." Asher replied, catching hold of his hand again and pressing his lips to the back of it quickly. "Happy learning children." The prince said as he turned on his heel and began making his way back to the palace.

"Say goodbye to the prince." Blossom said gently and the group shouted at Asher's retreating back a mixture of 'Goodbye your majesty' and 'goodbye master Asher'. The latter coming mostly from those who had signed up for weapons training with him.

Asher waved at them with a smile, and it wasn't until he heard quiet giggles and murmurings from his class that Blossom realised that he'd been waving back with a large smile on his own face. Blossom coughed and attempted to compose himself. "Okay everyone back to school, I want you in pairs as we were before."

He waited until the group had paired up, but as there were an uneven number of students there was one left standing alone. "Aelius, why don't you come to the front of the line and be part of my pair?"

The despondent child lit up instantly and hurried over to him. They set off at a slow walk, making sure that those with shorter legs could keep up. "I'm sorry master Blossom." Aelius said again and Blossom smiled down at him.

"There's no need to be sorry, you didn't know any better. I'm sorry for shouting." They lapsed back into silence again as they exited the gardens and began making their way down the blessing avenue. "Who told you about blessing transference Aelius?" Blossom asked, curious as to how such a young child knew how to perform such a complicated action.

"Mamma does it with me. She's sun blessed too." He replied.

"Ahh." Blossom said, that explained some of it. "But surely she told you never to do it without permission?"

Aelius thought for a second before shaking his head. "No. She never asked me if I wanted to do it."

Blossom felt his insides go cold at the words. He didn't want to worry any of the other children, so he let them file past him into the school, asking Aelius to stay with him for a moment. He crouched in front of him and asked. "Has your mother ever used it to hurt you?"

Aelius paused, looking down at his feet in shame. "Only when I've been bad." He said quietly. "Or when she wants me to be stronger."

Blossom swallowed, trying to clear the lump that had formed in his throat. How old had he been when Silas had first forced his power through him? He must have been at least 10 and here was this little 8-year-old who had also experienced it from blessers only knew what age. "Okay well, I just need you to know that she was wrong to do that to you. It doesn't matter how badly behaved you'd been she shouldn't have done that." He paused when he registered the second part of Aelius' sentence. "What do you mean make you stronger?"

Aelius looked up at him in confusion. "She said that the blessed become stronger when we endure our blessings. She said that it was to prepare me for when I came here. That I had to be strong enough for you to teach me."

Blossom stared at the child, his eyes wide. "Did you think that I would make you do that too?"

Aelius looked down, his face a mask of shame as he nodded. "She said that you are the strongest of us and that if I wanted to serve you then I had to be strong too." Aelius looked back up suddenly, his hands clasped pleadingly in front of him. "I swear I am strong enough master Blossom."

Blossom felt himself gaping in a mixture of shock and confusion as he tried to comprehend what Aelius was telling him. It dawned on him slowly what was happening and he rubbed a hand over his eyes. "Is your mother a Blossomite Aelius?"

Aelius nodded and Blossom sighed. He didn't know enough about their belief system to know exactly how much punishment this little boy had gone through, but if what Aelius was saying was true than there were more out there like him.

"Okay Aelius I want you to listen to me closely." The little boy leaned in as though Blossom was about to tell him a secret. "Pain is not what makes us stronger. Connection is what makes us strong. The connections that you make with other students, your teachers, and yes even me."

He hated the idea of playing into his own 'deity-ification' but right now he was more focused on ensuring that Aelius didn't continue along the path his mother had set for him. He reached out and placed his hands on Aelius' shoulders. "Every student here is strong in their own way, and you're all important to me." Aelius lit up at the statement and Blossom smiled back at him briefly. "But we don't hurt each other. Pain is not a good thing, I'm afraid your mother is wrong about that." He almost expected Aelius to disagree with him, but the small boy nodded.

"I think she might be wrong about a lot of things." He said quietly.

"What things?" Blossom asked, worry once again rising in him along with anger.

"She said that you didn't love the prince. That you were being forced to marry him. She said that you were his slave but that's not true, is it?"

Blossom blinked, whatever he had expected him to say it hadn't been that. "Not it isn't true." He said finally.

⌘

"Emma, can I ask you something?" Blossom asked, looking at Emma over the stacks of books piled between them. The school day had ended hours ago but they were both still in Emma's classroom, trying to catch up on the seemingly never-ending piles of marking that they had to get through.

"Of course you can petal. What's on your mind?" Emma responded, not looking up from her work.

"I've been meaning to ask for months now but it kept slipping my mind. Do you know anything about a group called 'the Blossomites'?"

Emma looked up suddenly, her face grave. "Where did you hear that word?"

"Asher told me, we saw some during the spring procession. I thought that they were nature blessed at first because they had hair the same colour as mine." Blossom was slightly surprised by Emma's sharp reaction but she seemed to school herself quickly.

"I wouldn't worry too much about them petal, they're a small group and for the most part harmless."

"Have you ever met one?" Blossom pressed.

"A few." Emma replied with a shrug. "I've mostly seen them around Kilan. I couldn't tell you much more than that. They don't deign to speak to unblessed, which is ironic as quite a few of them are unblessed themselves."

"How does that work?" Blossom asked, closing the book he'd been marking and looking at Emma expectantly.

"I think the unblessed among them were probably born into the group. They have their hair dyed very quickly so no one can tell."

Blossom thought for a moment, during which time Emma went back to her work. "Asher said that they'd only been around for a few years so the unblessed must be very young."

Emma seemed to be considering whether or not to speak again before finally sighing. "They've been around for a lot longer than that petal. I imagine they first formed when you were bought to the palace."

"Really?" Blossom asked in bewilderment.

"Well no one knew you existed before then."

"No that's not what I..." Blossom shook his head. Was it possible that the Blossomites were the reason for Silas' hatred towards him? "I'm surprised that they've been around for so long without me knowing about them."

Emma smiled at him. "It's not something that comes up in normal conversation petal. What made you think of it now?"

"One of the students is a Blossomite, or at least his mother is."

Emma gave up all pretence of trying to work, placing her pen down on the table with an air of finality. "Which one?"

"Aelius."

Emma thought for a moment. "Sun blessed?" She asked, to which

Blossom nodded. "How did you find out?" She continued and Blossom recounted the whole conversation that he'd had with the little novice. Once he'd finished Emma gave a thoughtful hum. "That is worrying. I had guessed that we'd get a Blossomite sooner or later but we'll need to have a look into whether or not this abuse is a common part of their rituals."

Before Blossom could think of a reply or try and determine why Emma didn't seem more shocked by his findings, Edwin appeared in the doorway.

"Hi Ed, what are you doing here?" Emma asked.

"Kara was looking for you, it's quite late." Edwin replied. "What were you two talking about?"

"Nothing much." Emma said definitively before Blossom could open his mouth.

Blossom frowned as Emma sent a look that he couldn't decipher his way. He wasn't sure if it was the look or something else that made him speak but before he knew it he was saying. "We were talking about Blossomites. One of the new students comes from a Blossomite family."

Emma heaved a weary sigh just as Edwin blurted out. "Really?"

Shocked by his sudden enthusiasm Blossom stuttered out an affirmative. Emma stood up and began trying to usher her brother out of the door as he gushed a litany of questions.

"How do you know they're a Blossomite? Were they injured or something? Did they tell you? What did they say?"

"Edwin hush." Emma snapped. "Like you said, it's late. Now is not the time for this discussion."

One of Edwin's questions stood out to Blossom, confusing him even more than Emma's blatant attempts to end the conversation. "What do you mean injured? What do you know?"

Edwin opened his mouth to reply but Emma shut him down quickly. "No." She practically shouted. "We are not having this conversation. Ed you are not going to fill his head with this nonsense." With a final shove she shut the door in Edwin's face and turned back to Blossom.

"What is going on? You said that you didn't know anything about the group. Why won't you tell me anything? If people are doing awful things in my name, then I should know about it."

Emma shook her head and walked over to him, taking hold of his hands she spoke gently. "That's exactly why Blossom. There's nothing you can do about it from here. You haven't done anything wrong, it's not your fault what they're doing."

That did nothing to reassure him, and Blossom was about to protest again when Emma continued.

"Just focus on your children. That's how you can help. Show them how they should be using their blessings. Show them how to treat each other."

"But..."

Emma fixed him with a look that he knew all too well. "No Blossom, no buts. When Asher is king then maybe things will change but right now there is nothing you can do. Forget that this conversation happened, focus on the long day celebration."

Blossom wanted to say more, wanted to push the matter until Emma told him everything but she swept him out of the room in much the same way that she had done Edwin. Having been raised by Emma he also knew when to pick his battles, she only ever used his given name when she was being deadly serious. He'd try again another day.

Over the next few days he tried multiple times to bring the topic up but Emma either changed the conversation or flat out ignored his questions. She'd evidently ordered everyone else to do the same thing as Edwin and Kara both suddenly became very busy whenever he tried to speak to them.

## Chapter 18

The King extended his tour up until the weekend before the summer solstice, a fact that both Asher and Blossom were informed of only on the day that he was supposed to return. Blossom had become so used to the freedom of having almost full run of the palace with Asher that the appearance of Silas at the breakfast table one morning caused an almost physical reaction in him. Asher also seemed surprised by his father's sudden return, but it was clear that nausea wasn't the reaction that hit him as he instantly piled his plate with bacon.

Blossom sat in his usual place in silence, his plate remaining empty as he tried to tamp down the gall rising in his throat. His injuries had healed well over the past two months thanks to his frequent trips to the rooftop but seeing the king in such close proximity caused phantom pains to lance up and down his spine.

"Was your tour successful father?" Asher asked brightly.

"Yes son, very successful." Silas wasn't looking at his son and was instead looking directly at him, and Blossom got the feeling that he wasn't just talking about the tour.

"So what was so important that you had to disappear so suddenly?" Asher asked, his tone still light as he took a sip of his coffee.

The king finally turned to look at him. "I don't have to explain myself to you." He snapped, his voice loud in the empty room. The court hadn't been reconvened yet and the king's statement seemed to bounce off of the walls around them.

Asher froze, a forkful of bacon halfway towards his mouth. "Of course not, I was just..."

"You have a lot to learn about ruling a kingdom Asher. Sometimes things come up that you have to deal with, and you don't have the luxury of wasting time. I had to leave the palace quickly because it was in the best interest of the kingdom and that is all." The king stood abruptly. "Now I must begin planning for the long day, or do you want to grill me about that as well before I leave?"

"No sir." Asher replied, still in shock. The king stormed out of the room with a sweep of his cloak. "What was that about?" Asher asked to which Blossom only shrugged. "I wasn't grilling him, was I?" He continued confusion clear on his face.

Blossom reached across the table, past the seat that the king had just exited and placed his hand over the prince's. "No you weren't. He's probably just tired from travel."

Asher placed his other hand atop Blossom's and smiled at him, looking as though he wanted to say something else. Blossom took a deep breath and stood up before he could, pulling his hand back out of the prince's grasp. He'd been reciprocating Asher's physical affection much more during the king's absence, which he knew hadn't gone unnoticed by the students and servants. He'd refrained from any open declaration of his feelings and still refused to kiss Asher despite how much he wanted to, but he'd allowed far more than he would have beforehand. A large part of him, probably the same part that had fought against the king's last punishment, wanted to continue letting Asher touch and hug him as much as the prince wanted, but that part wasn't quite as loud as the fear he'd always had. Fear that had instantly leapt to the forefront upon seeing the king's face again. "I have to get to class, but I'll see you at dinner." He said with a small smile. Asher smiled back at him, but it was tinged with a familiar sadness.

⌘

"Master Blossom?"

Blossom looked over at the doorway of the main blessing classroom where a palace guard was now stood, backlit by the sun. "Okay children keep trying, I'll be back in a moment." He said, gesturing to the students that he had been teaching to remain where they were sat. The sun blessed apprentices returned to their pots of soil and continued trying to combine their blessings into a form that would cause a sapling to sprout.

"Yes?" Blossom asked once he had walked over to the guard.

"The king wishes to speak with you." The guard said.

"Now?"

"Yes."

"I'm in the middle of a lesson right now, did he say what he wanted to speak to me about?"

The guard shifted uncomfortably. "No sir, only that you were to meet him in the royal hearth room."

Blossom sighed, a part of him wanted to send the guard away with a dismissive message. Tell the king that he would come after the school day was finished but he knew that the king would only take out his anger on the poor man.

"Okay, let me just wrap this up and I will be right with you." The guard nodded and remained in the doorway as Blossom returned to his class. Thankfully it was the last lesson of the day, so they weren't going to miss out on much more. "My apologies children but I have to leave you for now, the king has requested me. Please clear everything away and focus on independent study until the end of class." The students nodded and began to cart the pots and soil away to their shelves.

The walk to the hearth room was tense and silent and Blossom wondered if the guard knew what he was escorting him to. The man was clearly uncomfortable enough to know that he wasn't taking Blossom to a friendly chat with the king. "I can make it from here." Blossom said once they reached the palace doors. The guard looked as though he wanted to argue but Blossom laid a calming hand on his shoulder and gestured for him to return to his post. "I know the way, believe me."

The guard bowed. "Of course sir."

Blossom waited until the guard had walked out of sight before entering the palace. He looked up at the towering doorway, the grand entrance seeming cold and dark in comparison to the light and airy building that he had just left. He clenched his hands into fists and entered.

The king had his back to him when he finally entered the hearth room, staring pensively into the flames.

"You called for me your majesty?" Blossom asked, wondering what he could possibly have done wrong in the last 12 hours since the king had returned.

"Do you know why I left the palace boy?" Silas asked, his tone calm, still not turning to look at him.

Blossom frowned, was this a test? "I'm not sure your majesty. This morning you told Asher that some business had come up that you had to deal with. I guess I assumed that it had something to do with Lady Halberth and her daughter." He hated the memories that simply saying her name brought back for him, but they were nothing compared to the memories that seeing the king inspired.

Silas chuckled and the sound made the hairs on Blossom's arms stand on end. "Indeed that was a small part of it. That disappointing family have been dealt with." He said vaguely. "I also wanted to see if Asher would be fit to rule in my place whilst I was away." Silas turned to face him now. "And that you would still know your place."

Blossom didn't respond, only swallowed audibly in the sudden silence.

"Do you think that just because I'm not physically here that you can disobey me?"

"I'm sure I don't know what you mean." Blossom replied, although he had an idea what Silas was talking about. He'd been far less vigilant with rebuffing Asher's advances and flirtations over the past two months. He had even flirted back a couple of times safe in the knowledge that the king wouldn't find out. But now he realised how foolish he'd been, it had all been a test. One that he'd failed.

"Do not try and lie to me." The king stormed over, his face dark. "I have spies everywhere and they have told me of every single time that you have broken my trust. They've told me all about how you've been hanging off of my son like a brazen whore."

Blossom almost laughed but the anger on the king's face stalled him. Instead he sighed, suddenly tired of this game that they had been playing, tired of the pain that even now was crawling up his spine. "Has it ever occurred to you that maybe your plan isn't working? How long have we been trying to stop Asher from wanting me?"

King Silas growled a warning. "All I know is that no matter how many times I teach you a lesson, you still continue to disobey me. You've had two months of reprieve so don't expect this to be over with quickly." The king took another step towards him, and Blossom raised a hand to stop him.

"The summer solstice is in 2 days' time, you cannot leave a mark on me."

The king glared at him. "What makes you think that I care who sees? Why shouldn't I leave a mark on you?"

"Because he'll hate you if you do."

The king dropped his hand reluctantly, and there it was, the one thing that bound them to each other. The only reason why Silas had kept him in the palace after Queen Lila had died. The only reason why Blossom had endured his rage in silence. Their love for Asher.

"So be it." The king said finally, and Blossom breathed a sigh of relief. The relief was short lived however when Silas' hand shot out and grabbed a fistful of the hair at the back of his head. He was dragged forward and forced to his knees in front of the fire.

The king trailed his hand almost gently down the back of his neck in a way that made Blossom's skin crawl before pressing two fingers into the centre of his back. He placed his other hand flat on Blossom's stomach, directly above where the well of Fire's blessing rested. The two points of contact effectively stopping him from flinching away from the king's hands. Blossom took a deep breath and tried to relax as much as possible, it was always easier if he let the power flow through him without resistance.

"Just answer me one thing." He whispered, not sure if the lump that had formed in his throat was born of fear or sadness. The king didn't respond but he took the pause as permission to continue. "If I had been born within the borders of Vaten, would you have let him love me?"

He felt the king kneel behind him, a sure indication that this was going to last a while. "If you had been born as anything other than Castillan I would have encouraged it." Silas replied quietly.

Blossom closed his eyes as he felt himself crumble at the words. So there it was. There was nothing he could ever do to prove himself. Nothing he could do to please him. He would always end up here.

He felt the pulse of the king's blessing through his stomach first, aimed directly at the well of his own small reserve of Fire's blessing. His spine locked as the power flowed between the two points of contact that he had with the king, passing through his heart and lungs on its journey. He opened his mouth to scream but the chords of his throat were locked tight with pain and the only thing that came out was a steady plume of smoke. Out of the corner of his eyes he could see the king glowing as Silas asked for Fire's blessing, feeding his newly gifted power straight into Blossom's body in a never-ending stream.

⌘

His insides were on fire, every nerve and every muscle consumed by the force of Silas' power. He had no idea how long Silas had been cycling his power through him. The pain of the transference had kept him on the very edge of consciousness, and he knew nothing but it. His breathing was ragged as his chest struggled to expand without letting more fire flood through him. Silas was now supporting his weight entirely as he spasmed in his grip. The king ran the two fingers from the middle of his back up his spine, cupping the back of his head as he sent another wave through him, this time travelling up the length of his body to his brain. This was the final pulse that allowed Blossom to finally relinquish his hold on consciousness and his body slumped.

⌘

King Silas laid him back onto the cool flagstones and took his seat near the hearth, drawing fresh power from the flames to try and quell the coldness that had seeped into him. He watched the erratic rise and fall of the blesser's chest, each breath punctuated by a painful sounding 'huh' noise. His fingers were clenching and unclenching jerkily at his sides and his skin glowed a pale white as whatever blessing he had left tried desperately to heal the damage that Silas had caused.

Silas checked the clock on the wall, two hours he had pinned the boy beneath his hands, two hours he had fed the wrath of Fire's blessing through his body. It had been one of the longest sessions that he'd ever subjected him to and a rapidly growing part of him worried that maybe he'd gone too far.

There had been something different this time. Before, when the boy had meekly knelt for his punishments, there had always been that small trembling of fear that had kept him in check. Even last time when the boy had fought back, consumed with a rage that Silas couldn't help but admire, it had been enough to know that he still wouldn't cross him. But this time there had been nothing, just a quiet acceptance that scared Silas more than he cared to consider, and he'd let that fear control him.

The glow had dulled now, and the boys previously ashen skin had returned to its healthy bronzed hue. A colour that even Silas had to admit suited him, even if it did mark where he had come from. Marked him as an enemy.

As his eyes slowly fluttered open Silas schooled his features into a mask of indifference. The boy had to fear him, it was the only way. "The bell will be rung for dinner soon." He said, standing as he spoke. "I will make your excuses."

⌘

Blossom stared up at the ceiling as the king left, trying to catalogue the damage done to him and figure out how much blessing power it would take to heal. He could feel his reserves running low but at some point whilst he was unconscious his lungs had healed enough for him to take moderate, if not still painful breaths.

He let out a puff of smoke, watching it curl towards the ceiling as he tried to pinpoint what hurt the most. Coming to the conclusion that everything hurt the most, he decided to try and move. Nothing was going to get fixed if he stayed on the floor. With a hoarse groan he rolled over onto his hands and knees, pausing to catch his breath once there. That small action had almost caused him to black out again and every muscle in his body was screaming at him to just stay still. Part of him wondered if he was going into some kind of shock when he realised how calm he felt. There was no anger, no rage at what had happened to him. He placed a hand over his stomach in a mirror of how Silas had held him only a little while ago and waited to feel the indignity and violation that he always felt after one of these sessions but instead he just felt numb.

Maybe when the king had moved his hand to his head he had burnt through the part of his brain that felt shame. Or maybe the sheer length and intensity of the torture was too much to fully comprehend. In fact, now that he thought about it he was finding it hard to remember what had actually just happened. He knew it had been bad, his aching body was proof of that, but he didn't know anything else.

One thing he did know, he thought as he finally forced himself to his feet and stumbled towards the door, using the wall as a balance. It didn't matter what he did. It didn't matter how much he tried to please the king, how hard he tried to deny his love for Asher, or the prince's love for him. Silas was going to do the same thing, over and over again. He would always end up back in this room.

This was the worst he had to endure, the king couldn't kill him, or even incapacitate him properly without also sentencing Asher to death. So why should he keep pretending? Why should he continue to live this miserable life of lies? Why should he push Asher away?

⌘

"Where's Blossom?" Asher asked as he sat down next to his father. He'd spent most of the day sparring with the blessed students and half expected his father to admonish him on his bedraggled appearance, but the king made no mention of it. In fact, Silas didn't even seem to want to look at him.

"He's caught up at the school. Apparently there was some emergency to do with the students and the celebrations for the long day." His father replied with a shrug.

"Oh." Asher said despondently, he'd gotten so used to seeing Blossom every day that he'd forgotten how much time they used to spend apart when his father was around.

"You rely on that boy too much Asher. There may be a time when you cannot be joined at the hip with him."

Asher paused where he'd been filling his glass. "We're not joined at the hip. Why do you make it seem like wanting to have dinner with my betrothed is a bad thing? And if we're going to be married then if anything we'll be spending more time together."

The king's eyes narrowed, and he finally looked at his son. "A lot can change in a short time Asher."

Asher put his cup down with a defiant *thunk*, water sloshing over the brim. "You know you talk like that a lot. If I didn't know any better, I'd think that you didn't want Blossom and I to marry."

Silas sighed, a sigh that the prince had heard many times when he had been a child. The sigh of someone who was tired of dealing with a wilful prince's actions. "Don't be childish. Your mother was very adamant about you two being together, I will not be unfaithful to her memory."

Asher stared at him. "That's not an answer."

"There wasn't a question either." Silas responded snappily. "But as you've bought him up you have reminded me. I plan on sending another push into Castilla, the western border has grown weak over the past few years, so it is the perfect time. I would like you to lead the troops, you were very successful on your last campaign, and it would do our soldiers good to see you ride with them again."

Asher felt knocked off balance for the second or third time in this one conversation. "Hold on, why are you pushing into Castilla? We've been at peace with them for years."

"That's what you think. They have never accepted our claim over the nature blessed. Even though he was a peasant, they say that he is a son of Castilla and that he should be returned to them."

"Well they're not wrong, he is a son of Castilla."

The king glared at him. "So what would you suggest? That we just hand him over? You would give up your life because they are claiming their right over him? No, war is the only way."

Asher shook his head; the solution was so clear to him that he couldn't understand why his father couldn't see it. "No, we shouldn't just hand him over, also can we stop talking about Blossom like he's an object to be bargained with? There's a simple solution to this father."

"And what, in your expert opinion, is that?" Silas asked, clearly humouring him.

"Allow us to marry."

The king threw his hands up in exasperation. "Asher seriously, I've told you..."

"No, no, no hear me out." Asher flapped his arms at him. "Think of it as a union between Castilla and Vaten, after all that was what you had planned if the blessed who could save me had come from one of the other kingdoms. We would be honouring Castilla by raising one of theirs to the rank of prince. If they believe that he is being held here against his will, or as a slave or whatever they think we're doing to him let's prove them wrong. It could bring our kingdoms together with no need for bloodshed, we could have true peace with them for the first time."

The king paused at that, and Asher began to eat knowing better than to push now. "You have given me a lot to think about." Silas said at last. "I do not have an answer for you right now, but I will say one thing..." Asher watched him intently as the king seemed to struggle to find his words. "...What you have just said shows that you have more of a mind for politics than I ever gave you credit for."

⌘

He couldn't remember how exactly he had done it, having blacked out multiple times on the way, but Blossom had managed to drag himself back to his room. He had never been more happy that court had been disbanded so he hadn't had to explain his current state to any courtiers that would other whys have been in the guest wing. He knew that he wouldn't have the strength to climb onto the roof to ask for Moon's blessing properly, even now that he had moved back into his old room with his vines offering ample footholds, so he contented himself with the balcony. Slumping against the cool stone railing that surrounded it he looked up. The moon was a mere sliver in the sky at this time of the month but even so he felt the cool rush of its healing magic as he breathed Moon's word, and before he knew it the soothing flow of Moon's blessing lulled him into a deep sleep.

## Chapter 19

The main blessing chamber was crowded with the entire student body, their celebration robes sparkling in the light that was being refracted through the glass ceiling. The other blessing teachers bordered the walls, each one standing in front of their respective classroom, their own celebration robes rich with gemstones and embroidery. Only Emma's place was empty as this part of the celebration was reserved for the blessed only.

"Okay children to your places." Blossom said as he stood in the centre of the room, his voice carrying easily over the crowd.

The children calmly surrounded him and sat down, crossed-legged in a many ringed circle. Blossom could tell how excited they all were, there was a buzz of energy that rippled from them all, but the importance of the occasion had caused an almost reverent hush to fall over the crowd. The first circle consisted of the 7 water blessed in the school, behind them the 10 moon blessed, next 2 rows of fire blessed, 2 rows of sun blessed and finally 3 rows of earth blessed. Each circle larger than the one inside it until the final circle almost touched the perimeter of the chamber.

Blossom watched as they all held hands within their circle. They had practiced this enough times over the past few weeks, and many had experienced at least some variation of this in their own towns and villages that they moved without prompting.

With a smile he whispered. "Let us begin." Before closing his eyes and speaking natures word. "Ninehshim." He allowed his residual blessing to spread gently from him. Opening his still glowing eyes he pushed it outwards until it tapped into the power of the water blessed closest to him.

The water blessed spoke their word and began to glow, pale blue light emanating from them. The moon blessed followed, glowing white as they pushed their power outwards. Then the warm orange glow of the fire blessed joined, the yellow of the sun blessed and finally the green of the earth blessed.

Blossom could feel the crackling energy of the blessings in the air, mixing and mingling with each other as the blessed fed off of each other's power until the whole room was alive with light. He let it hang there for a few moments, his skin tingling as energy danced across it before letting his power dim. The students followed and the room grew dark again. One by one they all opened their eyes, blissed out smiles on their faces.

"Well done everyone." Blossom said quietly, not wanting to break the calm that had settled over the room. "Now we're going to go outside and get ready to head down to the lake. Can those of you who were chosen as banner bearers please collect your banners from the other teachers and can everyone else line up in their groups."

Still quiet and tranquil the students rose to their feet and followed their teachers outside. Blossom stayed in the blessing chamber for a few more minutes, letting the residual power of the group blessing mix and mingle in the air around him. He drew it inside himself with one more whisper of Nature's word and stepped out into the avenue. The avenue was much more rowdy than the blessing school had been, the fresh air and the excitement of what was to come breaking the spell that had temporarily fallen over the students moments before.

"Okay everyone, quiet please." Blossom clapped his hands twice and the 5 neat rows of students fell dutifully quiet. "We have rehearsed this, and I assume that everyone remembers what it is that they have to do?"

"Yes master Blossom." The students and teachers chanted.

"Good, now we are going to be walking to the blessing lake in just a moment but before we do does anyone need the toilet?"

A few of the younger students raised their hands and Blossom indicated for the relevant teachers to escort them to the bathrooms.

"I always think that the water blessed look so lonely compared to the other groups when we do this." Emma said from her spot next to him, indicating towards the 7 students dressed in blue.

Blossom had to agree, next to the large lines of other blessed children they did look small. Especially when compared to the earth blessed who were standing 3 abreast to prevent their line from being comically long. "Unfortunately that's not going to change until Water becomes less picky about who to lay its blessing upon." He answered as the teachers hurried back with the recently relieved children.

⌘

The blessing lake was almost unrecognisable by the time they reached it. Every inch of grass between the glittering water and its surrounding forest was covered in bright tents, bonfires and numerous tables stacked high with freshly prepared food. The shore of the lake itself was bordered by intricately carved wooden benches, each one emblazoned with symbols that indicated which of the blessed should sit there. The students were almost beside themselves with excitement, even those who'd seen a royal solstice celebration before. Blossom hadn't the heart to try and corral them, they were still mostly holding to their lines anyway and that was all he could ask for.

The king and Asher had arrived separately and were already stood by the lake. He wasn't sure if it was because he was now allowing himself to revel in his feelings for the prince but the sight of Asher in his formal regalia almost took his breath away. Asher was dressed in a long black robe cut similarly to a blessers robe, black jewels causing the light to glint off of him in a way that Blossom hadn't thought was possible. He hadn't acted upon his newfound resolve since the king had tortured him, mostly owing to how busy he had been and the fact that Asher hadn't made any recent advances, but it warmed his heart to know that he could.

The children all filled obediently down the hill and onto the benches that had been set up to bracket the lake, their respective banners stamped into the ground behind them, and Blossom made his way over to the king. He turned his back on Silas without a word and allowed the king to remove his spring robe. It had technically been summer for a number of weeks already but the changing of robes had become an important symbolic part of the royal celebration. He could tell from Asher's sulking face that he and the king had had their same old argument about who should be the one to assist Blossom in the ceremony.

Blossom stepped away from them and began making his way towards the water, he had removed his shoes before the walk to the lake and now stood in only his plain brown breeches. He called forth the reservoir of Moon's blessing that he'd taken the night before and sent it into the air in a white beam of light as 4 servants carried forward the flaming cauldron of coal from the royal hearth. He didn't hesitate this time to plunge his hands into the cauldron, Fire's blessing scorching through him seconds later. He tilted his head back and breathed out a torrent of fire into the sky.

The servants stepped back, carrying the cauldron away from him and he continued his slow walk towards the lake. As he focused on the feeling of the soft grass beneath his toes Blossom asked silently for Earth's blessing. He raised his hands as he walked, clenching his fists together and pillars of earth sprung up around him in a shower of dirt. He held the columns aloft for a few more steps before lowering his hands again, letting them sink back into the soil. He paused for a second once he'd stepped into the shallows of the lake, letting Water's blessing fill him as much as he was able, glowing brightly as he opened himself up to the full extent of his ability.

Taking a breath Blossom raised one foot out of the water and when he placed it down again it didn't sink below the lake, instead resting atop the clear liquid. He raised his other foot and began walking on the lakes surface until he reached the centre. The darkness and depth below him had been terrifying the first few times Blossom had performed this ritual but by now it was just another step.

Tilting his head back Blossom looked up at the sun hanging above him, he sighed in contentment as Sun's blessing warmed him and he allowed the power to radiate out from him in a bright glow. Taking the remnants of each blessing left inside of him, he allowed them to mix together until they became indistinguishable from one another and with a final shout of pure joy and exhilaration he let it burst from him. The blessing rolled out from him like a wave, a mixture of every colour imaginable rippling across the water.

People gasped in awe as the warmth of Nature's blessing washed over them, briefly filling everyone present with its power. As the last trickle of power left him Blossom felt the water beneath his feet give and he sucked in a breath as he was plunged beneath the surface.

⌘

It didn't matter how many times Asher had seen Blossom do this it was always amazing to him. As the remnants of Blossom's power brushed his skin, warming him briefly, he smiled. Asher then felt his stomach lurch as Blossom disappeared into the depths of the lake. This was also a feeling that never changed, the urge to run to the water's edge, to dive into the sacred lake and make sure that Blossom was okay. The sentiment was clearly shared by most of the students at the water's edge as they shifted in their seats, muttering in concern. Some even stood but stopped short of touching the water itself.

The worry didn't last long as a faint blue light began to emanate from the lake.

Glowing stronger as it moved towards the edge and a few seconds later Blossom's pink curls breached the surface, followed gradually by the rest of him, dripping wet but completely unharmed. Blossom walked calmly out of the lake and began to make his way towards the royal tent where King Silas had his summer robe slung over one arm.

Asher tried to remind himself that this was a sacred and serious occasion and fought not to dwell too much on the effect that being face to face with a dripping wet and half naked Blossom was having on him. Blossom glowed briefly again as he walked, this time with the warm yellow light of Sun's blessing and by the time he reached Asher and Silas he was completely dry.

He turned away from them once he drew level and the king stepped forward to drape the green and gold robe over his shoulders. Asher felt a rise of jealousy and indignation at the action, but the king had insisted that whilst they were still unwed Asher didn't have the right to assist Blossom in the ceremony. Blossom slipped his arms into the sleeves before spreading them wide and declaring. "And so, summer commences." To a thunderous applause.

⌘

"Another successful start to the celebrations."

Blossom turned at the king's words, absently doing up the buttons of his robe as he moved. "Indeed sire, thank you for your assistance." He replied dutifully, tying the golden sash at his waist with a flourish.

The king smiled at him and grasped his arm in what to many must have looked like a proud and friendly gesture, but the sudden searing heat that shot through him caused Blossom to stumble back in shock.

"Woah there, you must have overexerted yourself. Allow me to fix you a plate to help you regain your strength." The king patted him again and leant in to whisper in his ear. "Never presume to tell me when I can and cannot leave a mark on you again."

Blossom stared at his retreating back numbly as Asher walked over to him, his arm throbbing with a familiar ache.

"Another great success." The prince said brightly, and Blossom forced a smile onto his face trying to ignore how closely Asher's words had mirrored his fathers.

"Yes." He replied simply, turning his gaze to the flock of children that had gathered around the feast tables. "Come on, let's get something to eat." He said taking Asher's hand and leading him to a table away from the one the king was sitting at. "I'm starving."

⌘

The sun was beginning to dip towards the horizon when Emma escorted the students back towards the palace. They were going to have a solstice bonfire in the blessing garden that Blossom had promised to join them at later. He waved them off before joining Asher who was sat alone on the grass, gazing out over the lake.

"I asked my father if we could set a date for the wedding." The prince said, still staring at the setting sun.

Blossom laughed quietly as he sat down. "And how did that go?" He asked, smiling at him.

Asher finally looked at him, he pushed lightly at Blossom's shoulder before resting back on his hands. Returning Blossom's smile with one of his own he said. "It could have gone well, do you always have to be such a pessimist?"

"I'm not a pessimist, I'm a realist. And besides you know you love me." Blossom said absently, the words only sinking in when Asher's smile turned sad.

"Yeah, yeah I do." The prince responded, more to himself than anyone else, yanking a tuft of grass from the ground as he did so.

Blossom looked over his shoulder, feeling the raw skin on his arm as he stared at the king. King Silas had his back to them, laughing with a few of the visiting nobles. He was already a few cups deep into the ale barrels and far more dangerous for it. Blossom's eyes narrowed in a glare, he remembered the promise that he had made to himself and Asher, and despite the fear that continued to linger allowed the spark of rebellion that he had always tamped down to flair into life.

"Blossom can I ask you..."

"Come with me." Blossom interrupted, standing again and tugging on Asher's hand.

"Hey Blossom I'm trying to talk to you." The prince complained loudly as he was pulled to his feet.

"Shhh I know, just come with me for a second." Blossom sent a furtive look over his shoulder again and was relieved to see that the king's attention was still elsewhere, he hadn't even seemed to have heard his son's exclamation. He sighed in relief and gestured for Asher to follow him. He may be planning on disobeying the kings' orders, but Silas didn't need to know that, not yet at least.

He ushered Asher over to the secluded copse of trees that surrounded the lake, making sure that they were completely out of sight before rounding on the prince.

"Blossom what the fuck has gotten..."

He cut the prince off again, pressing their lips together in a gentle kiss. Before Asher had a chance to recover from his shock and reciprocate Blossom pulled back. Keeping his hands on Asher's cheeks he looked him in the eye and whispered. "I love you too."

There were a few tense moments where Asher didn't respond, just stared at Blossom in silent shock. Blossom opened his mouth, not sure what to say but desperate to break the suddenly awkward silence when Asher suddenly moved. The prince grabbed hold of the front of his robe, slamming his back into the nearest tree. Blossom coughed as the air was briefly driven out of him. "Asher what the..."

This time it was the prince that cut him off, locking their lips together in a searing kiss. Blossom clutched helplessly at the back of the prince's robe as Asher devoured him, stealing whatever breath he had managed to regain, leaving him gasping against the prince's lips. He broke the kiss when his lungs couldn't take anymore, resting his head back against the tree as Asher began peppering kisses down the length of his neck.

"Asher." He gasped out the word with a groan as the prince bit down gently on his collarbone. He hadn't foreseen this reaction and the sudden thought of them being caught if he let this continue caused him to tug sharply at Asher's dark hair. "Asher stop."

The prince growled, actually growled at him as his black eyes locked with Blossom's pink ones. The intensity of his gaze almost caused Blossom's legs to give out beneath him. "You're telling me to stop?" He asked, crowding Blossom harder against the tree. Asher pressed a thigh between his legs causing Blossom to gasp, clutching at the arms currently keeping him upright. "You tell me you love me. You give me everything I've wanted for so many years and then you tell me to stop?"

Blossom tried to grasp for words to respond with as Asher continued to press against him. "Yes." He finally gasped out.

Asher's gaze grew impossibly darker. "Why?" He ground out, finally removing his leg but thankfully keeping hold of Blossom's waist so that he didn't sink to the floor.

"We can't let the king know."

Asher stepped back in confusion. "What? Why would he care?"

Blossom shook his head mutely, grabbing for Asher as he moved away. He knew that he was sending mixed signals and being unfair, but he couldn't help it as he pulled the prince back in for another kiss.

"Tonight." He whispered against Asher's lips. "Meet me on the roof after the bonfire and I'll explain everything. I promise."

Asher sighed and rested his head against Blossom's shoulder. "Are you saying that I have to keep my hands off of you until tonight?"

"Afraid so."

Asher shook his head and, cupping Blossom's cheek, placed another passionate kiss on his lips. Blossom panicked briefly that the prince had ignored him and wouldn't stop but Asher pulled back after a few moments. Running his hand through Blossom's curls he said quietly. "You are contrary and cruel."

Blossom smiled back at him apologetically. "I know. But you still love me."

Asher chuckled and kissed him again. "Yes. And you love me."

"Yes I do."

## Chapter 20

Asher managed to convince his father that he should be allowed to accompany Blossom to the student's bonfire, a surprisingly easy task thanks to how deep the king was in his cups. As they crested the hill back towards the palace and the lake disappeared out of sight he reached out and laced his fingers with Blossom's. He half expected Blossom to pull away as he always had, proving to him that what had happened in the forest had only been a daydream, but Blossom simply looked at him out of the corner of his eye and said his name warningly.

"What? There's no one around. My father will never know that I committed the terrible crime of holding your hand." He retorted, relishing in Blossom's returning eye roll and chuckle. Something had changed at the lakeside, like a weight had been lifted off of his friend, he only wished he knew why Blossom had carried that weight for so long.

The warm orange glow of the blessing bonfire was looming bigger and bigger before them, peaking over the top of the garden wall, and just before they entered the blessing garden Asher pulled Blossom aside.

"What's wrong?" Blossom asked, looking around furtively for danger.

Asher smiled and took a breath. "Look, I know that you said you'd tell me after the bonfire and that I had to keep my hands off of you until then but..."

"Asher." Blossom said again, staring him down with his best teacher's expression. "Let's just enjoy the bonfire. I'll explain everything after."

"I know, I know it's not that." He said and Blossom leant back against the stone wall behind him. He swept his hand towards the prince in a 'go on' gesture and Asher swallowed, not used to having to ask this question with the very real option of it being answered with a yes. "Can I kiss you? Just one more time?"

Blossom laughed, sudden and loud enough that Asher stepped back in surprise. "Ash, less than an hour ago you had me pinned against a tree and seemed more than happy to kiss me whether I liked it or not and now you're asking for permission?"

Asher looked down at his feet, guilt and shame swirling uncomfortably in his gut. "And that was wrong of me. I should have stopped as soon as you said to, I shouldn't have grilled you or tried to force you. I just want to make sure this time, I don't want to do something that you don't want me to."

A hand touched his cheek and he looked up, Blossom was smiling at him gently. "My sweet Ash, you did stop when I wanted you to. You don't need to feel bad." The blesser sighed and looked away briefly. "I know I haven't told you why yet, but you at least know enough not to try anything when we're in public." When Asher didn't respond Blossom looked back at him. "The answer is yes by the way, you can kiss me."

Asher felt his heart swell and stepped in close, cupping Blossom's cheek and placing a gentle kiss on his lips, relishing in the enthusiasm that he felt in Blossom's reciprocation. He pulled back, content with simply being allowed to express his love in this way but before he could step back Blossom spoke again.

"Oh and for future reference." Blossom's smile turned mischievous, and he grasped a fistful of Asher's robe, pulling him close to whisper in his ear. "I quite like it when you're forceful."

Asher didn't give himself time to second guess Blossom's intentions and simply pressed him hard against the wall. Threading his fingers through soft pink locks as he licked his way into his mouth. He could feel Blossom smiling against him and strong arms wrapping around his shoulders as Blossom kissed back with equal fervour.

They kissed for a few more moments until Blossom gently pushed him away, a small and slightly blissed out smile on his face. "We should join the children." He said quietly, slipping past the prince and into the garden.

Asher followed with a large grin, his fingers still itching to grab Blossom and hold him close. When he entered the garden, he was met with a mixture of excited and very sleepy children. A small group of the older students had already caught hold of Blossom and he was dancing with them around the bonfire.

Asher made his way over to Emma who had a young fire blessed asleep on her lap. "Good evening your majesty." She said quietly, smiling up at him.

"Evening Emma."

"Have you had a good day?" She asked as he sat down next to her.

"Honestly this has probably been the best long day celebration I can remember having." Asher responded, smiling at the sight of Blossom spinning two children, one in either hand. "Look at how happy he is." He said more quietly, not intending for Emma to hear. He looked over when he felt a cool palm on his cheek.

Emma was smiling at him proudly and Asher felt his heart give a lurch, he hadn't seen that expression on anyone since his mother had died. "I know he can be hard to read at times, and that he makes its seem like he doesn't want you. But I hope you know just how much Blossom does love you."

Asher looked back at the bonfire, the ghost of their last kiss on his lips. "I think I'm starting too." He responded.

The song that had been playing ended and the band of servants began strumming a familiar tune, the ballad of courting. A slow steady beat that many of the children seemed unsure of how to dance to. Pushing himself off the bench Asher made his way over to Blossom.

"Shall we show them how it's done?" The prince asked, holding out his hand towards the other man. He expected Blossom to come up with some kind of excuse. This was probably within his definition of flirtations that he considered too much, but after a quick glance around Blossom shrugged and took hold of the offered hand.

"Why not. Although I'm not sure how much use they will get out of dance lessons."

Asher snorted but on the next beat stepped forward, raising their joined hands in the air as they stood almost nose to nose. He stepped back again on the next beat, Blossom mirroring his movements perfectly. He let go of the hand he had been holding and raised his other hand palm outwards, Blossom pressed their palms together and they side stepped twice before turning in a slow circle. They repeated these moves a few more times until the music began to speed up. Now instead of holding hands Asher wrapped an arm around Blossom's waist, Blossom placed his hand at the back of Asher's neck and leant forward until their foreheads touched.

"Not sure how to do the next bit with the bonfire in the way." He murmured and Blossom laughed quietly.

"Just go around, I'll deal with the rest." Blossom opened his eyes to look at him and Asher noticed the faint orange glow emanating from them.

He nodded his understanding and began to turn. They spun around the bonfire, their circles moving faster and faster as the music continued to speed up. Usually this dance was done by multiple couples all spinning around and past each other, but all of the students had stepped back from the fire to watch as they moved. Asher released Blossom on their second circuit of the bonfire and the man spun away from him, thrusting his hand out at the last moment for Asher to grasp. When they returned to their original position Blossom took the lead and took hold of Asher's waist turning them in the opposite direction.

"When I tell you to, jump with me." Blossom said, slightly breathless.

Asher nodded, too focused on where his feet were to be able to respond verbally. They completed one more circuit of the fire as the music reached its crescendo and he heard Blossom whisper "now."

They both leapt towards the fire, hand in hand, the flames parting at the last moment to allow them to make it to the other side unscathed. Blossom reached the other side first but lost his footing as he landed and, still holding onto Asher, tumbled to the floor. They ended up in a heap as they rolled away from the flames and Blossom lay giggling breathlessly beside him when they finally managed to untangle themselves from one another.

"That might have been a little unorthodox for the ballad of courting." He said, staring up at the sky as the students crowded around them in a mixture of excitement and concern.

"I dunno, I think I preferred it." Asher replied, standing up and brushing himself off. He held out a hand to help Blossom back onto his feet.

⌘

By the time that Blossom reached the rooftop later that night Asher was already there waiting for him. The prince had left the bonfire half an hour before him with a meaningful glance at the palace roof. Blossom had nodded his understanding but had also indicated his own unwillingness to leave the students just yet, he wanted to help the other teachers get the children back to their dorms safely.

Asher had chosen their childhood hiding spot, a space between two closely built chimney stacks on the northern side of the palace, and Blossom found him quickly.

He made his way over to his usual place against the stack opposite the prince but remembering that he no longer had to keep his distance he knelt in front of him instead and leant forward. He could feel Asher thread his fingers through his hair as their lips met.

After a few minutes, during which Blossom practically climbed into Asher's lap, the prince tugged gently on Blossom's hair, causing him to pull back with a quiet sigh. "As much as I'm enjoying your sudden change of heart you have something to tell me."

Blossom sighed again and placed another gentle kiss on Asher's lips before settling back against the original chimney. He let his head *thunk* back against the stone as he tried to organise his thoughts.

"Blossom." Asher said after a moment of silence. "Talk."

"Sorry there's...there's just a lot. It's hard to know where to begin." He looked down as he felt Asher nudge his foot with his own.

"How about I ask about what I want to know? You answer my questions and that way you only have to talk about a small bit at a time."

Blossom couldn't help but smile, looking at Asher with so much undisguised love that the prince visibly blushed. "Okay what do you want to know?"

"When did you fall in love with me?"

Blossom blinked in surprise, he hadn't expected that. "Technically the day we first met." It was Asher's turn to look surprised. Blossom shrugged and looked away. "That's kind of the thing when you have two people with spirits as closely linked as ours are. But I guess if you're asking when did I realised that it was romantic love? Our 16$^{th}$ birthday." He smiled at Asher. "The first time I used Water's blessing on you at the lake."

Asher chuckled. "Figures that it'd be the first time you saw me shirtless."

They both laughed quietly until Blossom spoke again. "When did you know? That you loved me I mean?"

"Do you remember when I told you that you were going to be my husband one day?"

Blossom straightened. "Then?"

Asher laughed again. "What did you think I meant when I told you that?"

Blossom raised his hands helplessly. "We were 10 Ash, I thought that you were just repeating what your mother told you."

Asher shook his head with a small smile. "She never told me that we were going to be married. She arranged it after I told her that I wanted to marry you."

Blossom sat back against the chimney stack, still in shock. "Huh, I always thought that our arrangement was just a way for your parents to keep me here."

"What do you mean keep you here? Did you want to leave?" Asher asked, suddenly concerned.

Blossom turned his head, avoiding the prince's gaze, instead staring at the slowly dimming glow of the blessing bonfire. "At first I did. I wanted to go home, I lost everything when they bought me here. This country and its people were foreign to me. Did you never wonder why your mother had to go and find me that day?"

Asher shrugged. "She never said, only that you and father had had a disagreement and that you needed space. I never realised that you'd tried to run away."

Blossom looked down at where his hands were resting in his lap.

"I don't think it was a proper attempt. I would never have left you if I'd been in my right mind. You were always the only thing keeping me here."

They sat in silence for a while whilst Asher mulled over what Blossom had said. "I guess I never looked at it from your perspective. For me I just gained a new friend that would always be there to play with me. I wouldn't be lonely or in pain anymore. I never considered what you lost, I'm sorry." Asher looked down at his own lap, suddenly ashamed.

Blossom cocked his head to the side with a smile. "We were children Ash, I don't blame you, I never did."

Asher looked back up at him. "That's not what you said before though."

Blossom sighed, this was the bit that he'd been dreading. "I know, but there had to be some reason for me to keep rejecting you. Your father figured that was the most believable."

"About that." Asher responded, eyes narrowing. "Why did you keep rejecting me? Why would my father want you to when he was the one who announced our betrothal to the kingdom?"

"Your father agreed to promise us to one another to hold me here, and after your mother died he didn't want to betray her memory by dissolving it. He hoped that you would change your mind as you got older. You can't tell me that you never noticed all of the young nobles that he threw at you."

Asher was staring at him with a mixture of shock and disbelief. "So you pretended not to love me back to make me change my mind?"

Blossom shrugged. "He made me."

Asher sat back, looking into the sky. "But why?"

"Because I'm Castillan. He didn't want you marrying a nobody from an enemy kingdom." Blossom blinked in surprise when Asher suddenly started laughing.

"No wonder it galled him so much when I said that we could use our marriage to unite our kingdoms."

Blossom blinked again before laughing too. "Oh blessing Asher you're a genius. That might actually make him change his mind."

They continued to laugh quietly for a few more moments before Asher spoke again. "So what made you decide to ignore his orders now?"

Blossom shrugged again, he still refused to tell Asher what exactly it was that the king had done to him. He wasn't ready to destroy the prince's image of his father. "I was tired of pretending, tired of how miserable it made me. Tired of hurting you."

Asher smiled gently at him and held his arms out, into which Blossom happily crawled. He tucked his head into the crook of Asher's shoulder, and they sat in a comfortable silence until Asher asked. "Why did you go along with it for so long?"

Blossom sighed, his breath tickling against the prince's neck. "Your father's terrifying Asher, and he can be very persuasive when he wants to be." He replied, refusing to elaborate past that.

Asher chuckled and continued to hold him. "Blossom?" He asked, running his hands through the blessers pink hair.

"I thought you'd run out of questions." Blossom grumbled in reply, pulling back to look Asher in the eyes.

The prince smiled. "Last one I promise."

"Fine, what do you want my love?" Blossom asked, grinning evilly as the new pet name caused Asher to turn bright red.

Asher cleared his throat, trying to compose himself. "Not that you ever have to worry about it but what would you have done if my father's plan had worked? What if I'd been put off by your rejection and chosen someone else?"

Blossom felt his heart squeeze and he looked down, staring resolutely at Asher's chest as he responded. "I promised myself that I would be happy for you. As long as you didn't banish me, and I could stay by your side as an advisor or something then I would content myself with that. But truthfully..." He looked up, tears in his eyes. "...I think it would have killed me."

"Oh flower." Asher whispered soothingly, kissing him with as much love and promise as he could muster. "That was cruel of me to ask, I'm sorry."

"I forgive you. Just hold me for now."

"Of course."

⌘

"I can't believe that the children are leaving the day after tomorrow. It feels like they only just got here." Blossom said quietly. The blessing bonfire had gone out about half an hour ago and the night was cool and quiet as they continued to sit, wrapped around each other, on the rooftop. Blossom had turned around in Asher's embrace and now sat with his back pressed against the prince's chest.

The prince rested his chin on Blossom's shoulder after pressing a quick kiss to his cheek. "You really do love them don't you." He said, his statement holding no judgment.

"It might sound crazy but I feel like they're mine. My children. I have to look after them."

"It's not crazy, you are probably the only one in the world that can relate to every single one of them. You bring them together, they are like a family when they're here." Asher kissed his cold cheek again before saying. "You're going to be a great father one day."

Blossom sank back against him even more, this was the first time that he was actually allowing himself to picture the future that Asher had planned for them. He imagined them both, on another solstice day many years in the future. Sat just as they were now but on the grass and not the roof, watching their children, two dark haired little girls playing by the blessing lake. He liked that image, but just as he was about to respond another image rose to mind. One of a young yellow-haired boy, rigid with pain as someone he trusted held him down, using his own blessing against him.

"There's a little boy here that I don't want to send back to his mother." He said instead.

"Is this about the sun blessed boy that you told Emma about?" Asher asked.

Blossom wasn't surprised that Asher had heard about Aelius. "Yes."

Asher sighed, kissing the crown of his head. "Blossom, I get that you care about these children but you can't dictate how their parents discipline them."

Blossom pulled away from the prince, turning to look at him in shock. "This isn't discipline Asher, this is torture." Asher sighed again as though he was being overly dramatic, and Blossom huffed. "Forget it, you wouldn't understand." He said, rising to his feet.

"Why, because I'm not blessed?" He heard from behind him as he turned his back on the prince.

He whirled again. "Yes Asher, that's exactly why. Because you're not blessed." He spat sarcastically.

"Then why don't you explain it to me? Or have you been forthright enough for one evening?"

He ignored the jab. "You wouldn't understand unless you'd been through it yourself." Blossom realised that he'd begun to shout but he couldn't stop himself.

Asher was on his feet as well now. "What and you've been through this?" He shouted back, clearly thinking this a rhetorical question.

"Yes." Blossom screamed.

They both froze as Blossom's statement sunk in.

"What?" Asher asked quietly, his expression an almost comical mixture of despair, worry and anger.

Blossom stepped back, looking around as thought trying to remember how he'd gotten there. "Nothing, never mind. Forget I said anything."

Asher shook his head. "Blossom, who did that to you?" He asked gently, as though speaking to a skittish animal.

Blossom stopped, staring at Asher with wide eyes. He couldn't tell him. Even after everything he couldn't tell him. "I can't." He breathed, and before Asher could say anything else he bolted.

## Chapter 21

Somehow Blossom successfully managed to avoid Asher for the next two days, mostly by actively ducking into rooms or alcoves when he spotted the prince. It had been a talent that he'd unfortunately had many years to perfect, so Blossom knew that he could do it indefinitely until he figured out what to do next. It wasn't until he was waving the last of the children's carriages off that the prince appeared beside him before he could bolt again. Blossom couldn't help the small flinch that went through him when Asher placed his hand on his lower back, or how much he hated the look of hurt that flashed over the other man's face at the action.

"If you're expecting me to apologise then you've got a long wait." He said by way of greeting.

Asher looked at him, his eyes sad. "I'm not expecting an apology flower. I came to apologise to you."

Blossom felt his shoulders go slack and he turned to the prince. Wrapping his arms around Asher's shoulders he hugged him silently, trying not to cry into his shoulder as the prince held him as tightly as he could.

"Come with me to the lake flower." Asher said quietly into his hair.

Blossom pulled back slightly. "Why?" He asked, his eyes flickering down to Asher's lips when he felt the prince's breath mingling with his own.

"Because we have two weeks to ourselves and I want to spend as much of that time with you as possible."

Blossom huffed out a small laugh. "Okay you win."

"And after you put up such a fight to." Asher responded with a laugh of his own, dropping his arms and stepping away from him.

He took hold of the hand that Asher held out to him, checking briefly to make sure that they weren't being watched or followed and they made their way down to the lake. There were only a few signs that the long day had ever even taken place, a few scorched patches of earth where the fires had been, a few scraps of food that hadn't been taken away by scavengers yet. Other than that the blessing lake looked much the same as it always had, sparkling and beautiful in the summer sun.

"Should we go for a swim?" Asher asked as they walked to the edge of the lake.

"I'd rather stay dry for now." Blossom replied taking off his boots as they stopped by the shoreline. "I don't mind just getting my feet wet though." He was very aware of the handprint shaped burn that was still on his upper arm. The king had found an excuse to grab him multiple times over the last few days, always in the same place. Just a silent reminder of his continued power over him, and what had started out as a tender patch of skin had now mutated into a blistered wound that he hadn't quite been able to heal. He hadn't been ordered back to the hearth room though, so Blossom was pretty sure that Silas didn't know how badly he'd disobeyed him yet, he was probably just angry at the lack of fear that Blossom now felt.

Asher tossed his own boots next to Blossom's and followed him into the shallows. "It's not like you to stay out of the water flower." He said absently, pulling off his tunic and rolling his breeches above his knees.

Blossom kicked at the water, his cheeks burning as he looked at Asher's toned and muscled back out of the corner of his eye. He was pretty sure that the prince wouldn't mind if he openly gawped at him, but old habits die hard it seemed.

"Come on, you can come in deeper than that." The prince called, now up to his knees in the cool water.

Blossom rolled his eyes with a smile and followed him out. "That's far enough Ash." He said without conviction as the prince caught hold of his hands and pulled him close. Asher smiled at him and kissed the backs of his hands, first one and then the other before leaning forward slowly. Blossom closed his eyes as he waited to feel the soft press of lips against his own, but he simply gasped in shock as he was suddenly pushed backwards and engulfed by the water of the lake.

He surged to the surface seconds later, sputtering in indignation, now thoroughly drenched. "Asher." He shouted as the prince simply grinned at him, his eyes alight with a playful mischief that Blossom remembered well from his childhood.

"Yes flower?" Asher asked innocently, causing Blossom to growl a profanity under his breath as he angrily brushed his wet locks out of his eyes.

He surged forward, tackling the prince at the waist. A move that Asher was clearly not expecting as he let out a surprised 'oof' and they both went sprawling into the water. The pair wrestled playfully in the lake for some time, their game taking them further and further from shore until they were up to their chests. Blossom clung to Asher's shoulders and kicked his feet up hoping that his weight would drag the other under, but Asher simply wrapped an arm under his legs and threw him, screeching, back beneath the water.

"This is so unfair, my robes are dragging me down." Blossom complained as he breached the surface again, treading water now that his feet couldn't quite touch the bottom.

"Then take them off." Asher laughed, not moved in the slightest by Blossom's plight.

Blossom splashed at him. "You'd like that wouldn't you." He continued to splash water at him as the prince raised his arms in an attempt to shield himself.

"I give up, I give up." He laughed, snatching out to grab Blossom's splashing hands.

Expecting to be dunked again Blossom struggled against his hold. He pressed his hands to Asher's chest, causing his arms to be pinned between them when Asher pulled him close and kissed him. Blossom relaxed almost instantly, sighing against his lips and letting Asher deepen the kiss as he wished.

"I love you." Asher whispered, breaking away from Blossom's lips only far enough to allow him to speak before diving back in again.

Unable and unwilling to pull away to respond verbally Blossom simply moaned. Sending gentle pulses of Water's blessing through their link, causing Asher to shudder as the power revived and relaxed him. After a while Blossom began to shiver in Asher's arms, the coldness of the water clinging to his clothes and seeping into his bones.

"Let's head back." Asher whispered against his lips, reluctant to pull away.

Blossom nodded at him silently and they swam back to shore. They both walked a short way up the hill until they were on unbroken grass, picking up their discarded clothes on the way. Asher took hold of his waist suddenly and tumbled him to the ground, pinning him beneath him with a triumphant grin. Blossom laughed as Asher covered him and began peppering his face with small, quick kisses.

"Asher you're soaking wet get off of me." He giggled, his words holding no conviction as he pushed ineffectively at the prince's shoulders.

"So are you. You can't get any wetter flower." Asher responded, rubbing his wet hair against Blossom's cheek until he shrieked.

"We'll catch our deaths my love, let me dry us." He said through his laughter, reaching a hand up past Asher to ask for Sun's blessing.

"Don't worry, I'll warm you up." Asher whispered, running his hands up and down Blossom's sides, rolling their hips together in a way that made Blossom gasp. Just as he made to begin undoing the buttons on Blossom's robe, kissing at his neck roughly the blesser stopped laughing. Asher pulled back as Blossom tensed beneath him. "What's wrong?" He asked, looking at Blossom in concern.

Blossom's eyes were alight with fear and his grip on Asher's wrists was turning his fingers white. "I can't." He gasped. "I'm sorry Asher I can't. Not yet." He had made his peace with what Silas might do to him if he found out that they had kissed but he couldn't even imagine what the king would do if he found out that they had lain together whilst unwed. What he might do to both of them. And if he was being honest with himself, he wasn't ready for them to take that step yet either.

"Okay, okay flower. Don't worry, we'll stop, we don't have to do anymore." Asher pulled away and sat next to him, gazing at him with worry. "Are you okay?" He asked as Blossom sat upright, his chest still heaving, but this time with residual panic.

Blossom nodded and drew his knees up to his chest. "I'm sorry." He said again.

"Blossom." He looked over at the prince in surprise at the sharpness in his voice. Asher took hold of his hands again, staring at him until Blossom looked him in the eyes. "Don't ever apologise for asking me to stop. Don't ever apologise for setting your boundaries."

Blossom smiled at him. "I love you." He said simply causing Asher to smile back.

"I know."

He leant forward and kissed him chastely on the lips. "Let me take Sun's blessing and I'll get us dry. I don't fancy explaining to your father why we're both in this state." Asher let go of his hands to allow him to stand and Blossom took a few steps forward, stretching his arms out and tilting his head back as Sun's blessing warmed and dried him.

"You're more powerful than him you know."

Blossom turned away from the lake to look at Asher in confusion. "Beg your pardon?"

Asher lent back on his elbows and gazed up at him. "My father. You're more powerful than him."

"So?"

"So why are you so afraid of him?"

Blossom couldn't help the small snort that escaped him. "Because he's the king Asher, and he's your father. You're physically stronger than him as well, does that mean that you're not intimidated by him?"

"Well no but I'm much less afraid of him than you are." Asher rose to his feet as he spoke.

Blossom stepped back as Asher moved towards him, absently touching his arm where the king had grabbed him. "I have plenty of reasons to be afraid of him." He said quietly as he looked out over the lake.

Asher zeroed in on Blossom's action, and before he could think to stop him the prince had grabbed his arm and pushed his sleeve up revealing the tender red handprint. "When did he...?" Asher trailed off as Blossom hurriedly pulled his sleeve back down.

"Two days ago, just after the solstice ceremony." Blossom rested his hand over the now covered mark again, refusing to look Asher in the eye.

The prince tipped his chin up with a finger. "How long has he been hurting you?"

Blossom's eyes flicked away, unable to keep Asher's suddenly intense gaze. "10 years or so? Ever since..." Blossom swallowed, unable to bring himself to finish the sentence.

"Ever since I told him that I wanted to marry you." Asher took a deep breath. "That's why you went along with his plan for so long. Did he hurt you every time I said or showed that I loved you?"

"Uhhh." Blossom stuttered but Asher spoke again before he had a chance to think of what to say.

"You said that you'd experienced blessing torture before like that little boy has, was that what he did to you?"

"Asher..." Blossom said desperately which seemed to be enough of an answer for Asher as he dropped his hand and spun on his heel, storming away. "Asher? Wait where are you going?"

The prince didn't answer so Blossom pulled his shoes on quickly, gathered up the rest of Asher's discarded clothes and followed him back to the palace. He finally caught up with him just as they entered the grand hallway.

"Asher wait please, you can't just..."

Asher whirled on him, his bare feet squeaking on the polished wooden floor of the hallway. "Why can't I?" He demanded. "So he can do it again? So that you can continue living in fear?"

Blossom clutched Asher's tunic tighter to his chest. "He's the king." He said finally, unable to explain past that.

"There are many kings flower." Asher said darkly. "But there's only one you." He turned away again leaving Blossom gaping in the hallway.

## Chapter 22

Asher threw open the doors to the throne room, not surprised to find it empty. With no courtiers to entertain the king hadn't been spending much time in the room since his return. He made his way quickly through the hall and around the back of the large stone seats. He automatically raised his hand to knock on the door located behind the thrones but forced himself to lower it again and opened the door without announcing himself.

"Asher." His father admonished, looking up from the map that he had been pouring over with his advisors. "I thought I'd taught you better than to enter here without knocking first." The king straightened and Asher noted with a grim satisfaction that even at his full height his father was still 2 inches shorter than him. Blossom was right, he thought as he looked the man over, even if they had been the same height, age and opulence had softened him physically. If this came down to a fight he had no doubt that he would win.

"I guess your lessons don't sink in as well when you can't burn them into your students." He snapped.

The king's eyes narrowed suspiciously, and he finally seemed to take in the state of his son. "What is this Asher? Why are you soaking wet? Where are the rest of your clothes?"

That was the moment that Blossom decided to enter the war room, still carrying Asher's boots and tunic. The king looked from Asher to Blossom and back again a few times, glowering as realisation began to dawn. "Gentlemen please excuse me for a moment, it appears that my son and I have something to discuss."

The advisors bowed and quietly exited the room, rolls of parchment clutched in their arms. Once they were alone Asher began to speak again. "Father I..."

"Put some clothes on, I refuse to speak to you until you are fully dressed."

Blossom handed him his tunic and knelt to help him on with his boots as he pulled it over his head. At some point during the walk here Blossom had dried the material and the tunic was still slightly warm with Sun's blessing. Asher looked down at the top of Blossom's bowed head with a frown, he hated how meek the blesser instantly became in the king's presence. He had hoped that Blossom's small act of rebellion would have allayed some of his fears, but he guessed not. Although the knowledge of what had been happening to him made the fear more understandable, and that thought reignited his own anger.

"Father." He spat once Blossom stood back up.

"Asher you are in a state, you should..."

"No, sit down and let me talk." Asher shouted, his father's obvious delay tactics infuriating him even more. Silas sat down, so surprised by his son's outburst that he obeyed without thinking about it. "How dare you lay a hand on my betrothed." He growled, gesturing to Blossom as though there could be any doubt about who he was referring to.

"Careful Asher, you are walking the line here." Silas responded, his voice infuriatingly calm.

"So you don't deny it?"

"As I don't know what it is that I am being accused of there is nothing for me to deny."

Asher glowered at him but took a breath to try and calm himself. He knew that his father would continue to be evasive if he continued to throw angry words out without thinking about them first.

"I am accusing you of torturing Blossom in an attempt to get me to call off our wedding." He said finally. "Do you deny it?"

The king sat back casually in his chair, fiddling with a pen that had been left on the table as though they were simply discussing the weather. "I do not deny that there have been times where I have had to discipline the boy, which is my right as his guardian."

Asher stared at him in shock. "What could he have possibly done to warrant such punishment?" He asked, aware that he was talking about Blossom as though he wasn't in the room.

"Laying a burn on his arm is nothing Asher. No different than when I laid a hand on you as a badly behaved child. I only disciplined him more than you because he was far more unruly."

He felt a hand on his arm, Blossom's fingers trembling as he clutched at his sleeve, ineffectually trying to pull him away. "You're lying." He said, disbelief colouring his words.

"What did you say to me?" Silas stood and rounded the table, all pretence at nonchalance gone as he stalked over to him.

"It wasn't just one burn on his arm, and I do not believe that Blossom was ever more unruly than I was."

The king shot an accusatory glance at Blossom who took a step back. "What lies has he been spewing?" He demanded.

"*He* is called Blossom." Asher responded, stepping in front of Blossom to shield him, worried that now that he had been found out that his father might strike him in front of him. "And he told me that you've been inflicting blessing torture on him for years now."

"And you believe him?" The king roared. "You believe the treason spewing from this commoner's mouth over my own?"

Asher tilted his chin up defiantly. "He may have been born in a farmhouse father, but Blossom's powers raised him to our level years ago. He has not been a commoner since he was bought here, and when we are married he will be a prince." Asher smiled without mirth as a thought suddenly occurred to him. "Maybe that is why you've been refusing to set a date, you're already so afraid of him that you can't bring yourself to allow him more power." He heard Blossom gasp behind him, the same shock in that sound as was mirrored on Silas' face.

"You may be my son Asher, but this is treason and I will not stand for it." The king responded finally.

Asher shrugged. "What are you going to do, disown me? I am your only son. You would be asking for war and revolution. You would be exposing yourself and your weakness to the whole kingdom." Asher had no idea where this confidence had come from. When he had woken up this morning, he would never have imagined that he would be confronting his father like this, nor would he have even wanted to. But it was like Blossom's revelation had removed a glamour from his father and now instead of seeing the great leader that he had been raised by he saw only a cowardly and cruel man.

Silas grabbed him by the collar and yanked him closer until they were standing face to face. "Do not push me Asher. I may not disown you yet, but I can dissolve your arrangement." He sent a meaningful look towards Blossom. "All those of noble birth require my permission to marry. I had hoped that you would come to your senses of your own accord, but this boy has clearly bewitched you beyond that. Maybe I'll do what I should have done years ago and promise you to a northern royal instead."

Asher smacked his hand away in disgust and stepped back. "If you do that then I'll give up my title and marry Blossom as a commoner. I'm sure that the farming village that you took him from would welcome us back."

The king stepped backwards as though Asher had just punched him. "You are willing to throw your life away, you are willing to throw your kingdom away because of this boy and his lies?" He spat.

Asher reached behind him and took hold of Blossom's still trembling hand. "There's nothing in this world more important to me than this man right here. I have worked my whole life to become someone that can rule this country fairly and strongly and I believe that I will do that better with Blossom by my side. I do not wish to plunge this country into war but if you make me choose between my birth right and the love of my life then you will not like my answer."

⌘

Blossom was near tears when Asher took his hand, he had known that Asher loved him, had heard him proclaim it multiple times over the years, but until now he had no idea just how strongly his affections ran.

"Oh and I know for a fact that it is you who is lying and not

Blossom." Asher said over his shoulder as he began to guide Blossom towards the door. "I saw the burns that covered him the night that his room was on fire, I heard the damage in his lungs."

Blossom knew that he should have been angry that Asher was still talking about him like he wasn't there, but he was too focused on what the prince was going to say next to care too much.

"The boy set his room on fire, of course he..."

"A blesser cannot be hurt by their own blessing." Asher cut in, his gaze cold. Blossom saw the king pale as he finally realised just how little control he had left. "He was burnt beforehand."

"Get out of my sight." Silas said, suddenly sounding exhausted.

"With pleasure, but before I leave this is my bargain. I will give you until our 21$^{st}$ birthday to announce a date for our wedding, you will support our union and you will never again lay a hand on Blossom. If you do not meet all of these conditions, then we will leave."

Blossom followed Asher out of the room. He had no idea how the prince was so calm, and he only made it to the end of the throne room before Blossom felt his legs give out beneath him.

"Blossom?" Asher knelt next to him. "What's wrong?"

"What have you done Ash?" He asked, his voice cracking as panic and the reality of what had just happened swept over him.

Asher looked at him, offended. "I protected you." He said like it was the most obvious thing in the world. "Unless you wanted to spend the rest of your life being tortured by that man."

"You're risking everything, everything you've ever wanted. You're risking it all for nothing Asher." He sobbed.

"Not for nothing, for you." The prince responded, making it sound like the easiest choice in the world. Asher wrapped his arms around him in a comforting hug.

Blossom sobbed into his shoulder, although he was now laughing as well, slightly hysterical. "He is going to kill me." He said.

"Then he'll have to kill me to." Asher responded. "Come on, let's get out of here before he decides that he'd not too old to sire another heir and actually disowns me."

Blossom laughed, properly this time, and followed him out of the throne room.

## Chapter 23

Deciding not to push their luck any further Blossom and Asher spent the rest of the day in the blessing school, tidying each of the classrooms and preparing them for the return of the students in two weeks time. Blossom hadn't anticipated Asher's help but the prince seemed more than happy to do anything that was needed and so they finished in record time. After packing away the last of the bedding for laundry they decided to order food to be bought to the blessing garden so that they wouldn't have to face the king in the dining hall.

"Do you think he'll give in?" Blossom asked, chewing on a piece of sliced apple absently.

"I don't see how he can't. I meant what I said though and I think he knows that."

Blossom pushed the, still mostly full, plate away. "I always knew that you'd make a great king Ash, but I don't think that I ever knew how good you are at diplomacy."

Asher laughed. "I wouldn't call that diplomacy."

Blossom took a sip of fruit juice before speaking again. "You presented him a choice, of which he would have to choose the option that you wanted or risk war. I think that's the very essence of diplomacy."

Asher hummed in thought before changing the subject. "Are you not going to eat anymore? You've hardly touched your food."

Blossom looked down at the spread in front of him and felt his stomach clench. "I'm not really hungry." He answered.

Asher watched him intensely for a few moments before giving in with a shrug, but Blossom got the feeling that he wanted to say more.

⌘

When Blossom went to bed that evening he half expected to be hauled from his room and dragged to the royal hearth for the final time, but the night passed without incident and he was woken by Emma the next morning as though nothing had happened.

Emma helped him out of his night shirt, tossing it onto a pile of clothes that she was going to be taking down to the laundry. "Any plans for today?" She asked as she passed him a pair of plain brown breeches.

"Not really. The school is all ready for when the children return. I thought it would take us much longer so I'm at a bit of a loss now."

"In that case how about I fit you for your autumn's robe? No time like the present, I'll get the fabric whilst you have breakfast." Emma said stuffing some stray articles of clothing into the large cloth bag that she'd brought with her.

"Sure." Blossom responded, sitting back down on his bed. "I'm not really in the mood for breakfast though, could you send up some tea instead?" He still didn't fancy having to face the king this morning and the knot in his stomach hadn't yet loosened enough for him to want to eat anything.

"Are you feeling okay petal?" Emma asked in concern, pressing the back of her hand to his forehead. "I know that you don't always eat as much as you should but it's not like you to miss breakfast completely."

Blossom shrugged, aiming for nonchalant and apparently failing because Emma continued to look at him in concern. "I feel fine, I'm sure I'll be hungry later."

⌘

Blossom dug through his deep wooden wardrobe, flinging clothes onto the floor behind him as he tried to locate something specific, he hadn't worn them in a while so Emma wouldn't have needed to take them to wash. "Emma have you seen my green riding trousers?" He asked from the depths of the wardrobe, he'd practically climbed into it during his search and was now encompassed on 3 sides by dark wood panelling.

"Maybe they're in this mountain of clothes that appears to have grown on your floor since yesterday."

Blossom poked his head out of the wardrobe at the sound of Asher's voice. "Oh hello, how long have you been there?" He asked.

"Long enough to have been hit by a few unfortunate articles of clothing. I'm just glad you don't wear anything with buckles." Asher responded with a smile. He took hold of Blossom's hand as he stepped gingerly over the mess that he'd created. Blossom smiled as Asher wrapped his arms around his middle and kissed him. "Also good morning." The prince said as he broke away.

"Good morning my love." Blossom replied, happy to see that his pet name still made the prince blush. He'd already started creating a list in his mind of other things to call him should it ever stop happening. "Let me clear this up."

"Do you want me to help?"

"Nah it won't take long." Asher sat down on Blossom's bed as he collected his things. "Any particular reason why you're here?" He asked, tossing his clothes into the wardrobe in an untidy heap and shutting the door, shoving his shoulder into the wood when it tried to swing open again.

"Not really, also I'm not surprised you can't find anything if that's how you store your clothes."

Blossom laughed at Asher's attempt at deflection. He knew that the prince had come to his room to act as a kind of bodyguard in case the king tried anything.

"Emma should be back in a moment, she wants to fit me for autumns robe."

"Already? Autumn isn't for another month."

Blossom shrugged, flopping onto the bed next to Asher and stretching out against the soft covers. "Pays to be prepared, my last one was getting quite ragged." He plucked at some of the fraying golden strands on the hem of his current robe. "And it's too big for me now for some reason."

The door opened again, and Emma entered the room carrying a pile of red fabric, another servant close behind her carrying a tea tray. "Oh good morning your majesty." She said. "Do you want me to come back later? This can always wait if you have something else to do." She turned her gaze from Asher to Blossom.

Blossom looked over at Asher questioningly from where he'd been pouring himself a cup of steaming hot tea, but the prince just waved his hand dismissively.

"I'm good here."

⌘

"What will you wear when we get married?" Asher asked, he was now sprawled out on Blossom's bed, staring at the canopy above him as he idly tossed one of Blossom's bedside candles from hand to hand.

"You do realise that you've never actually asked me to marry you right?" Blossom responded causing Asher to look over to him in confusion.

"What are you talking about I ask you all the time."

"No you don't. You tell me all the time. You say things like 'when we get married' but you've never actually proposed."

There was silence for a few moments, broken only by the sound of swishing cloth as Emma draped fabric over Blossom. He couldn't help but notice that she was being suspiciously quite about the whole conversation.

"But surely I asked you the first time." Asher said finally, his words trailing off as though he wasn't sure about himself.

Blossom looked at him over his shoulder with a smile. "No you didn't." His tone was light and teasing as he continued. "I distinctly remember you coming up to me and declaring that I was going to be your husband one day, it wasn't a question."

Asher stared up at the bed canopy above him before chuckling. "No wonder you kept rejecting me."

Blossom smiled at his reflection and was about to say something else when Asher spoke again.

"Oh well no need to break with tradition this late in the game, and I distinctly remember you saying that you like it when I'm forceful." A positively evil smile spread over the prince's face as Blossom stuttered in response, turning bright red as Emma looked at him in curiosity. Appearing to take pity on him Asher returned to his initial topic of conversation. "Anyway you haven't answered my question, what are you going to wear to our wedding?"

"Depends on the time of year I suppose." Blossom responded from his spot by the mirror, willing his face to return to its usual colour as he held out an arm for Emma to pin the material for his sleeve.

"You're not wearing a blessers robe to our wedding Blossom."

"Why not?" Blossom turned to the prince, offended at the statement.

Asher huffed good naturedly and sat upright. "Because it's a special occasion, you can't dress like it's just any normal day."

"I'll tell you what he's going to wear." Emma chimed in, not questioning Blossom's sudden lack of resistance to the conversation topic as she gripped him by the shoulders and turned him to face the mirror again. "He's going to wear white." She said decisively.

"Like winters robe?" Blossom asked.

"Something much more simple. White breeches and tunic I think."

"But why? That doesn't sound very special." Asher asked.

Emma shook her head with a small, indulgent smile. "Because that way it will make the contrast even more visible when you lay your black betrothal cloak on him. Don't you want the first time that Blossom is wearing your colour to be as spectacular as possible?"

The boys both looked at each other, remembering the night of the fire. Blossom couldn't help but blush slightly as Asher began to grin.

"Hang on. Why is Asher the one giving me his colour? Do I get to put a robe on him as well?"

Emma shook her head with a good-natured smile. "I'm afraid not petal."

"Why not?" They chorused in unison.

"I'm very glad that you're both suddenly so interested in this. And to answer your question that's just the way that it is. The one with the higher rank lays claim to the person with the lower rank. I took Kara's colour when we married because she is a knight and you will take Asher's because he is the prince."

Blossom scrunched his nose up at the thought whilst Asher chuckled again. "Don't worry flower, we'll think of some way for you to claim me as well."

Blossom watched as Asher made his way over to him, unsure if the prince was going to kiss him or not. He was also unsure if he wanted him to with Emma in the room. He didn't get an answer to either of those questions as Edwin chose that moment to knock on the door.

The quiet man poked his head into the room. "Sorry to intrude." He said meekly.

"Come on in Ed, we're nearly done." Emma replied, folding a piece of cloth near Blossom's shoulder to make his collar.

"I've come to retrieve the prince. The king has reconvened court and we are expected within the hour."

Asher and Blossom looked at each other.

"Do you think…?" Blossom didn't need to finish his sentence.

Asher nodded back at him, his hands in his pockets. "Yep, this is it." He replied, rocking back on his heels. "I'll see you down there flower."

"Has Blossom been asked as well? I'll need to get his court robes ready." Emma said, helping Blossom off with his half-finished robe, being careful not to accidentally stab him with the pins.

"We all have Em, he's convened official court and the whole servant body are to be there as well." Edwin replied.

"What's going on?" Emma asked as the implication of the statement sunk in. "Court hasn't been held officially since queen Lila was alive."

Edwin shrugged. "I wasn't told, you now know as much as I do."

The prince followed Edwin out of the room and as the door closed Emma turned to face him. "Blossom what's going on?"

"All I know is that one of two things is happening, either way everything is going to be different by tomorrow." Blossom replied vaguely, wincing apologetically as Emma opened his wardrobe and sent a disdainful look his way when she saw the mess inside.

Blossom allowed Emma to redress him in silence, for the first time in his life not caring about the stiff silks of his court robes. Either the king was about to announce their wedding date, or he was about to disown Asher in front of the entire court.

## Chapter 24

Blossom found Asher in front of the throne room doors, standing stiff and uncomfortable in his black brocade doublet. "Are you okay?" He asked, touching Asher's arm reassuringly. Emma had followed Edwin through the servant's doors, and they were alone in the hallway.

Asher nodded with a small hum. "Either way we won't be wondering anymore. I'll be glad to get it over with honestly. I'm just surprised that he managed to get court together so quickly."

"I doubt it's a full court, just the nobles that were already here and maybe a few from the capital." Blossom replied, more to fill the silence than anything as they waited to be announced.

After what felt like an age the doors to the throne room opened and an unnatural hush fell over the crowd within. Blossom had been wrong about the size of the court, and he had to wonder if Silas had planned on making some kind of announcement even before Asher had confronted him. He saw house colours and sigils of nobles from the farthest reaches of the kingdom, almost every house was represented in some capacity even those that hadn't attended court in years.

Asher and Blossom walked silently through the hall and up the dais to where King Silas was seated. They bowed before him as their names and titles were declared and took their seats. They sat on two smaller versions of the king's own throne, set back slightly on the platform, Asher on his right hand and Blossom on his left. Blossom looked over to where Asher was sitting, the prince looked at ease as though he knew he belonged there, the only tell of his nerves in the tight clenching of his hands. Blossom attempted to copy his posture, siting straighter in the uncomfortable seat, and placing his hands on his lap to hide how badly they were trembling.

"Honoured guests." The king said, his voice projecting effortlessly over the still silent crowd. He rose from his seat and spread his hands wide, light bouncing off of the many jewels that he had bedecked himself in. "As many of you will remember, ten years ago my son, the crown prince of Vaten and the world's only nature blessed were promised to each other."

There was a small smattering of stilted applause from the crowd as though the court was just as confused as Blossom and Asher were. The awkward atmosphere in the room helped Blossom to relax somewhat, part of him had been certain that this was a trick, one that the whole court was in on.

"Now 10 years is a long time for a betrothal, especially a royal one so it is understandable that many may have thought that their union would never go ahead. However I have simply been waiting for the right time to bond them together." Silas paused, allowing the court time to mutter amongst themselves.

Blossom looked over at Asher again in confusion, the prince simply rolled his eyes at him with a smile. *He's going to play this out as his idea.* The action said, but Blossom wasn't so sure.

"Many of you will have noticed the growing unrest in our western border. You may have even begun to anticipate another war with our Castillan neighbours, however you need not fear. Some of you will have forgotten that the royal blesser is himself a son of Castilla."

The king paused again, and Blossom felt almost all of the eyes in the hall land on him, and from the shiver that ran down his spine he was certain that many of the gazes were not overly friendly. He had always wondered what the nobles thought of him. They had always been courteous when he had been in court, but he had often heard whispers when his back was turned. Knowing that he hadn't simply been paranoid wasn't the relief that he had been expecting.

"My loyal citizens. Today I have called you all here to announce that on the eve of this year's harvest day, Prince Asher and Blossom will be wed, and in doing so they will form not only a personal union but a union of two kingdoms. When it comes time for them to take my place upon this throne it will be with the assurance that Vaten and Castilla will serve as allies."

The hall was silent for a few beats before a loud cheer erupted, Blossom was sure that he even saw a few of the nobles weeping. He sunk lower in his seat, unsettled by the courts easy switch of allegiance. Seconds ago most of these people had been viewing him as a hated outsider and now they were celebrating his being made one of them.

"As tradition dictates there will be a week of tournaments and feasts in celebration leading up to the wedding day. I expect every one of you to put forth a champion and to show our Castellan guests true Vaten hospitality."

Blossom wondered if anyone else heard the venom the king placed on the word guests but pushed the thought from his mind as he rose from his seat to meet Asher when Silas indicated for them both to join him.

Silas took Blossom's left hand and Asher's right. Blossom automatically braced himself for a pulse of heat, but the king simply placed their hands together in front of him and the crowd cheered again. Blossom looked at Asher in confusion, but the prince simply inclined his head towards the gathered nobles. They both turned towards the crowd and Asher raised their joined hands.

"To Vaten." He declared which received another round of cheers.

⌘

It took a while, but the nobles calmed down somewhat and Blossom and Asher began making their way around the crowd. Blossom had his arm looped through Asher's and the prince had kept a reassuring hand atop his own as he guided him around the room.

"Stop looking at him." Asher whispered out of the side of his mouth as Blossom glanced at the king once again. Silas had sat back in his throne and was watching their progress intensely, his eyes burning into the back of Blossom's head.

"Something doesn't seem right about this, we shouldn't have won so easily." He responded, smiling and bowing respectfully as an older lady in rich grey silks made her way over to them.

"I had hoped that I would live to see this day. I was there at court when the king made his first announcement, back when you two were just small children. I was beginning to think that it would never happen. This must be a sign from the Blessers." She took hold of Blossom's hand and smiled up at him, her eyes slightly fogged with blindness.

"Thank you, my lady." Blossom responded, not knowing what else to say. He really wanted to enjoy the evening but the discomfort growing in his chest was making it as though he was watching everything behind glass.

They made their way through more people, Blossom's unease threatening to bloom into a full panic until the king suddenly appeared behind them, placing a hand on his and Asher's shoulders. "I beg your pardon my lady, but I must steal these two for a moment. Lots to plan for." He smiled benevolently at the young noble that they had been talking to who bowed with a bright blush.

They followed the king through to his war room behind the throne, the din of the court disappearing as soon as the doors closed. Blossom had never noticed how well soundproofed this room was before, he guessed it made sense seeing as this was where all strategic meetings were held. The knowledge did little to sooth his nerves.

"There is much to be done before the wedding day." The king said, his tone as emotionless as if he was talking about what to have for dinner. "But there is one thing that I will demand of both of you right now." He rested his hands on the table and looked at them both intently. "As far as I am concerned this is a political union." He held up his hand as Asher opened his mouth to protest. "If you two see it as something more than so be it, many such arrangements have evolved into true courtships. My point is that until the day that you are married, I expect you both to act with proper decorum."

"I'm not sure what you are implying." Asher replied.

Blossom stayed silent, too surprised by the king's sudden change in demeanour to say anything.

"What I am saying Asher." Silas said, walking over to them. "Is that until you are married you will remain in separate beds, you will not embrace in public, and you will attend to your duties as normal. This..." He gestured to where Blossom and Asher's arms were still linked. "...is as much as I am willing to accept."

Blossom felt Asher squeeze his hand briefly before releasing it and he saw the king nod in satisfaction before changing the topic again.

"Asher I expect you to put on a good showing during the tournament. You will be representing not only this house but the strength of our kingdom as well. Many of the nobles have heard tales of your military prowess, it is time that you showed them the validity of those tales."

"Of course father."

Blossom was baffled, is this what a normal conversation with the king was like?

"Good, now I would have a word with your intended in private." Silas said, waving a hand at Asher in dismissal.

Asher was about to protest but Blossom placed a hand on his arm, glancing at the king briefly before turning to the prince.

"It's okay." He said quietly. Asher didn't look happy about it but after a pause and a warning look directed at his father he left. When Blossom turned back around the king was glaring at him hatefully. The expression actually causing him to relax somewhat, this was territory that he was familiar with.

"I'm sure that you think you've won." Silas said, his voice dark.

"In a sense." Blossom replied, figuring that there was no reason to lie now. "But you have turned this to your advantage, and you have made your son happy. Surely that counts for something."

King Silas laughed bitterly, looking down at the table in front of him. "My son is a fool. I am not about to let him throw everything away because of some childish notion of love."

"So you do not intend for the wedding to go ahead, all of that was a lie?" Blossom asked, he'd known that they weren't going to resolve this so easily, but he hadn't anticipated the king flat out lying to the entire court.

The king perched on the edge of the table and folded his arms. "Oh no, I fully intend for it to go ahead. Sometimes you must sacrifice a few battles in order to win the war."

"What war?" Blossom asked desperately. "The only one who has been fighting all these years is you. All I ever tried to do was please you. I did everything I could to be worthy. Why do you insist on seeing me as the enemy?"

Something about the king finally speaking to him as an equal caused every childhood hurt to rise to the surface, and all of a sudden he was once again that same orphan boy that had stood in the throne room 10 years ago. Heartbroken that the man who had taken him in refused to love him, refused to see him as anything other than a tool. He thought he'd given up the notion of Silas as a surrogate father years ago but the wrenching he could feel in his heart told him that it was not so.

The king stood up and cupped a hand around the back of his neck causing Blossom to finch. He was surprised that instead of the usual grim pleasure the king's eyes only reflected sadness at the movement.

"In another life I'm sure that I could have loved you like a son. I could have bought you into my family with joy. As it is you will only bring ruin to this house and this country, whether you mean to or not."

Blossom stared at him in confusion, somehow more perturbed by the gentleness with which he was being handled than he would have been if the king had struck him. "What are you saying?" He asked quietly. "I would never do anything to hurt him."

"I will make you a deal." Silas said finally, ignoring Blossom's question. He removed his hand from his neck and Blossom released the breath he didn't know he'd been holding. "I will allow you to marry Asher, with no tricks or punishments. But you will not bond with him."

"Why not?" Blossom couldn't help but ask.

Silas' eyes narrowed. "Swear it." He demanded. "Or so help me I will make all of your previous teachings feel like an ointment."

Blossom took an involuntary step back but stopped himself before he fled the room completely. He had told himself that he would no longer be afraid of this man, it was time to make good on that promise.

"Fine. I swear." He spat out, not meaning a word of it. As long as he didn't say anything the king would never know if they bonded or not. He turned on his heel and marched out of the war room, not waiting to be dismissed.

⌘

Asher was deep in conversation with a noble about which tournaments he would be entering when Blossom emerged from the king's war room, so he didn't see him until the blesser appeared by his side.

"Oh master Blossom, congratulations on your soon to be wedding. What an exciting announcement." The man said pleasantly when he noticed the new arrival.

"Thank you sir." Blossom responded with a smile that Asher was certain was fake, but he couldn't see any pain in it so he was fairly certain that his father hadn't yet broken his word.

"My child Phola is a student of yours, they haven't stopped gushing about their lessons since they came home and they can't wait to return next week."

Blossom visibly brightened at the mention of one of his students and Asher felt his shoulders relax slightly. "Oh yes Phola, they have made great progress already, they will be a very accomplished blesser before long. I would be happy to show you some of their creations if you would like, they have the makings of a master harvester."

"I would be delighted but alas I have to return home tomorrow and I think your evening is already full." He nodded over Blossom's shoulder and Asher turned to see a group of expectant faces watching them. "But maybe I will accompany them back for the second term and they can show me around before classes start. They are very insistent that I met their new friend Aelius."

The rest of the night passed in a blur of faces and handshakes and Asher was so tired by the time he finally made it back to his room that he forgot to ask Blossom about what the king had said to him.

## Chapter 25

Asher's original plan to spend as much time with Blossom as he could before the students returned was dashed almost instantly by the king. Silas gave both of them a seemingly unending list of preparations for the wedding, preparations which also coincidentally kept them apart. Despite the fact that there was at least another 2 months before the wedding date the palace had descended into a kind of chaos, and it became very rare to enter a room without someone running past in a state of busy panic. The only solace was that most of court had left after the king's announcement, returning to their own estates to prepare for the upcoming tournaments.

Asher stretched until his back gave a satisfying click, he'd been pouring over the list of entrants for the wedding tournaments for the last 3 hours. There were close to two hundred applicants so far and trying to devise a timetable of competitions where the combatants would be equally matched enough for a good show was proving to be almost impossible. He himself was going to compete in the jousting and sword fighting, but there was also archery, boxing, spear throwing and the foot races to organise. Not to mention the two hunts that the king was insisting he join. Asher was honestly finding it hard to imagine how they were going to fit so much into such a short amount of time. At this rate they would have to hold each competition back-to-back with no breaks for sleep.

He pushed away from the table, deciding to stretch his legs by seeing how the refurbishments to the training areas were coming along. For the past week they had been in the process of being transformed into the tournament grounds. This had the dual effect of preventing him from training and adding yet another job to his to-do-list. Through a series of careful manoeuvres he managed to make it out of the palace without being cornered. He had just stepped into the warm sunlight of the courtyard when a hand grabbed him roughly by the arm and he was dragged into one of the shadowed alleyways between the palace and the stables.

"What the…" He shouted but was shushed quickly by a giggling Blossom, who clamped a hand over his mouth. "Blossom? What's wrong?" He whispered, pulling his hand away.

Blossom shook his head, smiling despite the dark smudges that currently circled his eyes. "Nothing, I just escaped the seating chart meeting and thought that you might need to hide for a bit too. And yes, before you ask seating charts apparently require their own individual meeting."

Asher couldn't help but grin at Blossom's childish whispers and bumped their foreheads together gently. "Thank you flower."

"Also I wanted to give you this." Blossom lent forwards and Asher sucked in a sharp breath of air as he pressed his lips to the prince's neck, a surge of cool Moon's blessing running through his veins a second later. "I haven't been able to bless you since this started. That should hold for a while." Blossom said, his voice still a whisper, his breath ghosting over the prince's skin.

Asher looked down at Blossom as he pulled away, the prince was about to say something else when they were interrupted again.

"Master Blossom? Master Blossom." A voice called from the courtyard and Blossom sank further into the shadows.

"Ah shit." He hissed. "They've found me, I don't think I'll survive another conversation about napkin colours Asher."

Asher smiled and kissed him quickly on the cheek. "Duty calls." He said cheerfully before shoving him into the sunlight.

"Traitor." Blossom shouted back over his shoulder as the woman who had been searching for him waved him over, her face stern and unimpressed.

⌘

The whirlwind of wedding planning somehow seemed to drag on and fly past at the same time and the next thing Blossom knew the second school term had started. Now on top of endless meetings with nobles, tailors, chefs, and any other kind of artisan that he could think of every other waking moment was filled with lessons. He realised after the first two weeks of the final term that he hadn't even seen Asher except at dinners, and those had been fleeting and formal. Asher had made a passing comment during one of the few times that they'd crossed paths that they could meet up on the rooftop in the evenings, but all Blossom could do after forcing down his dinner was crawl into his bed and pass out.

One such evening when Blossom was vainly trying to remain awake, pouring over the invitation list for the final feast that was to be held before the wedding day there was a knock at the door. Blossom opened the door wearily, expecting to find Emma with yet another pot of tea but was instead face to face with Asher.

"Ash?" He asked quietly as the prince stepped into the room and closed the door behind him. The prince looked just as exhausted as he was, but his smile was warm and calm. "Why are you here? Is there something wrong?"

Asher didn't respond verbally to his question, instead he cupped the side of Blossom's face and drew him into a gentle kiss. Blossom smiled into the kiss and wrapped his arms around Asher's neck, dropping the invitation list unceremoniously on the floor as he lost himself in the moment.

"I've missed you." Asher whispered against his lips.

"And I you."

They stood that way for a while, trading small, sweet kisses, Asher's arms wrapped tightly around him until the prince pulled away. Resting their foreheads together Asher whispered. "I know that we are supposed to wait until our wedding, and there is no pressure if you don't want to, but may I share your bed tonight?" The prince ran his hand gently through Blossom's messy hair. "I just want to be close to you." He whispered.

Blossom paused for a second, trying to decide if he was ready or not, there wasn't that much that had really changed between the day at the lake and now. But when he looked into Asher's warm black eyes, he knew his answer instantly. Glancing at the closed door he answered the prince by way of another kiss, this one more heated than the last, pulling Asher as close to him as physically possible.

⌘

Asher wasted no time in walking Blossom backwards as soon as he realised that the blesser had said yes. He groped blindly for the buttons that held Blossom's robe closed, not noticing how much of the room they'd traversed until Blossom gave a startled yelp when the back of his knees hit the bed. He clung to Asher as his balance failed him, pulling the prince with him as they ended up in a heap on the bed, Blossom's robe half unbuttoned and hanging from his arms as Asher peppered kisses down his neck. Blossom was fairly certain that his heart was going to beat out of his chest and any previous exhaustion went out the window as Asher rolled their hips together.

"Asher." He moaned, digging his nails into the prince's still clothed back, not sure what exactly he wanted the other man to do, or what he was asking for but knowing that what they were currently doing wasn't enough.

Asher pulled back from his neck and dove in for another passionate kiss, kicking his boots off as he tried to shuffle them both further up the bed. An action that didn't work out as smoothly as either of them hoped when Blossom once again got caught up in his robe. As Blossom giggled breathlessly at their fumbling, Asher unbuttoned the rest of the fastenings and successfully managed to divest him of his robe, flinging it over his shoulder with a huff.

He paused for a moment to take in the sight of Blossom beneath him, his chest heaving and flushed, his eyes alight with joy, his breeches already tented in his excitement. He reached out and curled his fingers around the laces holding his breeches closed when a thought suddenly occurred to him. "Ah shit." He breathed.

Blossom froze at the exhalation. Had Asher suddenly changed

his mind? Was there something about him that had put him off? "What...what's wrong?" He asked, hating the way his words came out with a tremble to them.

Asher leant in and kissed him gently in reassurance, running his hands up and down Blossom's sides. "I was going to..." Asher trailed off, blushing deeply in sudden embarrassment. He let out a self-conscious laugh, not sure why it was suddenly so hard to tell Blossom what he wanted. "I was going to fuck you." He said at last.

"Do you not want to anymore?" Blossom asked, his voice small and nervous, his hands hovering uncertainly by his sides like he wasn't sure if he could touch him again.

Asher hadn't missed the shiver that had run through the other man at his original statement and feeling a new wave of confidence took hold of Blossom's hand as he kissed him again. He pressed Blossom's hand to the front of his trousers, relishing in his small gasp as he felt him for the first time. He leant close to Blossom's ear, remembering what he had said about liking it when he was forceful. "Do you feel how much I want you?" He asked taking Blossom's earlobe between his teeth and biting down gently.

"Then why...?" Blossom trailed off, shifting on the bed as his own arousal began to demand attention.

"I don't want to hurt you."

Realisation dawned on him, and Blossom reached over to his bedside table. He riffled through his drawer for a moment before returning to Asher. He sealed their lips together again as he pressed the jar that he had retrieved into the prince's hand.

"What's this?" Asher asked looking down at the jar in confusion, it was made of a dark brown glass and held no label that he could see.

"Oil." Blossom responded. "I use it to uhh..." He trailed off in embarrassment, waving his hand vaguely in the air. "...You know." He finished quietly.

Asher placed the jar on the covers, pulling his tunic over his head and tossing it behind him before kissing Blossom again. He gripped

Blossom by the hips and tugged him forward quickly so that the other man tipped backwards onto the bed.

Blossom hit the covers with a small exhalation of air but was quickly covered by the prince who set back to work unlacing his breeches, tugging the garment down his legs until they got caught in his boots. Laughing slightly at Asher's frustration Blossom helped him to take off the rest of his clothes, feeling Asher smiling in return as he kissed him again.

Asher ran his hand lightly back up his leg, caressing his thigh and squeezing his ass as he went back to biting and kissing at his neck. Blossom gasped as the prince pressed a finger against him and he felt Asher's hot breath against his ear. "Does that mean that you've touched yourself here?" He whispered.

Blossom didn't respond immediately, too busy trying to press down on the light touch. After getting no response Asher pulled back to look him in the eye, pressing harder until the tip of his finger breached him, and Blossom gasped again.

"Blossom." He said quietly and Blossom couldn't understand how the prince could so quickly go from awkward and fumbling one minute to cool and controlled the next.

He took a deep breath, trying to think of something to give himself back some semblance of control. "Yes." He finally breathed, catching hold of Asher's face as the prince leant in to kiss him again. "I imagine that it's you touching me." He added when the prince's eyes locked with his own.

Asher dropped his head onto Blossom's chest with a groan. "Fuck." He bit out, his voice suddenly strained.

"Ash?" Blossom asked, running his hand through the prince's hair.

Before he could ask what was wrong, Asher looked up at him again. "That almost finished me off and I haven't even really touched you yet."

Blossom laughed quietly and reached down to tug at the waistband of the prince's trousers. "Then you best get these off and hurry up."

⌘

Asher watched Blossom's sleeping face intently, once again noting the dark circles beneath his eyes that he was sure matched his own. Blossom seemed younger in his sleep, more peaceful than he'd seen him in a long time, his breath coming out in gentle huffs which ghosted over his face. He trailed his fingers down Blossom's bare arm before resting his hand on his side, his fingers slotting neatly between each prominent rib bone.

It had been something that he had noticed more and more over the past year or so, Blossom's half-full plates at the end of dinner, his absences from breakfast and lunch. Asher had never bought it up before, dismissing it each time as Blossom simply being too busy to sit for a meal or simply not hungry that day but now, without his loose robes to cover him, the prince could see just how thin he had become.

They had swum together regularly only two years before, during the last summer break and whilst Blossom had always been slim, never carrying the same muscle that Asher had honed through years of sparring, he had still seemed strong and well nourished, his bones never as prominent as they were now.

Blossom mumbled something in his sleep, a crease appearing between his eyebrows. Asher decided to put his worried thoughts to one side until morning and slid his hand further round Blossom's back, pulling the blesser closer to him and kissing the spot between his eyebrows until he felt him relax again.

"I'll look after you little flower." He whispered. "I'll take care of you, you won't have nightmares whilst I'm around."

## Chapter 26

Blossom groaned and tried to bury his face further into the curve of Asher's shoulder as the curtains to his windows were thrown open. He was thinking up a suitable curse to throw Emma's way when his brain caught up with him and the implication of Emma being in his room whilst the prince was still in his bed caused his to snap into wakefulness.

He shot upright, clutching the sheets around him in an attempt to hide his nakedness, despite the fact that Emma had already seen him undressed practically every day of his life. He wouldn't be able to explain this away the way that they had when she'd found them on the floor of Asher's room.

"Good morning." Emma said, an infuriatingly smug smile on her face as she turned her gaze from Blossom to Asher, who had been woken up by Blossom's sudden movements. "And good morning to you to your majesty."

"Morning Emma." Asher replied, still stretched out languorously on the bed. Not seeming in the least perturbed by the woman's discovery of their compromising position, or the fact that Blossom had stolen all of the covers from him.

"Emma it's..."

Emma's eyes snapped back to him and she frowned, her hands going to her hips. "Blossom, if you so much as think the words 'it's not what it looks like' I will slap you."

Blossom felt his cheeks warming as Asher laughed.

"Now I am thrilled that you two have finally come to the mature decision and fucked."

"Emma!" Blossom shouted, appalled as the woman casually began picking up some of the clothes strewn around the room. He turned his glare on Asher who seemed to be having trouble breathing through his laughter, how could the prince be acting so nonchalant about this?

"Oh come now Petal, we're all adults here."

"Yeah but..." Blossom trailed off, struggling through his mortification to explain why he didn't want the woman who had raised him speaking so openly about his newly discovered sex life.

Emma held up a hand to stop him. "All I'm saying is, that whilst I'm thrilled for you both. I'm sure that Asher would rather not explain why he is not in his own bed when my brother comes to dress him in a few minutes. Edwin's not well known for being able to keep a secret."

Asher stopped laughing suddenly, his face falling as the statement sank in. "Uhh, I should probably get going." He said, taking the clothes that Emma was holding out to him.

"I'll leave you alone to get dressed your majesty." She said with a smirk, wiggling her eyebrows suggestively at Blossom when Asher stood to pull his trousers on. "And I will prepare the bath for you petal." Emma sent a wink his way before walking into the bathroom.

Blossom was pretty sure that either his head or his heart was about to explode from mortification.

"Only a few weeks more and we will be allowed to wake without interruptions flower." Asher whispered against Blossom's hair as he leant over the bed, before placing a kiss to his soft curls. "I will see you at breakfast."

Blossom didn't respond initially, still in too much of a daze to say anything, but just as Asher made to open his bedroom door he leapt from the bed. Hurrying over to the prince, who was looking at him in shock at his sudden movement, he reached up and drew Asher into a sweet kiss.

"I love you." He said quietly once they parted, still relishing every time that he was allowed to say those words.

Once Asher had left, a radiant smile on his face, Blossom made his way into the bathroom where Emma was pouring relaxing lavender salts into the steaming bath water.

"Figured you'd need this after last night." She said, her evil smirk not dimming in the slightest.

Blossom ignored her and sank into the hot water with a sigh. His muscles were indeed aching, but he wasn't sure if that was because of what he and Asher had done or simply due to how tense he'd been over the last month.

"If you and Asher are going to keep doing this before the wedding day then you are going to have to be more careful."

Blossom rolled his eyes. "As long as he's back in his room before the servants come what does it matter? It's only for another few weeks and it's not like I can get pregnant."

"And right now that is indeed a blessing, but that wasn't what I was talking about." Emma handed him a small hand mirror which Blossom took with a confused frown, his eyes widening moments later when he took in the state of his neck. He was littered with bruises and small bite marks from his jaw to the edges of his collar bone.

"Curses." He breathed, pressing his fingers to one particularly dark bruise.

Emma hummed in agreement as she crouched beside the bath. "Just be thankful that your robes have a high collar to them. And maybe council Asher into being less rough with you next time."

Blossom felt his cheeks warming at the words, still transfixed on the marks decorating his neck. "Uh yeah, I'll do that."

He felt a gentle hand pet at his hair and looked over at his adoptive mother. "Seriously though Petal, he didn't hurt you did he?"

Blossom stared at her in shock but the look in Emma's eyes showed him that she was being completely serious.

"No." He said after a few minutes, placing the mirror on the ground next to the bath.

"Blossom." She responded, a warning in her tone.

Blossom sunk back into the water with an annoyed sigh. "What do you want me to say? It was uncomfortable to begin with sure, but he didn't hurt me."

The maid continued to watch him for a moment before relenting. "As long as you're sure." She said, pushing herself back into a standing position and beginning to tidy up around the room. Blossom's chambers had become increasingly messy over the last few weeks as other duties took priority, both he and Emma had been rushed of their feet with the return of the students.

Blossom couldn't help the snort that escaped him, more of a way to dispel nervous tension than anything else as he watched Emma piling a myriad of items into a woven basket. "What would you have done if he had hurt me?" He asked. His tone had been joking but Emma whirled on him, something dangerous flashing in her eyes. He shied away from her slightly as she advanced on him.

"If that boy ever does anything to truly hurt you, you don't want to know what I'd do."

"He's the prince Emma." Blossom didn't know why he was continuing with this conversation; Asher had never done anything to make him worry in that regard. He observed the fury on Emma's face with a kind of awe, confused as to why she was taking all of this so seriously.

"Yes, and his father is the king but that man's days are numbered as well."

Blossom looked around the room furtively, both thrilled and terrified at the treason falling from his mother's lips. "What are you talking about?" He hissed, sitting forward as Emma crouched in front of him again.

"I've bathed and dressed you every day for the last 10 years petal. Do you really think I haven't seen the marks?"

Blossom lurched forward at the comment sloshing bath water over the floor. "You knew?" He roared.

"Blossom calm down." She soothed, grabbing a soft towel to wrap him in as Blossom staggered out of the bath, catching him as he slipped on the water now spreading across the tiled floor.

"Calm down? Calm down? You knew, all this time you knew what he was doing to me, and you did nothing?"

"Did nothing?" Emma asked quietly. "I protected you as best I could. If I had done even half of the things I wanted to do to that man every time I saw a new burn, I would have been executed for sure and then where would you be?"

Blossom stopped ranting as the truth of that statement sunk in. "What did you do?" He asked and Emma smiled gently, her eyes pained.

"You don't want to know petal." She said rubbing at his shoulders through the towel. "I'm sorry that I never told you that I knew. I still don't know the details of exactly what has happened, but I should have been a shoulder of comfort for you."

For some reason this conversation reminded him of the night when he'd questioned her about the Blossomites. He couldn't help but wonder what else she had kept from him, what else she had done under the guise of protecting him. Blossom reached forward and hugged her, not ready to forgive her quite yet but far too tired to continue being angry.

"If you want to tell me the details then I'll be here for you." She said into his shoulder. "Do you want to talk about it petal?"

Blossom thought about it, refusing to let go of Emma as he did so. After a moment of standing in silence he simply said. "No."

⌘

"Emma where is my brush? Why can't I ever find anything in this place?" Blossom shouted, riffling through his drawer frantically. He'd been finding it hard to locate anything in his room lately and was becoming convinced that someone was stealing from him.

"Calm down petal it's right here." Emma said, handing him his hairbrush, a worried look on her face. "Sit down for a second, what's gotten into you?"

"Sorry Emma." Blossom could feel himself tearing up and tried to ignore it by roughly pulling the brush through his hair. "There's only two days before the tournaments start and the students have their last exams today. I haven't been focusing on them enough and I'm so worried that some of them are going to fail." Blossom slumped down onto his bed, cradling his head in his hands as he tried to fight off the tears, exhaustion pulling all of his emotions into overdrive. "I don't think I've slept in...I don't even know how long. How am I going to survive this next week?"

"Oh Blossom." Emma cooed, sitting down next to him and wrapping her arm around his shoulders. "It's only a few more days, you've done brilliantly petal. All of our scholars will pass with flying marks, I'm sure of it. And just think, there's the marriage tour after the wedding. Just you and Asher travelling the kingdom for two months, nothing to worry about except each other."

Blossom peaked at her through his fingers. "Did that come out the way you meant it?"

Emma laughed. "Not quite, but my point still stands."

As though he'd been summoned Asher chose that moment to poke his head through the door. "You coming to breakfast today or...what's wrong?" He asked as Emma gestured him over, he took her place beside Blossom as she stood up.

Blossom rested against him, relaxing slightly as Asher brushed his knuckles up and down the side of his neck. "Can you send breakfast up here Emma? I think my father will forgive us one meal together considering how much we still have to do."

Emma nodded and made her exit, throwing one last look Blossom's way before closing the door behind her.

"We don't have time for breakfast Ash, I have to get to the school."

"Blossom you are not leaving this room until you eat something." Asher demanded causing Blossom to look up at him in confusion. Asher looked back at him steadily. "You have to eat Blossom, I know we've been busy but I'm getting worried about you. You have to eat something." He moved his hand down to Blossom's side and pressed his fingers to his ribs through the red cloth of his robes to emphasise his point.

Blossom lowered his head and tried to push away from Asher's grip, but the prince kept his arm around him and tilted his chin up so that their eyes met. "Talk to me flower, is it just the stress or is there another reason why you're not eating?"

Blossom sighed and flicked his eyes to the side. He hadn't noticed Emma leaving the room but he was glad she had, he wasn't sure he could talk about this with both of them there. "Sometimes it is, sometimes it's just hard and I don't know why." He shrugged and leant forward, bumping his head against Asher's cheek. "I don't know how to explain it, sometimes I just can't eat and it gets worse when I'm stressed or scared."

Asher hugged him tighter, laying a kiss on his shoulder. "Okay. Will you tell me when it gets hard? I don't know if I can help but I'll try to."

Blossom made a noise of agreement followed by a hollow laugh. "I'm sure it's not pleasant trying to bed someone who looks like a skeleton."

Asher cupped his face and bought him into a fierce kiss, the intensity and suddenness of the movement causing Blossom to gasp. "I love you." The prince said, looking Blossom in the eye, trying to convey his seriousness through his gaze. "And I promise you that is not why I am bringing this up, I'm just worried about you."

Blossom held his gaze for a few seconds longer, his eyes searching, before finally nodding. "Okay." He said at last, relief flooding through him as Asher kissed him again.

"I love you." Asher repeated, letting Blossom rest his head on his shoulder again. Rocking him from side to side he waited for a response of some kind, but after a minute he realised that Blossom had fallen back asleep.

"This is going to be a long day." He said to himself, stroking a hand over Blossom's hollow cheek gently.

## Chapter 27

He needn't have been so worried about his students, as Emma had said every final year scholar passed their respective final tests with good marks and the graduation celebrations lasted long into the night. Blossom managed to stay awake for a few hours into the party but had to bow out early when Emma found him dozing against the wall of the blessing school.

The day after when Blossom waved the students off for the winter break that signalled the end of their school year, which had been started a week early to allow for the wedding, he didn't feel the sadness that normally accompanied the day. Instead he felt a tremendous surge of relief, now the only thing that he had to focus on was the wedding festivities.

Guests had been arriving since the early hours of the morning and the first feast was to be held tonight. He felt his stomach clench at the thought but tried to push past it by going to find the prince. He bumped into a few Castillan nobles as he made his way through the palace courtyard. The nobles bowed to him and greeted Blossom with a reverence that unnerved him in a way that he couldn't quite put his finger on. That was until he saw the insignia stitched into the backs of their tunics. It was the same one he'd seen on the pink haired Blossomites all those months ago.

Asher was in the stables when he found him, trying to calm down an irate valet who was insisting that his master's horse needed a much larger pen than he had been given.

"The pens are all the same size, and we have so many steeds here for the joust that there is not one space spare. I'm afraid you are going to have to use this one or return to the capital and house him there." Asher said through gritted teeth, and Blossom wondered why the prince was the one dealing with him instead of the head groom.

The valet entered into another tirade of demands about how his master shouldn't have to keep his horse in the same pen as a lesser noble, and how Castillan horses carried diseases that Vaten steeds couldn't fight when Blossom stepped next to Asher, linking his arm through the prince's. Asher smiled down at him. "Have the children gone?" He asked.

Blossom nodded. "The last one left a few moments ago, I came to see if you needed any help." He looked pointedly at the valet who had stopped talking as soon as he realised that he was no longer being listened too and instead stood fuming, his fists clenched at his sides.

"My good man. As I'm sure you can see, even the royal steeds are housed in pens the same size as this one. Rank has no bearing on how we treat our animals, and we will not provide an exception. Especially due to a flimsy excuse such as the evils of foreign horses. Now we have many other things to attend to before this evening, if you'll excuse us." Blossom said with an air of finality and an indication of exactly how absurd he thought the valets reasoning was. He subtly began pulling Asher towards the door as he did so.

Once they were outside, the cool autumn air sending a pleasant breeze over their skin, Asher's tense shoulders began to relax. "I think my heart might explode before the end of this week." He muttered causing Blossom to laugh. "I'm serious, or I may end up killing someone, possibly the next idiot who makes a stupid request like that."

Blossom ran his hand soothingly up and down Asher's arm. "You know how nobles are, always out to get as much as they can." He looked out across the courtyard and decided to steer the prince away from the arriving guests. They made their way out of the main grounds until they could see the tournament grounds spread out before them.

"I met some of the Castillans who have come for the tournament on the way here." Blossom said after a moment as they both stood watching the sun setting over the newly erected stands.

"How were they?" Asher asked.

"Nice." Blossom responded. "It was odd seeing people who looked like me." He added, gesturing to his warm caramel skin. "You know other than Emma and Edwin, it might be nice not being the shortest person around for once."

"There's no one in the world like you." Asher said, pulling him into a kiss.

"You're a sap." Blossom said with a loving smile, which dimmed slightly when he remembered the other thing that he'd found odd. "I think they were Blossomites."

"I thought we might bump into some, I'm sure many of them want to see what will happen when we marry. I think they think that something cataclysmic will happen."

"Sounds ominous, should we be worried?" Blossom asked, it wasn't lost on him that the king had said something very similar the night of the wedding announcement. Just one more thing to add to his pile of stress.

"I don't think so, did any of them have pink hair?"

Blossom shook his head.

"Then I'm sure we'll be fine. Only the fanatical ones dye their hair."

⌘

As soon as the sun had set completely they made their way back to the palace. There were now too many people in the palace to have dinner in the dining hall, and so long tables and benches had been set up in the grand hall instead. Many of the nobles raised cups to them as they entered, and Asher waved back theatrically as he guided Blossom to the high table.

As Blossom sat down next to Asher and the king he scanned the room for pink hair. His eyes landed briefly on a small group of people whose faces were covered with hoods but found no sigils on their clothes that he could see and so figured it must just be part of their noble dress. He was unhappy but not surprised to find the Vaten and Castillan nobles clumped together on separate tables, refusing to mingle with each other even as the night wore on and they all got more into their cups.

The servants had piled every table with such a wide variety of food that it was almost impossible to decide what to eat, and Blossom smiled thankfully up at Emma when she placed a plate filled with roasted lamb, potatoes, and cabbage in front of him.

"There you go petal." She said quietly so that only he could hear, ruffling his hair quickly before disappearing back into the shadows.

He poked and pushed at the food on his plate as the roar of so many people in such an enclosed space pressed in on him. He was sure that on any other day the sauce dripping from the lamb would have made his mouth water, but right now it just made him want to vomit.

"Just take a few bites." Asher whispered soothingly, squeezing his hand under the table.

Blossom gave him a wobbly smile and forced himself to take a bite of boiled potatoes. He grimaced as the soft potato lodged in his throat. Swallowing audibly he grabbed his glass and took a long swig of water.

He felt another squeeze to his hand and looked over at the prince, Asher tilted his head towards one of the back exits of the hall and stood. He watched as the prince slapped his father on the shoulder, making some kind of excuse before leaving the hall.

Blossom took another look around the room, absently sipping his water before also rising. "Excuse me a moment." He muttered to no one in particular as he pushed his chair back in. He turned on his heel and exited the hall through the same door that Asher had.

The quiet of the hallway hit him like a gust of air and he sighed in relief. He hadn't realised just how warm and stuffy the grand hall had been, the dimmed lights and the smoke from the fires causing the space to feel smaller than it was.

"Asher?" He called once he'd taken a few calming breaths.

The prince stepped out of the shadows. "You seemed to be struggling." He said, his hands folded behind his back.

Blossom nodded wordlessly, looking at Asher's hand in confusion when he held it out to him.

"Come with me for a second."

He took the proffered hand and allowed Asher to pull him into a small resting room a little further down the hallway. The room appeared to be mostly unused judging by the cold hearth and fine layer of dust over the furniture, in fact Blossom couldn't remember ever setting foot in it before.

"Hold this." Asher said, handing him something bundled in a large cloth napkin.

Blossom took it, surprised at the warmth that emanated from the package. "What is it?" He asked as the prince began moving chairs around until two were set in the centre of the room, a small table between them.

Asher gestured him over, taking the bundle from him again before pointing to the chair on the left. "Sit down and I'll show you."

Blossom complied and Asher placed the bundle on the table, undoing the loose knots that were tied in it allowing the corners of the napkin to flutter open. Blossom felt his breath hitch and tears build at the back of his eyes when he saw what was in the bundle.

"It was too crowded in there, so I thought that we could have dinner in here instead." Asher held out one of the 4 chicken legs that he had somehow smuggled out of the feast. "I would have brought some gravy too, but I thought it might leak through the napkin."

Blossom laughed warmly and took a bite of the chicken. It went down much smoother than the potato and he took 2 more bites before laying it back on the napkin.

"Is that all..." Asher never finished his sentence as Blossom rose and pulled him into a tight hug.

"Thank you." He whispered into the prince's shoulder, unashamed of the tears now rolling down his cheeks. He pulled back and cupped Asher's face with both hands. "Thank you." He said again, placing a kiss on his nose.

He settled back down in his seat and picked the half-eaten chicken leg back up, he managed two and a half more legs before declaring himself full. Asher looked like he wanted to push the issue but finally relented and they returned to the feast, Blossom's lamb and potatoes remaining untouched for the rest of the night.

⌘

The next day started as soon as the sun rose, and the first tournament was to be the joust. Asher had already been to the stables, making sure that everyone knew where they were going and that all of the horses were tacked and ready. He was now in the royal tent, the roar of the gathered crowd in the stands easily penetrating the canvas as Edwin finished securing the clasps of his armour. The valet stepped back to allow the prince to twist a few times, making sure that none of the plates pinched more than they should.

"Thanks Ed, seems like the smiths worked hard on this one, it already feels like I've broken it in." He said, swinging his right arm in slow circles.

His father had insisted on a fresh suit of pitch-black armour for the tournament, and it gleamed in the sunlight as he stepped out into the tournament ground, every plate buffed to perfection and free of scratches. Edwin followed him out, Asher's lance resting on his shoulder which he passed to him once the prince had mounted Coal. Coal had also received new armour for the tournament, his already impressive bulk accentuated by the shining black plates.

Asher rode out onto the jousting ground to a deafening roar. He circled Coal near the royal stand, bowing to his father and raising his fist to another cheer. His opponent was a noble from the southern part of the kingdom. His armour also shining and new, and by the way he held his lance Asher could tell it wasn't just new armour made for the tournament. He wouldn't be surprised if it was the first set of armour the man had ever worn.

He halted Coal at the right end of the list, where the horse pawed at the ground, huffing in excitement. He held his lance close to his side as the rules of the joust were read out. This was a show tournament and only direct hits to the shield were permitted, but he would be surprised if there wouldn't be at least a few broken bones by the end of the day.

The call to start came in the form of a flag drop and he kicked Coal into a gallop, lowering is lance as he charged down the length of the list. He unseated his opponent easily on the first turn and trotted back to his start position, handing his lance back to Edwin. There was a brief cheer but no one seemed overly impressed, not that he was surprised. The biggest celebrations came after a multiple round joust, and it always took a few rounds and a few opponents to warm the crowd. He returned briefly to the tent to change out of his armour before heading to the royal stand to watch the rest of the initial rounds. It would be at least 2 hours before he would be called to mount again.

"Well done." Blossom said, smiling up at him as he took his seat. The blesser still looked tired, but considerably less worn out than he had whilst the students had still been there.

"Hopefully you will have some kind of competition in the next round." His father said derisively. "I don't think that boy even knew how to sit a horse properly."

Asher sighed as he sunk back into his seat. "It wasn't done intentionally, his tournament list was very impressive. Although now I'm wondering if it was just a list of the ones he's visited and not ones he's competed in."

The king chuckled at that and they all settled back to watch the rest of the matches.

⌘

Asher's second opponent was not so easily unseated, and he took a few hits himself before finally landing the winning blow. The cheer that he got upon this victory was louder and far more genuine this time, enough that he could almost ignore the ache beginning to creep into his shoulders. Due to the sheer number of combatants, the final series of jousts didn't take place until the sun was setting. However Asher found this to his advantage as his pitch-black armour obscured him more than his final opponent, a behemoth of a man from the north.

He landed the first of the hits, but the other knight simply shrugged it off and when the second run down the list resulted in him very nearly toppling from Coal's back Asher realised that he might not win this one. A lucky blow to the centre of the other man's shield on the fourth run saved him though and he ended the day victorious. He leapt from his horse in triumph as Blossom and the king made their way over to him, the crowd deafening in their excitement.

He bowed to Blossom to allow him to lay a garland of flowers around his neck. "Do I get a kiss too?" He asked, smirking up at Blossom as he remained in his bow. He saw Blossom blush just as the king interrupted.

"Proper decorum Asher." He snapped and the prince straightened.

"Of course sir." He answered.

"May I be allowed to heal him?" Blossom asked as the king turned to leave.

Silas paused for a second before nodding, marching out of the tournament arena as Blossom sent Moon's blessing through Asher's stiff muscles.

⌘

Blossom found Asher outside his bedroom door when he opened it to head down to that night's feast. "Come to escort me?" He asked, pleasantly surprised. He'd half expected the prince to be carried off to the feast on a crowd of ecstatic nobles.

"And to claim my victory kiss." Asher responded, he was leant casually against the opposite wall, his smile easy and as charming as ever. It seemed almost impossible that only an hour earlier he had been caked in grime and sweat from a day of competition.

Blossom rolled his eyes in mock exasperation. "If I must." He said, grabbing a fistful of Asher's top and yanking him roughly towards him. The prince let out a surprised noise just before their lips collided. Blossom laughed against him as Asher stumbled forward, wrapping one arm around him and flinging the other out towards the wall to stop them both from falling back into Blossom's room.

"Never mind the other knights, I think you're trying to kill me." Asher said when they broke apart, resting their foreheads together with a smile.

"Come on, we can't be too late or the king will get suspicious." Blossom said by way of a reply, a small smile still on his face as they made their way down to the great hall.

Asher spent most of that evening being slapped on the back by an increasingly drunk entourage of other knights. This and the subsequent feasts were to be far less formal than the first and so the prince mingled happily with the other guests instead of staying seated at the high table. The ones that were scheduled to duel with him in the sword fights in the middle of the week seemed to be the most enthusiastic in their congratulations, and Blossom had to pull him away from multiple posturing contests.

Blossom pulled the cup of ale from Asher's hands as he raised it to ask for another refill and, after a quick glance around the room to check where the king was, leant in to whisper in the prince's ear. "If you stop now, I will allow you to come to my room tonight. Then I can reward you properly for your victory."

He watched with satisfaction as a blush formed over the princes' cheeks so severe that it reached his ears. They hadn't slept together since that first night, both being too tired and too busy to do anything other than sleep when they reached their respective rooms. He knew that it would be safer and more proper to wait just another 4 days where they wouldn't have to risk being caught, but there was something about the illicit nature of what they were doing that made it all the more exciting.

Asher stood up suddenly and turned to face him. Using the darkness and crush of the hall as cover he tipped forward, and Blossom felt himself reddening when the prince's teeth sunk into his earlobe.

"Promise?" Asher husked into his ear, his black eyes intense when he pulled back to look at him.

Blossom gulped, trying to tamp down his sudden arousal as he nodded.

## Chapter 28

Blossom gasped awake, his heart pounding as he bolted upright. His eyes raked over the room as he tried to ground himself in the familiar sights and scents of his bedroom. He felt his heartbeat slowing and his breathing return to normal as his hands skimmed the soft sheets. He looked down in surprise when his hand met warm flesh, his still slightly addled mind taking a few extra moments to comprehend the form lying next to him.

He jolted when the hand that he'd brushed against slid gently up his arm, squeezing slightly before the prince whispered. "Are you okay?"

Blossom looked down at him, running a hand through his sleep mused hair as he took another deep breath. "Yeah." He finally whispered back before lying back down.

Asher studied his face in silence for a moment before asking. "Is it always the same dream?"

"It used to be." Blossom replied. "But now it keeps changing."

"Do you want to talk about it?"

Blossom shook his head. "No, I just want to go back to sleep."

Asher looked like he was about to press the point but then seemed to think better of it as he pulled Blossom close, letting him rest his head against his shoulder as he ran a gentle hand up and down his back.

"If you change your mind I'm here."

Blossom couldn't help but smile sleepily at the comment and simply burrowed deeper under the covers as his mind replayed the dream he'd just woken from. He didn't have the energy or the patience to try and comprehend why his memory was changing. Why instead of his mother screaming at him to run it was Emma, why one of the guards now wore the king's face. Why instead of the rolling green fields from his childhood, the cottage was now backed by sweeping ocean, or what the shadow shrouded island in the middle of that ocean meant.

"Do you remember the day that we met?" Blossom asked quietly, not quite ready to fall back asleep again with his nightmares waiting for him.

The room was silent for a moment, during which time Blossom began to wonder if Asher had drifted off before the prince spoke. "Not really." Asher yawned, his intake of breath nudging Blossom's head. "If I'm honest I don't remember much from that time. All of my memories have you in them, there aren't any from before."

Blossom wasn't really surprised, Asher had been in so much pain and so close to death for the first 8 years of his life it would be a miracle if he remembered anything.

"Do you?"

Blossom nodded against Asher's chest. "I do." He remembered everything from that day. How scared he'd been when he'd been bought before the royal family. How that fear had vanished the instant he'd seen Asher. How small the prince had looked amongst the pillows and blankets of his sick bed. How he'd instinctively known what to do to make him better. The flood of the prince's pain when he'd inadvertently opened their connection just that little bit too far, almost bonding their spirits right then and there.

It was that final thought that caused Blossom to push himself slightly more upright, looking Asher in the eye. He'd been meaning to bring the bond up ever since the king had forbidden him from reforming it. Asher deserved to know what had been taken from them.

"How about the day when I tried to run away, do you remember that?" He asked, his voice still quiet in the stillness of the bedroom.

Asher looked pensive for a moment, tucking the hand that wasn't currently running up and down Blossom's back behind his head. "I remember waking up and knowing that something was wrong. I don't really know how to explain it, but before then I had always had a sense of where you were, even if I couldn't see you. That was the first day that I couldn't sense you, I thought something awful had happened."

Blossom found that he wasn't surprised to learn that Asher had also noticed the loss of their bond. "Something did happen." He felt Asher's hold on him tighten.

"That was the first time my father punished you."

"Well yes but..." Blossom placed a hand firmly on Asher's chest as the prince made to rise.

"What else did he do?"

"Calm down my love." Blossom soothed, rolling so that he was led more fully on top of Asher. "I'm sorry for bringing that up but it'll help me explain. You know how we were able to feel each other's emotions a few months back, after I had to use more power than normal to deal with the death mark?"

Asher nodded, confusion clear on his face.

"Well before the day when I tried to leave that was kind of the constant state of existence for us. It's one of the reasons why you always knew where I was."

"I guess that makes sense, you were young so you didn't have full control of your blessings yet. I'm not surprised that you used too much."

Blossom looked at him in confusion until he remembered the lie he'd told to explain the bond beforehand. "Oh yeah, well you see the thing is, that wasn't because of a residual bit of power like I said."

Asher pushed himself into a sitting position, pulling Blossom with him so that the blesser was effectively sitting in his lap. "You had better start making some kind of sense Blossom, and soon."

Blossom groaned, tipping his head back as he tried to think of an easy way to explain himself. "Okay here goes. You and I have spirits that resonate with each other more than normal, that's why I'm able to cure your death mark."

"Following you so far." Asher said, still watching him intently.

"The thing with resonant spirits is that when they are as close and as similar as ours they can do something called bonding. If I was to push enough of my power through our connection I could bond our spirits together so that they effectively share the same space." Blossom threaded the fingers of his right hand with the fingers of his left. "It's something that I almost did by accident when we first met, I never bonded us fully but we were connected enough to share emotions. It was something I almost did again that night on the rooftop, it's why your death mark has never grown bigger than that night."

Asher stared at Blossom's intwined fingers, trying to wrap his head around what he was being told. "So wait, if you nearly bonded us when we were children why did we stop sharing emotions? Why did the mark begin growing again?"

Blossom sighed, his shoulders slumping slightly. "The king found out. It took a few years but when he realised what I had done he..." Blossom pulled his hands apart. "...burnt away the connection." He felt a hand take his. "And then he made sure to keep it that way."

"By torturing you."

Blossom cupped a hand to Asher's cheek, kissing him quickly. "I'm not telling you this to hurt you." He said, rubbing his thumb over Asher's cheekbone. "I'm telling you because now that you know he can't do it again." Blossom took a deep breath, finally ready to take that final step that would forever mark him as the king's enemy, even more so than he already was. "Because I can reopen the connection and bond us fully, if you want me to."

## Chapter 29

Blossom found the next two days to be rather dull, he had no interest in watching people race each other across a large field and he had never been very good at hunting. He did however enjoy watching Emma's wife Kara practically obliterate every other opponent in the archery competition. The only other upside was that as Asher wasn't competing in the races or the archery they spent the days in the royal stall together, even if the king insisted on sitting between them to 'keep up appearances'.

Blossom couldn't even bring himself to care about the king's blatant attempts to keep them separate. Asher had readily and enthusiastically agreed to Blossom's proposal to bond them, even insisting that he do it that night. Blossom had declined only on the grounds that he had a better time and place in mind, and he hadn't found it hard to distract the prince with other activities for the rest of the night.

It was the fourth day of the tournament that Blossom was really looking forward to. Whilst he had enjoyed watching Asher in the joust, he was much more excited to see him in the sword fighting which is where he had always excelled. He settled in the same seat that he'd been sat in for the past two days as the king fumed silently beside him. Despite the success that the tournament had been so far the king seemed to be becoming more tense and snappy as the week had been going on, and Blossom had a feeling that his and Asher's increasing happiness was only making it worse. And for the first time in his life he was content with that, in fact he was more than happy to make it worse.

Just as he was having that thought the prince entered the sparring ring. Asher looked resplendent in his black shining armour as he paraded around the ring, holding his newly forged sword above his head to thunderous applause. His opponent stepped into the ring after him, his lower rank meaning that he came second on the billing but the cheer he received was just as loud as Asher's. He was a giant of a Castillan noble, would be considered tall even by the Vatens and he towered over Asher even from a distance.

Blossom wasn't that concerned about the other contestant. Sure he looked big but Asher was swift and well-practiced, Blossom had seen him take down opponents twice his size many times. He clapped and cheered along with the rest of the crowd who were tossing flowers and favours into the ring until the ground was a blanket of bright colour. A thought occurred to him as the contending knight received a personal favour of a white handkerchief from one of the noble ladies on the opposite stand. Leaning on the railing in front of him he called Asher over to him.

The prince strode over, an easy smile on his face as he vaulted the ring fence, looking more at home in his plates than he ever had in his court attire. "Please tell me that you have a dainty handkerchief to give me as a token of your affection." He said with a wink.

Blossom shook his head, smiling even as he felt his cheeks heating. He could also feel the weight of the king's eyes on him but the day when that would have stopped him had long since passed. "I have something better." He said, beckoning Asher closer still with a wave of his hand.

The prince approached curiously until he was standing as close to Blossom as the railing would allow. Bringing the Sun's blessing that he had taken earlier that day to his lips Blossom leant down and pressed a kiss to Asher's cheek. Asher gasped as Blossom sent the blessing into him, warmth spreading through him at the touch.

Blossom made sure to allow as much of the blessing to bleed out of him as possible so that he briefly illuminated the whole arena. The crowd, which had already been in a state of excitement went wild.

"Sun's blessing to give you luck." Blossom said quietly. "Now go and get him your majesty." He added with a wink of his own.

He was about to pull away and take his seat again when Asher reached out and grabbed the collar of his robe, pulling him into a proper kiss. Blossom had to grip the railing hard to stop from falling over the edge.

"You're a menace." Asher whispered against his lips before letting him go.

"Says you." Blossom responded as he straightened, his response almost lost to the increasingly loud roar from the crowd.

"I love you flower." Asher said simply, closing the visor of his helmet and turning back to face his opponent.

"You will pay for that." He heard from his right, but Blossom refused to take his eyes off of the fight that was just about to start. Too busy watching Asher circle his rival slowly as the announcer shouted the rules.

"I'm sure I will." He replied calmly, and he could almost feel the king deflating beside him.

The call to fight was sounded and the Castillan knight stormed forward, his giant sword raised high as he charged. Asher deflected the first few blows easily, his opponent had an aggressive fighting style and seemed to be playing hard and fast with the rules which was something he wasn't used to, but he also relied too heavily on his strength and height and had no technique of which to speak of.

They were only a few moments into the fight and there were already large rents in the dirt where the other knight had swung down and gotten his sword lodged in the ground. Asher spun away from another heavy blow, the sword once again landing in the dirt with a *thunk*. Finding his footing easily he swung at his opponent's back, using the opening of him being distracted with dislodging his sword, landing the first blow of the match.

It wasn't a lethal or even an overly hard hit, but it seemed to enrage his opponent and, having finally retrieved his sword from the grounds grip he swung wide, almost connecting with Asher's head. There was a collective gasp from the crowd as Asher ducked into a crouch, dropping his shield in favour of having the use of both of his hands. He tucked his feet beneath him and surged back up again with a grunt, hitting the other man under the arm. His opponent dropped his sword with a roar and Asher kicked it swiftly away. There was a raucous cheer and Asher raised his hands in victory. Disarmament was always the more noble way of winning and he could see the respect that it inspired in the crowd.

Blossom had been ecstatically clapping and cheering along with the rest but suddenly gave a shout of horror as the other knight surged at Asher knocking him to the ground. "Somebody stop him." He shouted as the two knights wrestled on the ground, swords forgotten.

"Sit down boy." King Silas said and Blossom turned to him in shock.

"The match is at an end, this is just a brawl. One that Asher isn't going to win." Silas stared him down, but Blossom refused to break eye contact. "He's you son." He said finally, shocked that he was even having to use that argument.

Silas crossed his arms and Blossom turned back around, his throat dry as he tried to comprehend what this meant. Asher's helmet had been knocked off and he was intently trying to protect his face as the other man rained blows down on him. He was no longer attempting to fight back and seemed to simply be trying to outlast his opponent's rage. Did the king really think that Asher was going to be able to fight a man of that size hand to hand?

The opposing knight paused in his assault to reach into his boot and Asher used that opportunity to wiggle out from under him. He'd just rolled onto his stomach to try and stand when the Castillan pulled out a large, shining dagger.

Blossom gasped and attempted to run back to the railing but Silas caught hold of his robe. He looked back at the king briefly, Silas was staring at the sparring ring as though enraptured by the spectacle before him.

"He's going to kill him." Blossom cried as the knight raised the dagger above his head, taking aim at Asher's now exposed back. The prince seemed oblivious to the danger that he was in as he attempted to stagger upright.

"Sit down." Silas said again.

Realisation dawned on him as he took in the almost manic glint in the king's eyes. He felt a chill run through his body, somehow Silas had planned this. He was sacrificing his own son and with Asher's death would have full backing from the kingdom to wage war on Castilla. That was why he hadn't fought to stop the wedding, he'd never intended for it to happen in the first place.

Blossom sent one last glare at the king, ripping his robe from his grasp before vaulting over the railing. He summoned the full force of Sun's blessing to his hands as he strode over to the fighting pair, feeling an extra rush of power as the sun replenished his stores as he walked. He flung his hands out in front of him, sending a blinding ray of light that hit the man on top of Asher like a punch. The man gave a cry of pain as he toppled backwards, dropping the dagger and clutching at his face as he fell. Blossom scooped his hands under Asher's arms and helped him to scrabble backwards whilst the other knight stumbled to his feet. Throwing his helmet off in fury the Castillan noble began advancing on them again.

"Stop. The match is over." Blossom shouted, holding out a hand towards him, his eyes glowing with residual blessing as a warning.

The knight stopped, a look of confusion crossing his face. "You're protecting him?" He asked, his accent thick enough that Blossom almost struggled to understand him.

Blossom turned to look at Asher and then back again at the knight. "Of course I am." He replied, equally as confused. "You think I'd sit and watch the man I love be beaten to death?"

The knight took another step forward and Blossom felt Asher crowding closer to him, his aura threatening as he placed his hands on Blossom's waist. The knight glared briefly at the prince before looking back to Blossom. "I was freeing you from this tyrant's clutches."

Blossom looked around in confusion, he hadn't expected the man to admit to treason so openly, and the confession didn't match with what he was sure the king had planned. As he surveyed the stands, he noticed a large contingent of Castillan nobles crowding the railings, watching him intently. With a sinking heart he also noticed the sigils embroidered on all of their clothes, sigils that were mirrored in the metal of the knight's armour, the circular nature tree.

One of two things was happening he realised. Either the king was in league with the Blossomites and had planned this as an excuse to start a war, or the Blossomites had their own agenda and the king was simply turning it to his advantage.

He turned to face Asher, not breaking the grip the prince had on his waist. His gaze flickered over the other man's face, the bruises already rising around his eyes, the blood trickling from his nose down past his chin. He cupped the prince's face, gently wiping away the blood with his thumb. "I can fix this with Moon's blessing, you'll be fine by tonight." He whispered quietly, placing a small kiss on Asher's nose, and then smiling apologetically as the prince winced at the action.

"You think that I am being forced to marry this man against my will?" He asked, turning back to the nobles. There was no reply but the silence and the confused looks that were being shared amongst the group was answer enough. He sighed and, turning in a slow circle addressed the whole tournament crowd. The unnatural hush that had fallen over the arena making it so that he didn't even have to raise his voice to be heard.

"Listen everybody, for those of you thinking that this is simply a marriage of a political nature or that I am being held here against my will then hear this. I love this man." He pointed at Asher. "And I am certain that he loves me." Asher nodded, taking the hand that was being pointed at him and giving it a squeeze. "And I give myself to him freely and without reservation." He ended his speech by staring directly at the king. "And anyone trying to prevent that union will not be well received."

## Chapter 30

Blossom was already awake when Emma came to dress him, his knees pulled up to his chest as he surveyed his sparse room. Emma and Edwin had spent most of the previous day moving his belongings across the palace to Asher's room, but it still hadn't quite sunk in that this was to be the last time that he would wake up in this bed.

"Did you sleep at all last night?" Emma asked, hanging the tunic and breeches that he would soon be wearing on the door of the wardrobe.

"If I did it wasn't much." Blossom answered, scrubbing a hand over his face with a yawn as Emma wandered into the bathing room to start his bath.

"Are you having second thoughts?" Emma asked when she returned.

Blossom shook his head, pushing himself off the bed and tugging off his sleep clothes. "No, I think I was worried that if I fell asleep this would all turn out to be a dream, and to be honest I think it was excitement more than anything that kept me awake. Like when I was a child and couldn't sleep before harvest day because I was too busy wondering what gifts I would get."

Emma smiled indulgently at him as she followed him into the bathing room. "Well at least today you know the gift that you're getting. And it's a gift that you've already tried out a few times so you know it's good." She finished with a smirk.

"Is that judgement I hear?" Blossom asked, scrubbing himself rigorously in an attempt to wash the tiredness away. That and he wouldn't have time for a long bath this morning if he was to be ready in time.

"Of course not petal, I've always thought it silly that these Vaten insist on waiting until marriage to have sex. Imagine bonding yourself to someone for life and then finding out that you're not compatible after the fact."

Blossom hummed in agreement, he was aware that Castillan tradi-
tions were different in that respect but had never paid it much mind.
As far as he was concerned, he wasn't really Castillan anymore anyway
having spent more time here than there, and he certainly wouldn't be
after today.

⌘

"I can't believe the day has finally come." Emma said breathlessly as
she adjusted the collar of Blossom's plain white tunic.

She stepped back once she was satisfied and gestured for him to
look in the mirror. From head to toe he was dressed in plain but
expensive white fabric, a tunic tucked into well fitted white breeches
and white boots. Despite being fully clothed Blossom couldn't help but
feel a little naked without his robe. He hadn't been in public without a
blessers robe since being bought to the palace and he already missed its
comforting weight. He consoled himself with the knowledge that he'd
be wearing a cloak in the not-too-distant future but still felt himself
blush at the thought of entering the crowded great hall in just this.

"Are you going to cry?" Blossom asked with a smile and a teasing
jab to Emma's side, half in an attempt to distract himself and half in an
attempt to distract her.

Emma smiled back at him. "I'm not ashamed to say that I am on the
verge." Any cheeky remark that Blossom was going to say died in his
throat as Emma placed a hand on his cheek. "I love you so much petal,
and I have never been happier for you."

Blossom hugged her, feeling his own eyes tearing up as she squeezed
him back. "I love you too Emma, and I'm so happy to have my mother
there for my wedding."

This time Emma did begin crying and it took them both another
15 minutes before they were composed enough to head down to the
great hall.

The great hall was packed with guests and Blossom stopped briefly
when the doors were opened to him. He had never seen so many people
in one place before, he hadn't even thought that the great hall could
hold this many people. Blossom's impromptu speech had spread to the

rest of the kingdom and even people why had initially rejected their invitations, or had never been formally invited, had turned up.

Asher was already stood on the raised dais at the end of the hall next to a woman that Blossom recognised as the royal officiant, though in his current state of shock and nerves he completely blanked on her name. The prince was in a rich black tunic embroidered with onyx and obsidian beads, resting on his shoulders was the equally ornate black betrothal cloak that Blossom would soon be draped in.

Blossom once again felt severely underdressed, but the way that Asher was looking at him as he made his way down the aisle that had formed in the middle of the hall allayed any worries he might have had that he didn't look the part. He ascended the steps to the dais slowly, resolutely ignoring the dark glare that he was receiving from the front row.

"You look beautiful." Asher whispered when they came face to face.

"You're one to talk." Blossom responded and they both smiled at each other, uncharacteristically bashful.

The only thing that Blossom was wearing that was of any special decadence was the silver circlet that had been placed on his curls, 5 small gems representing each deity set into the metal. The prince wore a similar crown but formed of gold and set with black gems, the same crown that he had been presented with during his coming-of-age ceremony.

"Let us begin." The officiant said as she held her hands out. "Exalted guests, we are gathered here today to witness the union between Asher, crown prince of Vaten and Blossom, nature blessed of Castilla."

Blossom chanced a look around the hall as the officiant continued speaking, his eyes resting on a small group of hooded figures in the far-right corner. He turned resolutely back to face Asher as the officiant reached the end of her speech, he would not let a group of overzealous sycophants ruin this day for him.

"Do you two give yourselves freely to one another?" The officiant asked.

"I do." Asher responded.

"I do." Blossom echoed a second later.

At a gesture from the officiant Blossom turned his back and knelt in front of the prince, keeping his head bowed as he had been instructed to do during their rehearsals. Asher unclipped the chain holding the black cloak on his own shoulders and holding it in front of him, recited his oath. "With this cloak I cover you, protect you and bring you under my care. From this day forward we will be one family, by the deities of my house and yours I swear it."

Blossom felt the weight of the cloak settle over his shoulders and looked up just as Asher bent to secure the clasps of the chain. The prince smiled at him and placed a kiss on his forehead. The officiate gestured for him to rise and was about to begin reciting the final declaration of their marriage when Asher held up a hand.

"Is there a problem your majesty?" She asked quietly, her hands falling to her side.

"No problem my good lady." He replied. "Blossom and I simply wish to make equal vows to each other. I have claimed him as my own by laying my colour on him. It is his turn."

The officiant appeared to be mulling it over whilst the attendants began murmuring in their seats, changes to tradition didn't often go over smoothly in the royal court. Blossom didn't have to look at the royal bench to know what expression Silas would be directing at him right now and he took a dark pleasure in his last act of disobedience.

"It is not what is usually done but I see no harm in it." The officiant said finally before gesturing towards Blossom. "Master Blossom have you prepared a vow?" She asked.

Blossom nodded. "I have indeed." He took hold of Asher's hands as the officiant gestured for him to continue. Stepping closer he locked eyes with the prince and began to speak. "I have no cloak to offer you and no material item with which to pledge my love." Asher smiled at him. "But what I have at my disposal I offer freely. I carry all of Nature's blessings." He released Asher's hands to cup his face. "And with this kiss I give them to you, and as such bind us forever."

He drew Asher into a deep kiss, pouring his power through their connection. Breaking down all of the barriers that he'd built whilst he did so. Binding them together in the way that Silas had forbidden him from doing.

⌘

Asher felt the flow of Blossom's blessing stronger than he ever had before, wrapping his arms around the other man he realised that he was also getting a flood of his emotions. The outpouring of love and protection from Blossom was so strong that it felt like an almost physical being. It was then that he realised that Blossom must have destroyed the blockages that he'd told him about, he was bonding them together spiritually just as Asher had bonded them in marriage by laying his cloak on him.

He had his eyes closed but could tell from the sparks flashing behind his eyelids that Blossom was glowing, and he couldn't help but smile at the image as he pulled him even closer, not caring how many people were watching, not wanting the kiss to end just yet.

There was some kind of commotion from the crowd as Blossom's power dimmed and he was suddenly wrenched away from him.

"Stop!" His father boomed as he shoved both of them violently away from one another. Asher stared at him in shock as Silas rounded on Blossom. "What have you done?" He shouted accusingly but Blossom simply looked at the king in surprise, taking a step back as Silas continued to advance on him.

"Father what are you doing?" Asher demanded, stepping around the king and attempting to shield Blossom with his body.

Silas grabbed him by the collar of his shirt and Asher reached up, grasping his wrist as he braced himself in preparation for the king to try and pull him aside, but Silas simply moved the fabric to one side and inspected his neck where his death mark was.

The king shut his eyes and his shoulders slumped briefly. "Look at what you've done." He growled, turning Asher so that Blossom could see.

Asher blanched for a second, had the power surge caused his mark to grow? But the sudden delight on Blossom's face and the surge of relief that washed through their connection calmed him.

"It's gone." Blossom said before looking Asher in the eye. "Asher the mark is gone."

Asher placed a hand against his neck where the mark had been, branded into his skin since before he could remember. Now that he thought about it the constant ache that he'd felt his whole life was also gone.

Blossom looked from Asher to the king in sudden confusion. "Why are you acting like this is a bad thing?" He asked. "Did you know this was going to happen? Is that why you didn't want me to bond with him?"

The king advanced on him, furious beyond anything Asher had ever seen before. "Do you have any idea what you've done you stupid child." He boomed.

Asher placed himself between the two again, pulling Blossom close to him. "Do not speak to my husband that way." He demanded.

The king paused, taken aback by his sudden defiance. "And so it begins." Silas said finally.

"And so what begins father? You're not making any sense. I'm cured, why is that a bad thing?" Asher had released Blossom whilst he was talking and turned to face his father properly.

"Fine, I'll show you." Silas growled. He moved lightning fast, shoving Asher out of the way and slapping Blossom across the face. The slap landed so hard and was so sudden that Blossom was knocked to the floor.

Asher heard himself shout as fury and worry rose within him. He ran at his father, throwing his hands out to grab him but instead what appeared to be black shadows leapt from his fingers. He felt the same dark force that had bucked against Blossom's blessing on the rooftop so many months ago rising inside of him as the tendrils wrapped themselves around the king.

⌘

Blossom stared in a mixture of horror and awe as darkness poured from Asher's hands and coiled itself around the king. He looked up into the king's eyes, still cradling his stinging cheek, as the man glared at him in pure hatred.

"See what you've done." He spat just as the blackness enveloped him fully.

He stumbled to his feet and edged around the void like cloud, being careful not to touch it. "Asher." He called gently when he reached him.

Asher wrenched his gaze away from the black smoke, fear and confusion in his eyes. "What's happening? What have I done?" He cried, desperation causing his words to sound small and childlike.

"I don't know." Blossom answered, his words equally choked. He grasped Asher's outstretched wrists and gently lowered them. "I don't know my love." He said again as the darkness stopped pouring from him. He pulled Asher into a hug just as the attendants who had been previously frozen in shock erupted into a volley of panicked shouts. Shouts which grew louder and angrier as the blackness that had engulfed the king disappeared and his now lifeless body crumpled to the floor.

Blossom instinctively clutched Asher closer to himself, a hand at the back of his head to prevent him from turning and seeing what he had inadvertently done. The king's face was unnaturally grey, like it had been leached of colour and his once bright eyes and hair had darkened to a pitch black. Blossom staggered backwards, pulling Asher with him, every instinct in his body telling him to get them both as far away from the body as possible.

"Asher we have to get out of here." He said, his voice pleading as he held Asher's head in his hands, keeping his eyes fixed on him.

The crowd was beginning to surge on the dais, braying for retribution or simply caught up in the madness that had transpired. This and the panic that was surging through their bond was what caused Asher to finally break free of Blossom's grip and turn.

Blossom's heart squeezed painfully at the sound, unlike anything he had ever heard before, that seemed to tear itself from Asher's throat. Asher dropped to his knees, tears pouring down his face as he keened again. Blossom dropped beside him, wrapping an arm around his shoulders which Asher didn't seem to feel, too intent on the sight of his father's lifeless body.

"Blossom, Asher we need to leave. We have to go now, this isn't safe." At some point during the commotion Emma had appeared beside them. Her hands grasped Blossom by the shoulders and tried to tug him upright, but his sole focus was on Asher who appeared to be blind to everything but his sudden and all-consuming grief.

The prince stretched out a hand as though to try and touch the king but seemed to think better of it and simply wrapped his arms around himself, rocking backwards and forwards as he sobbed loudly.

Blossom looked up at Emma helplessly, the press of the crowd growing louder as they got closer, the sheer number of them preventing anyone from reaching them quite yet. "What do we do?"

She shook her head and opened her mouth to say something but closed it again as the hall suddenly fell silent.

A hooded figure had pushed their way to the front of the crowd and now stood with their hands raised and their back to Blossom and Asher. Blossom pulled the still weeping prince closer to him as he recognised the sigil on the back of the figures cloak. Just as he had suspected, a Blossomite.

"It has begun." The figure said, their voice loud and clear. "The curse has been released, the end has come and it is time for the rightful heir to take control."

"We have to go." Emma hissed in Blossom's ear and Blossom nodded, whatever was happening here it wouldn't end well.

He wrapped his arms tightly around Asher and hauled him to his feet, backing away slowly to one of the servant's entrances behind him. They didn't get far before the Blossomite whirled around, her hood falling as she did so and Blossom felt his whole world crumble.

She raised a finger and pointed directly at him. "Chosen son of nature, king of the blessed. It is time to take your place."

He didn't hear the rest of the speech as Emma suddenly cried.

"Now!" and the hall erupted in a flurry of fire and light. She pushed Blossom and Asher through the door, slamming it behind her.

"Emma what..."

"I'll explain later, for now just run." She demanded, taking off down the hallway.

Blossom and Asher followed, the prince having recovered enough to move unassisted even if his face was still contorted with grief and pain.

"Emma that was..." Blossom gasped as Emma led them through a series of servant's hallways and staircases. She appeared to be heading downward towards the catacombs. The burial place of every Vaten ruler that lay beneath the palace.

"I know, just keep running."

Blossom did, trying to piece together the truth of what had just happened as Emma threw open the heavy doors to the catacombs. Blossom was too deep in thought to question why the doors had been unlocked. Too panicked by the increasing noise of the mob that was still following them to ask why Emma seemed to know her way through the dark hallways so easily.

It was impossible and yet it must also be true. The woman who had just declared him king. The living blossomite that was also somehow someone he knew to be dead. The face he hadn't seen in 12 years and yet could never forget. His mother.

The End

9 781399 927581